The Loyal

Jacquie Rogers

For Peter,
and
for the people of Scotland

"They make a desolation and call it peace."

Tacitus, *The Agricola*

"The whole people must be wiped out of existence, with none to shed a tear for them, leaving no trace."

From Homer's *Iliad*, as quoted by Septimius Severus to his troops when about to invade Scotland, in AD 210.

THE LOYAL CENTURION

Prologue

AD 122
Northern Britannia

My name is Centurion Lucius Saturninus, primus pilus of the mighty Ninth Hispana legion, and I have failed.

I've failed my legate, Sextius Florentinus, who was cut down as the tide of battle turned against us. I failed my century, and the junior officers I held as friends. Failed my family and all my ancestors, that long line of Saturnini legionaries who fought for the Roman empire in deserts, through forest and bogs, across the seas, until all the world became Roman. I've failed the gods — and worst of all, I've failed my emperor Hadrian. They say even now he is on his way to Britannia, to take personal control of building the strongest wall the empire has ever seen. It's the wall that will save the province of Britannia from the savage northern barbarians.

But that wall will come too late for my legion, now annihilated in the bogs and hillsides of Caledonia.

I may be the only senior officer left. After Sextius Florentinus fell, run through from behind by a leaf-shaped thrusting spear that burst his chest open, the two remaining tribunes ordered a final desperate horn-blast from the cornicines. It was to summon the final remnant, the dregs of our proud legion. A last great charge, with gladiuses raised, to break through the circle of Caledonians. Those of us who could move, crawled and staggered to gather on the low summit of a knoll. The end of the short northern day was approaching, and all I could see below us was a dark mass of half-naked warriors, occasionally raising a spear or longsword to menace us. We waited; they waited too. We looked ever south for the relief force coming from our Tungrian comrades at Vindolanda. We looked, but they did not come. Perhaps all our riders have failed too, the hastily written messages lying trodden and bloodied where the rider was ambushed?

I am still on my feet, though the blood drips down my sleeve

1

from a gash on my shoulder. The wound is throbbing now rather than burning, but I refuse to look at it; I still have another hand to raise my sword for the last charge. I have that hand, I have two feet, and I have my pride — what more does a legionary need?

Then, as the dimmed red disc of the sun sinks into the western mists, the barbarian masses fall still. Their terrible shouts are silenced in the dank evening air. The clash of longswords against round shields ceases, and the night grows oppressive.

A lone man approaches the foot of our knoll, a path opening before him. A huge warrior, breeched, with a plaid cloak slung over his bare shoulder. He stalks through his host, men lowering their heads as he passes. When he reaches the front of the besieging ring, he lifts his head to glare directly at me, and bellows something. I don't understand the words, but what need? It's obvious: he is ordering our deaths. I prepare for the attack, all my attention focussed on the slope before me. I tighten my grip on my sword, and prepare my soul to meet the gods.

This is my biggest failure: I allow myself to be distracted by the huge chieftain, as he clearly intends. The attack comes from another direction. A hurled shout from behind, then, and the mass shifts shape. A wedge of Caledonians detaches and surges uphill towards us. Too late, I see the peril. Not to us — we are dead men already. But right in the path of this swirling onslaught stands our aquilifer, Marcus Galienus, and raised high and proud in his hands is the standard of our eagle. The golden heart of our legion, the ultimate symbol of Rome. As I swivel towards him, yelling a warning, a long Caledonian blade sweeps through the wooden standard, and on, irresistibly, to slice into Galienus. He drops with half his torso cut away, dead before he hits the ground. The standard drops, shattered. The eagle — ah, the eagle! I am already in motion, impelled by the spirit of the legion and my oath to the emperor, running full tilt. The eagle bounces onto the turf at my feet, and I catch it as it rebounds.

I will never forget the agony of that catch, tearing anew my shoulder wound. But my legs carry me on, pushing a passage through the startled warriors, on past their massed ranks, away into the Caledonian mists. On I go, feeling only white pain and my legs driving beneath me, as if impelled by Jupiter himself to save the precious eagle. On into the dark bogs until, slowing at last, I run straight into a solid form, striking it so hard I am knocked over. I lose my bearings, and my feet. A hand reaches down to drag me up. I have found a horse, a Roman mount, bearing the last of our messengers: my friend Brutus Quartinus.

He dismounts, and somehow pushes me up onto the mare.

'Leave! Hide in the woods, then get the eagle to safety.'

'But you, Brutus? Where are you going?'

He grins then, a gleam of white teeth in the gloom. 'I go to avenge the legion. There is no way to get a message out, Lucius, they have us surrounded for many miles. But as long as the eagle survives in Roman hands, the legion survives. Remember that!'

He steps back and slaps the mare hard on the rump to make her jump away. The last I see of my best friend in the world is the flicker of his gladius, as he runs up to join our dead comrades on that nameless knoll.

So now I have failed my friend. All that is left is the eagle. But I swear by all the gods, I *will* save the eagle of the Ninth.

Chapter One

December AD 224

Lagentium

Two soldiers, wrapped in heavy hooded cloaks, rode side by side in companionable silence along the highway from Danum. The ground was iron-hard, and their horses' hooves clacked in the frozen air. As the afternoon dimmed into dusk, the shorter of the two, wearing a phalera disc for bravery on his chest, spotted a milestone in the cropped verge.

'Only a mile more to Lagentium, sir,' he called cheerfully.

'Good,' returned the Governor's Man. 'A bathhouse and dinner at the mansio are just what we need, Tiro. Let's pick up the pace.'

Quintus Valerius, senior beneficiarius consularis to the Governor of Britannia Superior, squeezed his legs lightly against his horse and clicked his tongue. The well-trained animal responded with a faster trot. They approached the industrial outskirts of Lagentium, passing lime kilns, a spoon works, and a glassmaking factory. Fortunately only one of the kilns was alight, and the foul fumes blew well away from them.

Lagentium was the final stopover on their long journey north from Londinium. As they entered the town, Quintus briefly reflected on the mission taking them on to Eboracum. At their last meeting in Londinium, Governor Aradius Rufinus had sounded anxious for the security of Britannia, both for their own wealthy southern province and here in northern Britannia Inferior. Quintus shared his concerns. It was one of the peculiarities of Britannia that Governor Rufinus, being the commander of two legions, was superior in rank to the new governor in Eboracum. Crescens was also ranked as legate, in command of the Sixth Victrix legion based at Eboracum. But Londinium was a long way from Eboracum, and even further from the Aelian Wall which separated Britannia from the barbarians.

Lagentium was a busy little town, clearly prospering from its

4

many trades. The settlement had begun life as an invasion fort guarding a strategic crossing of the river Aire, but the army had long since moved north to Eboracum and the Wall, leaving only a local policing station. The town's large two-winged mansio was right next to the market square. Quintus resigned himself to what he guessed would be a disturbed night, with travellers and post messengers coming and going and traders setting up their nearby market stalls before dawn. He showed his travel warrant at the desk, while Tiro took their tired post-horses to the stables.

'Something up?' he asked when Tiro joined him, wearing a frown.

'Oh, just a plonker of a head ostler. There was a lad helping with the horses, nice boy, eager but limping and struggling a bit to get around. He's got a withered hand, too. I had to sort out the stable man when he started setting about the poor lad.'

Quintus recognised the fierce look on Tiro's face, and pitied the foolish head ostler. Quintus had seen that look before, generally when the two men were called upon to investigate a serious crime, or even tackle the threat of assassination and insurrection. Tiro didn't always come out on top in a scrap, but woe betide whoever affronted his sense of fair play.

They made a good pair, the thoughtful patrician Valerius and his tough optio Tiro. Like chalk and cheese they were, but both loyal to the core when it came to pursuing justice and protecting the Empire.

'I'm sure you did the business,' Quintus said, a smile lighting his grey eyes.

'He won't go picking on Nicomedes again, not when I'm around. I gave him a proper fist in the face.'

Quintus held back a laugh.

They walked to the handsome limestone bathhouse, a sturdy and popular legacy from the long-departed Ninth Hispana legion who had built the original fort. There they soaked in hot water until even Quintus felt warmed through. He'd lived in Britannia long enough to be resigned to the cold dark winters, but it had been a while since he'd been in this hardy northern province of the island.

He lifted himself reluctantly out of the heated pool in the apse of the caldarium, and was heading through to the frigidarium for a final fresh plunge when he noticed someone watching him. He paused, considering. The man was fully dressed, so not here to bathe or exercise.

Tiro caught Quintus up.

'Know that bloke, boss?'

'No. But he seems to know me. What do you think?'

'Dunno, he looks pretty ordinary. A clerk, or a merchant. He's not wearing a toga, so he's not a town bigwig.'

'Look beyond his clothes. What else?'

'Brownish — no, dark red hair. Tall, long legs. His skin is very white, and those pale eyes… Got it! One of those Caledonians. Big buggers. I used to see them being sold on the slaver's block in Londinium.' Tiro nodded with satisfaction.

'I think you're right. If I'm not mistaken, life has taken him a long way from home. Here he comes.'

The stranger came towards them, nodded slightly, pausing to say under his breath, 'Beneficiarius, let me buy you and your optio a drink. On Governor Rufinus. I'll wait outside while you dress.' Quintus wondered how the man knew who they were. He disliked being caught unawares.

The northerner honoured his offer. Once they were sitting in the taproom of the mansio with cups of wine in front of them — in Tiro's case, a mug of local Brigantian beer — accompanied by hot fresh bread and a generous round of salted cream cheese, served with olive oil and a tiny pitcher of dark honey, the man reached into his leather shoulder bag for a wooden tablet. It was fastened by a wax seal that Quintus recognised. Quintus broke the seal and quickly scanned the message inside before passing the tablet to Tiro, who ran his finger along the crabbed lines rather more slowly.

'Well, Lossio Veda, it seems we work for the same master,' said Quintus.

'Indeed we do. Although your profession of Governor's chief investigator, unlike mine, is declared openly through your uniform and the hasta badge on your baldric.' As Veda smiled, his light hazel eyes creased at the corners.

'Governor Rufinus certifies your position as a speculator, assigned to him by the Castra Peregrina in Rome. Yet I suspect your parentage is closer than Italy.'

Veda nodded. 'My mother was a Venicone: she was proud of her old tribe in Fiv. Their main centre was at Cair Pol on the Tausa, before the Romans built the fortress of Horrea Classis there. By then, of course, the Venicones had thrown in their lot with Rome. My father came as a boy from the northern mountains beyond the central valley, before the campaigns of Emperor Septimius Severus. Our governor tells me you were involved in that fighting, Beneficiarius?'

Quintus nodded but said nothing. His wounds from that war still ached; his losses felt difficult to bear, even after many years.

Tiro saw the rigidity of his boss's face, and broke in.

'Governor Rufinus writes you have news of the Painted People. I thought they were just a tale out of the northern mountains and glens, painted monsters to frighten small children?'

Lossio Veda stopped smiling. 'So did I, once. I was surprised when Governor Rufinus asked me to travel so far beyond the Aelian Wall. There's been peace for a generation and more beyond the Wall, bought with Roman silver ever since Emperor Caracalla made peace with the Caledonians. Our allies, the Venicones of Fife and the Votadini tribe of Dunpeldyr, prize silver above anything. We've always kept an eye on the tribes close to the Wall, of course. I myself spent several years based in a lowland fort, until I married a southern girl who wanted to move back to Camulodunum.' The Caledonian smiled again, sadly, perhaps picturing his persuasive wife. 'Since my wife died, I've come and gone, acting as Governor Rufinus's representative attending locus meetings, mostly at Locus Trimontium and Locus Manavi. I have recent intelligence that will affect your mission.'

'You'll need to explain, Lossio. When I met the governor recently for this mission briefing, he said nothing about matters north of Eboracum, let alone beyond the Aelian Wall.'

Quintus felt a little testy. He saw the inexorable call of duty approaching to change his plans. The governor knew he was travelling to Eboracum to spend some time with his wife, at Julia's maternal home there. He was as anxious as he was keen to be with Julia for the birth of his second child, due in a month or so.

Quintus thought back to his conversation with Aradius Rufinus in Londinium a few weeks earlier. It was largely due to the actions of Quintus and Tiro at the battle of Corinium the previous spring that Aradius had become governor, and he had rewarded them with promotions, and his trust. Their efforts to protect his cousin Ulpian in the blazing Roman summer had further won his gratitude and friendship. Sending Quintus to build bridges with the recently-posted Marius Crescens seemed an ideal opportunity, as Quintus was already planning a long visit to Eboracum.

Julia had left their Summer Country home some weeks ago to take charge of a complex family legacy in Eboracum. Her maternal aunt had died there, wealthy and aged beyond the norm.

Quintus had mixed emotions about the northern city, where as a neophyte Praetorian guard in AD 210 he had been sent to recuperate from a serious wound during the Caledonian wars. There he had met and wooed the young Julia. And lost her, or so he thought at the time. Now that his life was stable and his marriage content, he was happy to go back.

But it was one thing to meet Legate Marius Crescens, to sum him up and report back to Aradius Rufinus. It was quite another to travel beyond the Aelian Wall, roaming that bleak, empty landscape to gather intelligence of an invisible potential enemy. Quintus had no intention of getting into any more trouble in the remote north of Britannia. That was the role of the armed forces at the disposal of Legate Crescens. He shoved memory aside, listening as Lossio Veda explained why he had come to intercept them now: because the governor was puzzled by conflicting reports from the north. Aradius Rufinus wasn't as sure as Legate Crescens that peace reigned beyond the Aelian Wall.

Lossio went on, 'What we call the locuses are meeting places where the tribes near our boundary gather at regular intervals with Roman officials from the border forts. Organising these meetings is easiest if we hold them at places sacred to the tribes, like Locus

Maponi and Locus Manavi. Thus the tribes near our border govern themselves, we offer them protection from their enemies further north and west, and we keep a good notion of what is going on from the Wall as far as the river Tausa.'

Tiro had been drumming his fingers during this explanation, perhaps because his beer cup was empty.

'Well, this all sounds as it should: under the control of Roman officers. And your spies,' he said, nodding at Lossio. 'But Governor Rufinus says in this letter that he's heard disturbing reports. So what more do you know?'

The Veniconian clicked his fingers for the serving girl, and Tiro had to wait while the cups were refilled. He didn't seem to mind the pause too much, Quintus noted, as Tiro sucked down the new beer.

'The trouble is,' continued Lossio, 'these locus meetings are too far south to give us the full picture. And of course the lowland tribes have been allies of Rome for many generations, and are well rewarded with Roman silver. It's what's happening beyond Tuesis, the river the locals call Tausa, that worries Governor Rufinus.'

He paused, and now it was his fingers that drummed on the table. Quintus felt a sinking sensation. He doubted what was to come would be good news.

'Before I moved my family south, I set up a string of speculatores out of Vindolanda to operate beyond the Wall, even beyond the great mountains towards the north coast. They are no longer based at the fort, but well embedded into sensitive locations. I trained them myself, and they have faithfully reported back over the years since Emperor Caracalla carried out his father's wishes before returning to Rome.'

'Carried out his father's wishes?' echoed Tiro, perking up.

'You know of the dying emperor's instructions, surely?' Lossio's eyebrows were raised.

'I'm not a Caledonian. I'm from Londinium!' Tiro hated to be exposed as ignorant.

Lossio explained. 'You see, Optio, on his deathbed the old emperor instructed his army to wipe the whole people out of existence. By that he meant the two tribes who had combined to break the emperor's treaty and bring new rebellion against Rome: the Caledonians and their allies the Maeatae. And that's what happened. Emperor Caracalla exterminated every warrior, every wife, every bairn he could find beyond the Earthen Wall of Emperor Antoninus Pius. The only ones spared were lads too young to take up arms. These were captured and enslaved, or sent to serve in Rome's cohorts at the ends of the empire.'

Tiro stiffened, looking at Quintus. The beneficiarius sighed, saying, 'I was near death myself when that order was given. I heard later that a terrible campaign of killing had been carried out.'

Lossio nodded gravely. 'My own distant mountain kin included. I once went scouting as far as my father's old village. It was empty, bereft of life, not even a chicken scratching in the dirt. It was a severe punishment.'

All three fell silent, the two older men staring into their wine. Tiro gulped down the last of his beer.

Quintus stirred. 'Why then is Aradius Rufinus concerned? After such horrors, it's likely that the land between our allies the Votadini and the highlands of the Mounth remains empty. And the Votadini are still being paid good silver to protect the south from northern marauders.'

Lossio looked up. 'No longer, it seems. That is a fertile region, long a bread basket, with a wealth of fish and grazing stock. In contrast, the peoples of the far north — the tattooed ones — live a mean life of harsh weather and thin crops in the mountains and coasts beyond. The northern tribes have been on the move since we decommissioned the last of our forts. The worry is they are moving south to fill the vacuum left by Caracalla, settling in villages and working the rich land.'

'Why is that a problem? With all the warrior chieftains so recently dead, how can a few farmers pose a danger?'

The Veniconian leaned forward across the table. His long craggy face looked serious, as his voice sank.

'Because these incomers, the Painted People, are led by a great new chieftain. I've had word he has left his mountain stronghold to join his people. And coming south with him are all his warriors.

They have never met our Roman forces, remaining all this time beyond the great highlands. But now this supreme chieftain, whom they call Athair and worship like a god, has come south with his untamed soldiers.'

Sudden loud voices rose outside, and the tavern wench ran to the door. Quintus saw a blur of commotion through the windows, and stood up to peer through the thick green glass.

'Tiro,' he called, 'you're needed!'

Outside, a thin lopsided-looking boy, barely in his teens, was trying desperately to gain entrance to the tavern. He was hampered in his efforts, lacking some use of his right hand, which he kept tucked into his long tunic sleeve.

'Sir, Tiro sir!' he piped in a reedy voice. 'Oh please, w-won't you come?'

The maid hustled over to shut him out, but Tiro and Quintus were faster. They got Nicomedes in through the door.

'Well, boy? What is it? More trouble with the ostler?' asked Quintus.

The boy turned to Tiro. His face was deathly white, and Quintus saw he was trembling so badly he surely could not stay much longer on his feet.

'It's all right, Nico,' Tiro said gently. 'This is my superior officer, Beneficiarius Quintus Valerius. Any trouble, the boss'll see to it.'

The boy cast about as if searching for more help. Quintus crouched down by him, his face now level with the boy's large dark-fringed eyes.

'How can we help, Nico?'

Nicomedes drew a long sob to speak in a faltering voice.

'It's my friend, Sacra. She works here in the mansio. I get so hungry, and she always — she always keeps some food back for me. Most days I come to meet her behind the kitchen. Today I waited and waited at the usual time, but she never came. Then the scullery slave w-went to draw water from the well in the courtyard, and — and...'

Tiro grasped him by the shoulders. 'Tell us, so we can fix it.'

11

A wail broke from the lad, and he awkwardly scrubbed at the tears scudding down his grubby face. 'No-one can fix Sacra, not ever. They j-just pulled her out of the well. She's dead!'

Chapter Two

Eboracum

Julia swept back a lock of fair hair from her forehead, and tried once more to make sense of the figures on the wax tablet before her. Her back was aching, the baby was apparently turning somersaults in her swollen belly, and she was infuriated with the Roman numbering system. Surely there was an easier way to represent amounts, especially when one needed to add and multiply?

She wished she'd brought Demetrios with her to Eboracum. She reminded herself that her highly-educated Greek estate manager was needed more at Bo Gwelt, her villa far away south in the Summer Country. Demetrios was essential not just to run the estate, but also to keep an avuncular eye on her headstrong daughter, Aurelia. Who was, no doubt, hurtling round the Polden Hills on her high-bred stallion accompanied by her friend Drusus, the son of their neighbour Magistrate Agrippa Sorio.

A buxom young woman came into the room carrying a tray with candles and drinks, and Julia remembered she had at least one person here to be grateful for.

'Now then, mistress, time to stop squinting at your accounts. Put your feet up with a drink for a while.' Julia's housekeeper and oldest friend, Britta, spoke briskly as ever and waved at the slavegirl with her. 'Get these candles lit, and some more coals in that brazier, and quick about it! The poor mistress is near frozen.'

The girl scuttled round, head down, disappearing once her tasks were done.

'Britta, that was unkind. The poor girl doesn't yet know how soft-hearted you really are.'

'Soft-hearted? Me? You're the one who's soft-headed. Must be that baby of yours, Julia!'

Julia stood up to leave her work, stretching her back and rubbing her bulge.

'Well, you're certainly right about one thing, Britta. I need a

13

break. Let's go for a walk instead, and maybe drop in at the library of the Serapeum. I think we'll find Corellia Velva there this afternoon.'

The Serapeum was in the north-west of the civilian area of Eboracum, standing in its own walled precinct. The painted walls were bright with colour. The temple had been built only a few years ago in honour of Emperor Septimius Severus, famously devoted to the Graeco-Egyptian god Serapis.

The two women walked across a masterly mosaic pavement featuring a bull with a fishtail — strange to their British eyes — and entered the library. They found Corellia, a woman in her late twenties, medium height and dark haired, in animated chat with a younger strikingly beautiful girl.

Corellia smiled at Julia in greeting, her eyebrows raised in pleasure. 'Julia, Britta, how timely! I've been wanting to introduce you to my dear friend, Placidia Septimia.'

The dark girl greeted them shyly. She was richly-dressed, wearing a stola expensively embroidered round the neckline with gold thread. As she lifted her hand to Julia's, the tinkle of several elaborate bangles chimed softly. Julia noticed one in particular, shaped of gold and silver wires bound into a circlet, which flashed as the girl moved. Julia judged Placidia to be more than a decade younger than herself, still a teenager in fact. She embraced the girl, noticing an exotic scent of cinnamon in her tightly-curled black hair.

'This is my friend, Britta,' Julia continued, patting Britta on the arm. Britta gave her warmest smile, but Placidia, perhaps overwhelmed by these confident new acquaintances, dropped her gaze.

'It's all right, Placidia,' said Corellia, tucking her arm through Placidia's. 'Julia is an old, trusted friend. We were trainees together here in the Serapeum, when we were even younger than you are now.'

Placidia coloured, but lifted her face to look more openly at Julia. Corellia went on, 'Julia, Placidia is the wife of our legate Marius Crescens, so Britannia is still very new to her.'

Julia was surprised, knowing Crescens to be a mature man of determined reputation. It wasn't unusual for powerful men to marry much younger women, but Placidia might well feel out of her depth, so far from home.

'I hope you're finding our city to your taste, Placidia? Am I right in guessing that you are of the imperial family, given your family name? It's a long voyage indeed from Leptis Magna to Britannia Inferior.'

Placidia nodded, looking encouraged by Julia's easy manner. 'I met my husband only a few months ago, when my mother, who was cousin to the divine Caracalla, took me to visit relatives in Rome. Marius was recently widowed, you see, and the Empress Mamaea arranged our marriage. Mother was delighted. It all seemed to happen so swiftly! And then, of course, when my husband was appointed legate here, I sailed with him from Rome. But Marius can be stern at times. And I do so miss my family and my friends in Africa.'

Her beautiful face drooped at the mention of her home. Julia exchanged glances with Britta, feeling sorry for this girl barely out of childhood, married off to a much older man for dynastic purposes. Being part of the extended imperial family was, Julia guessed, no great blessing. Placidia, with her striking dark looks and high family status, would have been a pearl of marriageability.

'Do you come here today to seek the god's blessing for a child?' As soon as the words were out of Julia's mouth she regretted them. She had spoken innocently, forgetting for the moment that Corellia herself visited the shrine of Serapis frequently to pray for a pregnancy, after more than ten years of childless marriage to her beloved husband, Aurelius Mercurialis. Julia turned apologetically to Corellia, who gave her a warm glance, saying, 'Indeed, Julia, Serapis is most gracious to all women who seek his wise blessing. No doubt he has his hand outheld to you, too, for safe delivery of a healthy child soon.'

Julia grasped Corellia's hand, the slight squeeze communicating apology for her clumsiness. Turning back to Placidia, she saw with consternation that the girl looked distraught, mouth visibly trembling and the blood retreating from her face, leaving a strange pallor under her dark complexion.

'What is it, Placidia?' asked Britta kindly. 'Is something wrong?'

'Oh, no,' Placidia replied too quickly. 'I'm sure the god will look on all of us kindly.'

Corellia shook her head, looking gratefully at Britta when she suggested they go out into the temple precinct. There they could make a suitable offering to Serapis at his altar, watched over by a small pillar-mounted bronze of the sacred bull Apis. Placidia seemed to cheer up after the little offering of wine, and asked the others to accompany her over the bridge to the legate's praetorium, where she wanted to offer them refreshments. Julia was inclined to demur, as her feet were beginning to hurt. But she saw the eager look on Britta's face and gave in silently. Britta would enjoy seeing inside the prestigious imperial palace, built and embellished as the residence of the Emperor's family only fifteen years earlier. It was the closest any ordinary Briton would come to experiencing the marvels of Rome itself.

As they walked, Julia tried to look with Placidia's eyes at the city's solid gritstone buildings. The thinly-cut sandstone roof tiles of Eboracum were distinctively different from the red ceramic tiles so common throughout the empire. Constant evidence of manufacturing came from all parts of the city: the noisy hammering of metalworking, the stink of leather tanneries, and everywhere the sounds of corralled horses. Eboracum was still a military city at heart, having been initially built as a garrison town. After a century and a half it remained the residence of the Sixth Victrix legion, and was now the proud capital of the northern British province. And still home to far more men than women, she realised, hearing on the river breeze the stamp of boots and shouted calls as the soldiers in the large fortress manoeuvred in unison, obeying the drill orders of their officers.

Outside the legate's palace, imposing on a ridge facing south-east across the river Isura, Julia was pleased to see a look of joy on Placidia's face. She often felt this way herself after communing with her own special goddess, the wise and benevolent Sulis

Minerva. Her relief was short-lived. She saw a young man coming out of a nearby doorway, turning towards them. He was a striking sight, dressed in an expensive version of the standard tribune's uniform with a finely-woven white woollen cloak flung elegantly over one shoulder. His leggings were so tightly fitted, she was astonished he could walk comfortably. He was unlikely to be a native Briton; apart from his prohibitively extravagant clothes and his swagger, his olive-toned countenance surely indicated Mediterranean origins. As he neared she noted with a sinking heart the rather blank expression on his even-featured face. Maybe she was being unkind, but she saw none of the intelligence and leadership of her own noble Roman husband, Quintus Valerius. Actually, the tribune's flashing dark eyes were rather too vague to be pleasing. Julia looked at Placidia, and felt unhappy resignation at the adoration on the girl's face. The young officer paused, inclining his head gracefully. His eyes sought Placidia's, whose heightened flush revealed her feelings.

Corellia tactfully intervened.

'Ah, Tribune Gaius Laelianus, well met! May I make you known to Lady Julia Aureliana of the Durotriges? And her companion, Britta.'

The officer looked at Julia, seeming to lose interest as soon as he registered her advanced pregnancy. He barely glanced at Britta. Julia felt rather than saw her friend's quick ire rising, and jumped in hastily.

'A pleasure to meet you, Tribune. Are you newly posted to Britannia?'

He slowly dragged his gaze back, saying, 'Yes, Lady Julia. I accompanied the legate and his wife on their voyage here.'

Placidia interrupted. 'But the tribune was already such an old friend, Julia! Just imagine, my family and his know each other well in Leptis Magna. It was a surprise to meet Gaius again in Rome, and then to find he had been assigned to Marius's staff. Such a lucky coincidence, don't you think?'

Julia thought grimly that it was neither coincidental, nor lucky; not for Placidia at least. It seemed clear to her that this spoilt scion of an ambitious senatorial family was not a suitable friend for the

17

legate's young and impressionable wife. Julia foresaw rocky shoals ahead.

Corellia said briskly, 'We mustn't keep you from your duties, Tribune.' She took possession of Placidia's hand, despite her wistful departing look at Gaius, and managed to steer the group out of range of his hungry stare without seeming to be rude.

Julia took very little notice of the magnificent legate's palace, as they sat and chatted politely long enough to accept glasses of watered wine, and tiny honey and almond cakes. Her feet were now throbbing, and she felt horribly weary. She had a sinking feeling that Quintus would expect her to intervene to end the inappropriate connection between the peacocky tribune and little Placidia. She was grateful when Britta soon rose, thanking Placidia for her hospitality and saying her mistress was tired and needed to rest.

Placidia immediately bade them a pretty goodbye, as Corellia also made her excuses. They were ushered out of the vast building by an arrogantly stalking steward in a long gold-edged tunic.

Once outside, Corellia said, 'Oh dear. I knew about Tribune Laelianus and his family's hopes, but I had not imagined he would continue his flirtations once Placidia was married.' Julia was intrigued. Corellia's connections were impeccable, and here was more evidence that she had her finger on every pulse in Eboracum.

'Go on, Domina,' said Britta bluntly. 'You'd better tell us it all. What trouble is that girl in?'

Corellia sighed. 'Straight to the point as ever, Britta. The truth is, Placidia *has* confided in me. She fancied herself in love with Gaius Laelianus even before he joined the new legate's staff. His family in Africa pulled strings to send him to Rome, and then to get him appointed to the Sixth Victrix legion. Their influence stretched as far as having him assigned a berth on the legate's own galley. He spent the whole voyage, from what I can tell, in Placidia's pocket.'

'Surely just a girlish crush on her part?' suggested Julia.

Corellia sighed. 'It's worse than that, Julia. You may not know that this is the third marriage for Marius Crescens. Both his previous wives turned out to be unable to give him a child. His first wife died of unknown causes, one hears. Marius divorced the other within two years, blaming her infertility. Placidia is already becoming frightened, as it's over a year since they married. I have heard he can be violent when crossed. I myself have seen bruises on her arms and even, once, round her throat, but when I asked she just laughed it off.'

'No sign of an heir yet?' Britta's tone was grim.

'No.'

Julia was thoughtful. 'No wonder Placidia goes frequently to worship at the Serapeum. Serapis is her only hope, if the fault indeed lies with her husband. Of course, she can never say so. Poor girl! And still carrying a torch for that foolish young tribune. With him also assigned to Eboracum, living right next door, it's a recipe for disaster.'

The three walked in silence to Julia's townhouse, which was pleasantly sited on an exclusive terrace with a fine view of the river. As she lay down to rest, Julia hoped the uneasy feeling in her belly was due to the babe turning, and not to her sharply-honed instinct for trouble.

Chapter Three

Lagentium

In the courtyard of the inn a small crowd had gathered. A dumpy middle-aged woman, presumably the scullery slave, was sitting on the ground, well into an unhelpful fit of hysterics. Quintus nodded to Tiro, who went over to the woman with Lossio. The pair patiently supported her up onto her feet, and took her, still wailing, into the inn.

Quintus turned his attention first to the body. The stable manager had been sufficiently distracted from bullying Tiro's little lad to lend a hand when the scullery maid began screaming. The mansio-keeper had joined him, a stout man in a dirty apron, with a birthmark disfiguring an otherwise genial face. He now stood by, wringing his hands helplessly, talking in a low voice to the stable manager. Two of the ostlers had retrieved the dead woman from the well, and dragged her over the retaining wall to lay her out on the cobbled yard. Looking rather sick-faced, they were doing their best to arrange her limbs respectfully. This was difficult as the body and its clothes were saturated and slippery. They moved away with evident relief as Quintus approached.

Quintus looked around. Nico was hovering nearby, and limped over readily when Quintus crooked a finger at him.

'Are you all right to help me with Sacra? I know she was your friend.'

The boy nodded eagerly, showing an unexpected resolve. Quintus looked carefully at Sacra's face. She had been a pretty woman; he now saw that she was still young. The skin of her face was pale, no mottling as yet. He pulled up one eyelid, looking for signs of mortification. The lens of the eye was clouded, and he felt some stiffening in the muscles of her face. He picked up a hand — it was still limp. The skin was wrinkled.

'May I ask, sir, what are you looking for?'

Quintus regarded the boy, Nicomedes, seeing intelligence and moral strength in his look. He noted that the right side of his face seemed to have slipped somehow, but he evidently could speak clearly enough, with sometimes a slight halt.

'I'm looking for signs that might tell us how long Sacra has been dead. For example, if her body had gone completely stiff, that would normally mean she was killed more than two hours ago, but less than a full day and night.'

'Does her b-being in water make a difference, sir?'

Quintus was struck by the boy's calm questions, and gave him a considering look.

'Yes, well guessed, Nicomedes. The fact that the water is very cold in winter will also have slowed down any changes since death. Can you help me turn her head to face you, Nico?' The boy swallowed, but helped competently, lifting his friend's head with his left hand, and turning it with care towards himself. Quintus immediately saw how she had been killed. Her skull was crushed in at the back, with obvious bone fragments visible. He laid her head gently down so Nico could not see the hideous wound. He wondered whether to share what he had found with the young boy, deciding that he had enough strength of character, and needed to know.

'Thank you, Nico. I know what killed Sacra, and it seems very likely she was attacked during the night. She was hit hard on the back of her head, before she was put into the well. She would not have felt anything, or been able to call out. Unfortunately my wife Julia, a healer with expertise in severe injuries, isn't here with us to confirm. But from my own long experience, I believe Sacra was attacked from behind. She died instantly, and would not have known anything about her murder. Or her killer.'

He said the last words almost to himself. His eye had drifted back to her hand, from which the long wet sleeve had been drawn back. He picked her hand up again, turning it over carefully. There were weals around her wrist, old calluses where layer upon layer of tender skin had been rubbed away, then healed, building hard scars. He reached for her other hand, examining that wrist too. He sighed, laying both hands at rest across Sacra's chest. He sent Nico, shivering with delayed shock and cold, inside to warm up. Tiro would know what to do with the lad.

Next Quintus examined the well. A good size and solidly built, it had a low protective wall round the outside, and was surmounted by a thick windlass on a horizontal bar, propped across two solid timber supports. Being the main water supply for a large mansio in a busy town, the well was sturdy and much used. The windlass had been kept smooth and moved easily, especially when two strong men were operating it, as now. The rope looked almost new. He searched in vain for marks of a struggle at the well's edge; he had not expected them. He did find something else, which he picked up and slipped into his pouch.

He glanced once more round the courtyard. He would look again by broad daylight, though in all probability there would be nothing more to find. Then he too went inside, feeling uncomfortable about the picture beginning to form in his mind.

Tiro had done a competent job of corralling and questioning all possible witnesses at the inn. He'd requisitioned a quiet interview room, normally used as a snug for private parties. As Quintus entered, Lossio caught his eye, saying, 'We sent the stable lad off to bed. He told us he had been helping you. He looked too tired and upset to tell us much more tonight, anyway.'

'Thank you, Lossio. Anything useful from the others?'

'We've drawn a blank with the few guests who hadn't already moved on. And no one saw anything suspicious, or noticed Sacra in conversation with strangers. The ostlers had nothing useful to add. The scullery maid is in with Tiro now.'

'Right. Keep the innkeeper on alert, would you? I'll want to speak to him tonight.'

Quintus quietly entered the room. Tiro nodded at him, still listening to the upset scullery maid. She had evidently calmed down somewhat, no doubt helped by wine drunk from the empty jar at her elbow. Judiciously supplied by Tiro, Quintus guessed. None knew better than his optio how to loosen the tongue with wine.

'The bucket must have been let down before she went into the well. When I tried to draw water, I felt the bucket was so heavy, too heavy…I couldn't turn the windlass at all. She must have been

22

stuck, and I couldn't raise the bucket, nohow. So I called the stable lads to help, thinking a dog or something had fallen in. And when they eventually got the bucket up, there she was...' The slave broke down afresh.

Quintus waited tactfully, then asked, 'Did you know Sacra well? How long had she been working here?'

'Dunno, sir,' the woman sobbed, face blotchy with tears, emotion and snot, which she wiped off with her sleeve. 'She were a nice lass, good with our snap. Tasty. But I'm new here mesel' so I really didn't know her that well.'

Quintus, guessing "snap" referred to Sacra's cooking ability, rose to usher her politely out. At the door she turned, saying, 'There were one thing I noticed. She spoke a bit funny.'

'Funny?' echoed Tiro, quirking an eyebrow at Quintus, who was content to let his native British colleague pursue this.

'A bit. Like them tribes in Cambria.'

'Silurian, eh?'

'Yes, like enough. Only...' she hesitated, evidently pondering. 'Only she sounded old-fashioned to my ear.'

The inn-keeper had little more to add about his dead cook. He looked harassed, as he undoubtedly was. A body in the well might draw in a few curious tongue-waggers, but the incident was unlikely to do the reputation of his establishment much good. He clearly wanted rid of Sacra, the murder investigation, and the investigators themselves, as soon as possible.

He told them how she had turned up a few weeks ago, looking thin and travel-worn, and begging for a job. As it happened, his previous cook had run off that very day with a passing soldier she had taken an instant fancy to.

'Up on one of them bloody frozen Wall forts, wishing hersel' back 'ere, I don't doubt,' he said with moody relish. Sacra had quickly shown herself to be a good cook, and had soon been given control of the kitchens, and her own little room to sleep in.

Tiro broke in. 'I had a look in Sacra's cubicle, sir. Nothing there. She had virtually no belongings, poor girl.'

Quintus was satisfied with that. Tiro had a very sharp eye. If he said Sacra's cubicle was empty, then there had been nothing to find there.

'Kept hersel' to hersel'. That's how I wanted it. We're a respectable house 'ere. No whores, no bedbugs, good food, and the best beer.'

Quintus thought the existence or otherwise of bedbugs was yet to be proven, but he was clearly going to draw a blank on the subject of Sacra's background before Lagentium.

He asked about recent guests, hoping something significant might emerge, though it was a forlorn hope in such a busy mansio.

'The usual mix, sir. Merchants, tax collectors, soldiers, a couple of families with maids and tutors in tow.'

Thinking of the weals on Sacra's wrists, Quintus asked, 'Soldiers? From which fort?'

The innkeeper scratched his nose and then his abundant belly, evidently searching his fragmented memory. 'Now, let me see — we had a pair come in, bit unusual. Cavalry, but with bows not swords… Never did see horsemen shoot while riding. Must be tricky, that.'

'When was this? Did you notice anything particular about them?'

'Just the funny bows, sort of curly-like they were. Nothing like we hunt with round these parts. Reminds me of that time years ago — we had the imperial party pass through, all foreign folks you know. When our Nico's mother came here and died, poor lady. So sad, that were, lovely lass and all —.'

Quintus saw he would get nothing more coherent from the innkeeper, who was a better host than he was a witness.

Once they had let the landlord go, Lossio joined them in the little snug.

'Well, sir,' said Tiro, 'I have to say I've rarely come across someone working with so many people, who knew her so little.'

'Yes, I was thinking much the same,' admitted Quintus. He stretched his bad leg towards the smouldering fire, wishing he hadn't spent so long crouched in the cold outside. 'There is one more thing, though I'm damned if I know what it signifies.'

He reached into his pouch and brought out a small silver disc, hung on a fine broken chain. On the disc was inscribed a symbol. The others peered at it.

'An amulet? Inscribed with a crescent moon, maybe some local goddess? Or could that be "V" for "Victory"?' offered Tiro.

Lossio was silent. He took the necklet from Quintus, looking long at the little disc. He seemed struck with sudden melancholy, as if a deeply-hidden wound had been exposed to light.

Quintus waited, sensing that Lossio was struggling with a sad memory. The Veniconian stirred, and eventually spoke.

'I told you earlier that my father came from the far north of Caledonia, fleeing as a youngster to the lands of the Venicones where he met my mother. What I didn't tell you was that my father claimed to come of a royal family. They ruled the lands between the mountains and the sea, far north of the old Roman forts, north even of the great deep loch which splits the highlands in two. He said he was the survivor of a clan feud, smuggled away by his family when their rule was overturned by a fierce new tribe. The newcomers had come ravening out of the mountains to move into our sea-facing lands. The same new clan had united the bickering northern tribes under one rule, and had begun to be called the Painted People.

'Some years later, our Veniconian lands, too, were threatened by the northerners. Father went back up north, taking only a few warriors as bodyguard. He said he would use his royal position to negotiate with the Painted People; come to an arrangement to keep the tribes content to live alongside each other in peace.'

'What happened?' asked Tiro.

'I don't know. He never returned. Neither did his men.'

Lossio fell silent, and after a while Quintus stood to ease his grumbling leg. He leaned over to toss another log onto the foundering fire.

'What has this to do with the symbols on the dead girl's necklet?'

'Before he left, my father had tried to share with me what was left of our heritage from his family line. He would draw strange marks in the dirt, symbols which he said were his people's way of writing words.' Lossio blinked momentarily, then handed the necklet back to Quintus.

Quintus sat back, staring at the little marks. 'It was this symbol, wasn't it?'

'Yes. He said it meant his tribe, the name of his family. The two lines of the V, these that look like poles with finials — the left one is a spear, representing the warriors of our people. The other pole of the V is a trident, meaning our skills as fishermen living on the long north coast where the sea provides in abundance.'

'And the crescent moon behind the V sign?'

'It means our goddess, the Moon Lady we worship, who holds us in her protection. Or did, until the Great Pict came.'

The final log on the hearth broke with a sharp noise, scattering sparks onto the tiled floor.

Quintus felt his back prickling, and turned to Tiro with sudden intent. 'Tiro, your little lad, with the crooked arm and leg — he said he was friends with Sacra. Do you suppose he might know more that might help us understand? We have to find out whatever we can about this poor dead girl. There's more going on here than the random killing of an unfortunate servant. If there's any connection between the girl and Lossio's news, we need to know urgently. When I inspected the body I found unmistakeable marks of shackles round her wrists. Not the raw wounds made by the iron manacles of slavers, I would judge. I don't think Sacra is a common escaped slave. The marks look more like weals from being routinely tied up with leather or rope hand-cuffs. I wonder about the landlord's soldier guests, but they'll be long gone now. I want to know where this girl came from, and what, or who, she was running from. I'm reluctant to wake poor Nicomedes, he's had a hard enough day, but we can't wait. Fetch him, would you, Tiro? Time may not be on our side.'

Chapter Four

Lagentium

Nico came into the dimly lit snug, looking sleepy. His limp was noticeable, and when he spoke his mouth and tongue seemed occasionally reluctant to work smoothly. But his brain was obviously active, and he was eager to help.

'Sacra was my friend. I want to help catch her killer. I'll t-tell you whatever I can.'

'Good boy! You can start with explaining how you come to be here yourself,' said Quintus warmly. He patted the settle in front of the fire; Tiro had tossed another log on, and the small room was the warmer and brighter for it.

'I've lived here in the mansio all my life. Since my m-mother died when I was born. She was a foreigner, coming from Eboracum with the Augusta after the Caledonian wars. They were heading south to take ship back to Rome. They told me I was born nearly dead, c-cord wrapped round my neck. It took an age to get me out, and then my mother started bleeding. They couldn't stop the bleeding, and she died. I w-was left with my right side like this.'

He pulled up his sleeve to show them his palsied right hand. It was a common enough story, but Quintus was struck by how strong this boy must be to have survived his bad start in life. Nico continued, 'I was lucky. The old mistress was g-good to me. She had no children of her own, and I suppose she felt sorry for me. She insisted I wasn't put out to d-die on the rubbish heap. She begged the master to keep me on, saying I could pay my way when I got older. He wasn't keen, but when she died herself, the master carried on g-giving me food and lodgings and let me work at what I love. It's the horses, you see. I'm mad d-daft about horses. They seem to trust and understand me. I can get a horse to d-do what no-one else can. So I stayed here, and worked in the stables. But all my life, I've never really had a friend, not to speak of. The ostlers and other stable lads often bully me, calling me names and saying I'm blighted by the gods. Till S-Sacra came along. It was me who saw her come into the courtyard, looking for food and a place to stay. I knew the c-cook had run off that very morning with a soldier going north. So I helped Sacra wash off her travel dirt, and took her to the master. He was at his wit's end, with a b-big party of travellers due in that s-same night. Sacra went straight into the kitchen, cooked a wonderful meal, and got herself a job here. She never spoke of where she had come from, or why.'

Tiro leaned forward. 'So Sacra never told you why someone might want to find her?'

'Not to say, *told me*. She k-kept apart from the others, and didn't talk to anyone, much. I noticed that she was shy of strangers, and sometimes when C-Caledonians passed through the inn she would disappear all day. I think she was hiding from someone she feared. But I s-saw her necklace one day when she was leaning over a trough, washing her hair. She told me the signs weren't just pictures, but she wouldn't say what they meant. Another t-time, she described where she lived as a young girl. She told me about seals basking on long white beaches, and great red deer roaming the mountains, and eagles flying so high! And once, when I asked about the m-marks on her wrists, she said it was a terrible secret, and if the bad men who had tied her up ever found her, they would kill her. And me too, for knowing.'

'Thank you, Nico. What you've told us will help us avenge Sacra. Go back to bed now.'

The boy nodded, stifled a yawn, and shuffled out of the room. Lossio shook his head and Tiro too was looking troubled. Quintus recognised the signs, as Tiro opened and shut his mouth to speak without actually saying anything.

'Out with it, Tiro. I suppose you're worried about Nico?'

'I am sir, now you mention it. I think if Sacra's killer is still around, Nico could also be in danger. I don't like to leave him here. Anyway, sir, he's certainly a bright lad, and a dab hand with the horses. We could do with some help — with the horses, I mean.'

Quintus nodded, his mind running on the dead girl, her necklet, the scars on her wrists.

'All right, Tiro,' he said. 'I'll speak to the inn-keeper in the morning.'

He didn't say so, but a fierce desire to save this boy from danger and a dismal life of hard work had arisen in him. Tiro wasn't the only one with a soft heart, he thought ruefully.

In the morning, having gained the consent — for a price — of the innkeeper, they took a delighted and now wide-awake Nicomedes with them, adding a fifth horse to their train. Tiro, in deference to his own sense of decency and the feelings of their new horse-boy, had quietly made arrangements with the local army unit for Sacra to be properly buried beyond the town boundaries.

Lossio had decided to go north with the two investigators. He explained why, as they trotted along the impressive embankment of the straight road running north out of Lagentium, heading towards the village of Calcaria. 'My role remains to gather intelligence from beyond the Aelian Wall, and to keep Governor Rufinus informed with regular reports. I have more reason than ever to come with you, at least some of the way. I've been thinking about how the scullery slave described Sacra's accent.'

'Yes?'

'She said Sacra spoke in an "old-fashioned way, like a Cambrian".'

'What of it?

'Cambria is a long way from here, many weeks travel to the south-west beyond Deva. I think it unlikely a penniless Cambrian woman, fleeing in desperate circumstances, would have come as far as Lagentium. No, I think Sacra was from somewhere else entirely. Again, I have memories of my father to help. He too spoke with a particular accent, the same British words for the most part as Tiro and me, but sounding softer than the Veniconian speech. It's the British tongue all right, but I guess the Cambrians and the people of northern Britannia had a close relationship once. I suspect Sacra was also from the far north.'

'In fact,' said Quintus slowly, 'you think Sacra may have been Pictish herself?'

Tiro, looking puzzled, said, 'But why had she come so far south? Why the scars on her wrists, as if she had spent long periods tied up? And who was she fleeing — surely not her own people?'

'Who indeed?' answered Lossio, his hazel eyes focussed in thought. 'Quintus, I wonder whether there is a connection between Sacra being here, and the reports I'm getting from my scouts about Athair and his people moving south. My source in Trimontium has reported refugees fleeing from well-established settlements along the bank of the Tausa. We don't yet know why, or who they fear, but tied together with my intelligence reports about the Picts, there is no doubt in my mind that Athair will be looking to take over strongholds all along his line of march into the prosperous southern lands.'

'No way of knowing yet,' Quintus said, 'but I'm sure Legate Crescens in Eboracum will be able to tell us more. He's expecting us, and I have a high-level mandate from Governor Rufinus to discuss the implications of your intelligence reports and to work with the legate to improve the security of both our provinces. I expect he will assign a decent-sized body of troopers to help us do just that. Rome cannot ignore the rise of a substantial new threat to our Wall garrisons, with all the risks to the prosperous lands they exist to protect.'

Lossio shook his head, looking sceptical, but Quintus saw no reason why the legate of the Sixth Victrix, who also commanded large forces arrayed along the mighty Roman Wall, would refuse Governor Rufinus's request to assist Quintus to his fullest ability. It was in the interests of the whole island of Britannia.

On the other hand, Quintus was beginning to wish he'd acceded to the begging of his keen deputy, Centurion Marcellus Crispus, commander of their small force in Aquae Sulis, to be allowed to bring an honour guard in company with Quintus.

Marcellus had pleaded. 'You are a senior officer, Quintus, representing our governor in talks with the new legate of the Sixth Victrix legion. It's only fitting that I accompany you.' Quintus had smiled, knowing how eager his bright young deputy was to see more of their country, and to show off his well-trained men.

'Governor Rufinus wishes me to conduct informal talks merely to support and reassure Legate Crescens as he settles in, and to pick up what tidings I can from our scouts in the north. The border has long been peaceful, and I am sure the roads of the northern province will be perfectly safe for Tiro and me to travel along. Anyway, Marcellus, you know I'm planning to stay in Eboracum with Julia until our child is born. That would be far too long for the Summer Country to be left unguarded and unpoliced. I rely on you to keep an eye on our people here, and my daughter, too. You can't have forgotten how recently you had to intervene to protect Aurelia from Fulminata?'

Marcellus had eventually conceded the point, having indeed a lively recollection of the narrow escape Aurelia had from the murderous actress Fulminata before Quintus had returned from Rome the previous summer.

So now Quintus felt obliged to express his confidence in Legate Crescens in front of Tiro and Lossio. But Crescens had not long arrived from Rome, and was rumoured to have recently married a distant relative of Emperor Alexander Severus. Quintus was unlikely ever to forget his own encounters with the boy emperor, and his realisation on that blazing August day in the imperial palace that the poor well-meaning youngster was surrounded by a court of deadly snakes. Not least Alexander Severus's own scheming mother, Augusta Mamaea.

While he put on an air of confidence in front of his companions, Quintus was by no means as sure as he sounded.

Chapter Five

Eboracum

'Corellia, if I hear one more drunken idiot wishing me *Io Saturnalia!* I shall scream.'

Julia's doorman grinned at Corellia Velva as Julia and her friend passed under the red-berried garland hung over the front door. Julia lowered herself, groaning, onto a couch in the vestibule.

'Let me help you, Domina,' the old slave insisted. Julia gratefully allowed Fronto to take off her pattens, as she could no longer reach over easily to do so herself. Fronto had known her since she was a young girl coming on trips from her Durotrigan home in the Summer Country, staying with her Brigantian grandmother and aunt. Now Julia was the owner of this rather gaudy Eboracum property, with all the complexities her aunt's extended business and land holdings had bequeathed. She knew she shouldn't begrudge the legacy, which would leave the Aurelianus family even more wealthy and influential. She just wished this windfall hadn't come her way so shortly before her child was due.

Britta followed the two ladies inside, shaking mud off Julia's thick mantle, and removing her Saturnalia mask. 'You've only yourself to blame if you're tired, mistress,' she grumbled. 'What were you and Corellia Velva thinking, going out tonight when all the silly slaves of Eboracum are out and about, drunk as lords?' She added to Fronto, 'They'll soon remember their place when they have to come back to work with stinking hangovers tomorrow. At least you kept your wits, Fronto.'

The doorman smiled, saying, 'I've had my foolish years of Saturnalia carousing, Britta. Nowadays I prefer to stay at home in front of a nice bit of fire. And someone has to guard Lady Julia's door, and make sure all the young merrymakers get in safely.'

Fronto bowed in Corellia, then bolted the door. Julia thanked him as Corellia unwrapped her enveloping palla and mantle, saying a little wistfully, 'It was fun tonight, though, wasn't it? And the feast here was wonderful, Julia! Especially that delicious suckling pig.'

As Corellia spoke, a loud bang came at the door, making them all jump. The urgent knock was immediately repeated, before Fronto could even drag back the bolts. Corellia frowned.

'Now who's that so late, I wonder? A friend with Saturnalia trinkets to present, perhaps, Julia?'

But the young female who practically fell through the door was neither a friend, nor bearing seasonal gifts. She was a richly dressed, dark-skinned slave, who tore off her silken fringed mask in panic. As soon as she spoke, Julia registered the north African accent.

'Lady Julia, Domina Corellia — you must help me! It's my mistress!'

'Salvia? What's wrong?' asked Julia, recognising the personal maid of Placidia Septimia. Corellia led the distraught slave by her arm into the salon, where the hypocaust and braziers kept the room warmer than the draughty vestibule.

Salvia drew a ragged breath, and took the offered seat before beginning her tale.

'The domina and I went out in her litter after our household feast was over, and all the palace servants had left to enjoy the festivities. My lady Placidia was so eager to enjoy the street parties. And... umm...and it's her first Saturnalia away from her family.' The girl paused, keeping her eyes lowered. She seemed to have lost her nerve. Julia glanced at Corellia, who nodded back.

Julia spoke for them both. 'You'll need to do better than that, Salvia. If you want us to help Placidia Septimia, you *must* be truthful and tell us the rest of it. It wasn't just an innocent desire to celebrate Saturnalia, was it?'

Julia kept her voice firm, although she felt sorry for the young slave who was accustomed to the careful guardianship of a large noble establishment in Leptis Magna. The rough streets of this muddy British city, perpetually under reconstruction and full of loud soldiers and bustling merchants, must feel like another planet to the poor girl. And how could Salvia prevent her high-born mistress from acting foolishly? Nevertheless, she watched with a stern look as the girl turned her face mask nervously around in her hands.

Julia tried again. 'I think I can guess what has happened.' Salvia looked surprised.

'The two of you dressed yourselves in bright Saturnalia clothes, covered your faces with masks, waited till the palace staff had enjoyed their feast, and then disappeared away to join the street crowds with your identities hidden like everyone else. I suppose the legate was not at home? Maybe he'd already gone out, perhaps on cult duties to conduct the official observations of Saturn's festival?'

'No, Lady Julia. The dominus is spending the whole festival on a tour of the Wall garrisons. He won't be back for at least another two days. But you're right about the rest. Though we did take the litter, to begin with.'

'And left it where?' asked Corellia.

'Across the bridge, Domina. By the fort.'

Corellia slammed her hand palm down on the low table.

'You mean by the gateway to the Tribune's houses, don't you? Loitering by the Dextra gate like two common lovesick street girls waiting for soldiers!'

'No, Domina, it wasn't like that,' the girl protested, tears brimming at Corellia's scathing tone. But the attack had worked; Salvia now told the full story. Placidia had fallen for the pretty boy Gaius Laelianus when they were barely more than children in Leptis Magna, and had fancied herself in love with him ever since. He had done nothing to turn her attentions away, no doubt flattered to have won the heart of a member of the imperial family. Even after Placidia had married and come to Britannia, Laelianus had pursued his flirtation. Salvia had not been in on the evening's plan, but as they arrived at the fort, Placidia told her that she had sent her lover a bangle of twisted gold and silver. It was a prearranged signal, alerting Tribune Laelianus that Placidia Septimia was leaving her marital home to elope with him.

But the Tribune wasn't at the agreed meeting point outside the fort. Placidia had become anxious, sending her maid to look for him. She herself would gain admittance to the fort. Surely the guards at the gate would recognise her high status, and help her find her officer? When Salvia returned after a fruitless traipse through the crowded streets of the celebrating city, the litter remained, but the bearers had gone and Placidia was nowhere to be found. The heavily armed soldiers at the gate merely laughed at her, and then seemed inclined to banter with the pretty slave girl. Salvia left in confusion, imagining that Placidia had already met her swain and fled the city.

'I didn't know where else to come for help, Lady Julia!' Salvia broke down again into weeping, while Julia wished profoundly this hadn't happened. The linen bands supporting her belly had rolled up and were beginning to rub her skin; she was tired; and she had no idea how to manage this situation. Mentally she dismissed the foolish Placidia to her just desserts, knowing nevertheless that she would have to try to salvage this scandal. Quintus, a most loyal subject of Placidia's cousin the emperor, would no doubt expect Julia to do something to save the girl from herself. For a moment, Julia's resentment was diverted towards her own husband, who was never around when she needed him. Then she thought of her mentor goddess, Minerva the ever-merciful and just, and knew that Lady Minerva would expect Julia to take action.

Corellia sat unmoving, with deep frown marks between her straight dark brows, while Britta excused herself to leave the room. Julia kept thinking about Placidia, inexperienced and new to Britannia. Even as a mature native woman herself, of substantial position and means, Julia knew how difficult it was to live life here as an independent woman worthy of respect. How much worse would the outcome be for Placidia, young and naive, having come from a pampered life in Africa? Marius Crescens was also said to be ambitious and ruthless, and thus unlikely to act magnanimously when he discovered his prestigious wife was missing.

They would have to act quickly, if Placidia was to be saved from the consequences of her own actions. Julia heaved herself back onto her sore feet, saying firmly, 'We must go after Placidia now to stop this madness. If we can get her home before the palace household returns tonight, we may be able to stop a scandal developing and save Placidia from herself. And from that foolish puppy, Gaius Laelianus!' She rang peremptorily for Fronto, as Britta came back in bearing thick cloaks and a pair of lanterns.

'Fronto, get a stout stick, and dress warmly to accompany us out, please. We have an emergency: our friend the governor's wife Placidia Septimia has mislaid her way in the city. We need to find her, discreetly. Lock the house up, please. If any of our people come home early, they'll just have to wait on the garden terrace till we get back.'

She glanced at Salvia, thinking she would be more hindrance than help out in the city; the girl had gone completely to pieces. She had better stay here until there was news of her missing mistress. Fronto, loyal old servant that he was, kept his peace while he bustled around. The look of worry on his face was eloquent enough. Attempting to locate a single masked woman on the very night of the year when every slave, employee and commoner was out getting drunk and creating mayhem — it was the definition of madness.

Julia loved her husband, the senior Governor's Man in Britannia, and valued his optio, Tiro, immensely. But she didn't need Britta hissing in her ear as the four of them left the house, swaddled and masked, 'We should wait till the master and Tiro are here, my lady. This is no task for you. If you end up dropping that baby into the gutter, what shall I tell Dominus Quintus?'

Julia was just relieved that her child had for once paused the perpetual internal kicking and roiling. She walked on steadily, knowing she looked more like a wallowing corbita under full sail than any kind of authority figure. 'Curse you, Placidia,' she said under her breath, 'and curse your puerile lover and harsh husband too!'

The streets of Eboracum were even more chaotic than when they'd left them an hour earlier. They struggled against the revelling crowds, taking care to avoid the many guttering candles held aloft in unsteady hands. Fronto led them confidently along alleyways and smaller passages to avoid the more raucous merrymakers, crossing the bridge to the legionary fortress.

'No, Domina,' insisted the guard at the porta praetoria, wiping his dripping red nose and stamping hobnailed boots to keep some feeling in his feet, 'no civilians have entered the fortress tonight. Even on Saturnalia — especially on Saturnalia — we keep a careful watch. Some of the men are inclined, with a few drinks taken, to bring in ladies of the town, begging your pardon, Domina. And that's something the praefectus castrorum don't allow nohow.'

'More's the pity,' echoed his companion in a lugubrious voice. 'Might just brighten up the evening for us what's left on duty, bit of chat with some pretty girls.'

'Pretty! With all our boys out throwing their money around in the taverns and brothels, any whores left free to come here peddling their wares are bound to be the scrapings of the barrel.'

Britta stifled a giggle, and the guard seemed suddenly to remember who he was addressing. He subsided into a mutter, saying that with the legate out of town, the martinet who ran the camp in his absence was spoiling everyone's fun by insisting on a tight ship, all rosters of guards and sentries fully manned, at full attention. And absolutely no civilian visitors permitted.

'Could you tell me whether Tribune Gaius Laelianus is in the fort tonight?' asked Julia, determined to persevere.

The second guard answered in the negative. 'I believe the tribune is off-duty, Domina. Leastways, we saw him leave the camp at sunset, and he's not come back yet. The senior officers are all out, barring the camp prefect.' This was said so resentfully that Julia had to hide a smile. She thanked the two sentries, and turned away, saying to her companions, 'Well, that's pretty much what I expected to hear. At least we know Placidia didn't get inside the fort.'

'I don't see how that helps at all,' said Corellia, sounding exasperated. 'We could spend all evening staggering around the streets till we're dying of fatigue and cold, and only find Placidia by falling over her.'

Julia said, 'Look, why don't we split into pairs? We can cover the ground twice as fast. How about Britta and I go east, and you two go west? Search the streets around the fort, and then meet us at the bridge in, say, half an hour? We'll begin combing through the colonia once we've ruled out the streets round the fortress.'

They parted as Julia had suggested, each pair taking a lantern to head in opposite directions. But there was no need to wait long to meet up. Barely a minute later, Britta grabbed Julia's arm. Julia heard Corellia's distinctive voice, raised to a strained pitch, coming from the next street.

'Julia! Britta! Come quickly!' Britta gathered up her skirts and set off at full tilt, running with surprisingly light feet along the narrow gravelled street. Julia did her best, but couldn't keep up with Britta. She was puffing badly by the time she rounded the corner into the fitful light of the lanterns, both held high, where the multangular tower of the fortress masked the immediate view beyond. She found three people gathered together, leaning over an ominously still bundle tucked into the dark crevice between the tower and the fort's dextra wall. Julia slowed, struggling to walk.

'My lady,' said Britta in a shaky voice, 'we've found her. But I'm afraid...Julia, she's dead!' Corellia had knelt down by the bundle, her face white and scared in the lantern's beams. Fronto turned to Julia, puzzled, as his mistress halted.

Julia was suddenly obliged to lean against the tower, feeling the cold bricks mercifully solid under her trembling hands. She couldn't move, and she knew only the wall was keeping her upright. Her legs were wet with a gush of warm fluid. *No, no, not now!* she thought in despair, as an irresistible wave rose and then crashed through her, tying her whole body into a knot of hard agony for what felt like an eternity. When she could draw breath again, she gasped, 'Britta, I'm sorry! Fronto, can you — can you help me...' Britta caught her as she collapsed. Corellia, who had crouched to check Placidia's body for signs of life, turned as two mounted soldiers emerged from the shadows of the cobbled street. They clattered towards the three women and the old man.

'*Deodamnatus!*' said a voice Julia knew and loved. 'What in Hades is going on here?'

Chapter Six

Eboracum

Tiro didn't know where to put himself. The whole house was in turmoil. Some lady called Corellia, together with Britta and the female slaves, had formed a women-only huddle and was ordering the men of the household around. And the boss was looking as if the three Furies were plucking at him with their brass-studded scourges.

It was all so bloody unfair! They'd arrived in the city at the end of a long cold journey, and by the time they reached Julia's house only Nico was still amused by the street parties. They'd pushed their struggling horses past drunks and whores, through beer and vomit, to find the house dark and deserted apart from an unknown slavegirl. At the sight of the four of them she started up such a caterwauling that Tiro would cheerfully have smacked her. If he wasn't such a gentleman, that is, and if Quintus hadn't taken the girl firmly by the shoulders, asking in his calm voice where everyone was. She stopped screeching long enough to tell them that Domina Julia had gone out late, with Britta and another lady, to find the missing legate's wife. Taking as their only protection some old bloke waving a stick, when Saturn himself knew the streets were packed full of boozing louts.

'What's all this about the legate's wife, sir? If Legate Crescens has lost his missus, why is it Lady Julia who's out looking for her, instead of him and his squaddies?'

Quintus merely shrugged, his face hard. It wasn't an expression Tiro liked to see, as it invariably meant they were about to pile into trouble. He was in hearty agreement, therefore, when Quintus brusquely told Nicomedes to stay behind. The boy looked crestfallen, until Quintus added more gently, 'I need you here, Nico, to take charge of the house in case my wife and the other ladies come back and need your help. Can I rely on you?' The boy nodded, holding his weary body straighter, and the three men, having checked their weapons, remounted and rode off towards the bridge.

It was a good job they'd gone so smartly. They arrived outside the walls of the fort to find Britta struggling to hold Julia, who was coming round from a faint. The other lady — Corellia Velva, who turned out to be a friend of both Lady Julia and the legate's wife — was sitting on the filthy cobbles, silent with shock, her arms round the dead Placidia Septimia.

Tiro left Quintus to look after Julia, who was clearly in great pain and strangely disinclined to greet her lord with affection. Britta made shooing-away gestures to Tiro. It was quite a relief to get let off, thought Tiro, not a man who felt at ease round whelping women. He persuaded Corellia to let him look at the dead girl. The poor lass was limp but not yet cold, and at first he could not tell how she had died. It was only when Quintus momentarily swapped his living, cursing, wife for the dead woman that they made a discovery.

There was faint pinpoint bruising to her face, especially the eyelids. No signs on her throat yet, but as Lossio said under his breath to Tiro, highly likely to be strangulation. The fort surgeon would have to confirm the cause of death as the bruises emerged over the next few hours. Tiro also noted the mask in her hand, her undisturbed clothes, and the fortune she was wearing in exotic jewellery.

Quintus hurried back to Julia. Tiro went with Lossio Veda to the fortress gate, where they persuaded the guards to report the death of the legate's wife. That set the cat among the pigeons, too, with well-oiled legionaries running round shouting at each other until, mercifully, the praefectus castrorum, a grizzled veteran with many years' service under his belt, came striding out and put an immediate stop to the panic. Tiro told him briefly about the girl's presenting bruises and what little more the women had reported of the incident, leaving him to organise a party to collect the girl and bring her home to the palace. Tiro reckoned that was the end of his responsibilities to Placidia, for now at least. He foresaw they would get dragged back into that mess soon enough, but he needed to arrange urgent transport home for his own lady.

There was no chance of heaving Julia onto a horse in her present condition. Fortunately Camp Prefect Antonius Gargilianus was responsive to Tiro's urgent request, and let them borrow a litter from the fort. It wasn't long before they'd got Julia, breathing fast and folding over in pain every few minutes, on board the litter. Leaving Corellia and Britta to follow them with a couple of likewise-borrowed soldiers to manage the horses and lanterns, the four men heaved up the litter and carried the panting Julia home.

And ever since, Tiro thought resentfully, he'd been like a spare part at a wedding.

The rest of the night should have passed quickly for Tiro, who was able to sleep through anything and was feeling worn out. But Britta thought otherwise, and made a point of waking him in the black reaches of the night, telling him sharply to run to the Serapeum, to fetch the wise women skilled in childbirth.

'Corellia is doing what she can, but we need the trained Sisters. The baby is turned wrong, and poor Julia is tiring and in great pain. Get over there as fast as you can; don't come back without the Sisters.' If Britta hadn't looked so tired and pale herself, so obviously on the edge of tears, Tiro might have had something to say at this peremptory order. The thought of Julia's danger and what Quintus must be going through was enough to add wings to his feet. He'd barely turned the first corner when he heard the rat-a-tat of swift hooves, catching him up quickly. He looked round as little Nico, awake, saddled, mounted and in skilful control of Pegasus, the fiercest of Julia's hunters, surged past. The boy waved and cantered out of sight, taking the next sharp bend with consummate ease. Tiro had time to wonder how the midwife would fare on the tall hunter, but guessed Nico would be in command of that, too.

Once the senior Sister was safely landed from Nico's returning horse and in charge of Julia's room with two younger assistants, the house went very quiet. Tiro hoped the slaves had all crept back unnoticed from the Saturnalia celebrations and simply gone to bed. He feared rather that everyone was fully aware of the drama taking place upstairs, and that the house was holding its collective breath.

Quintus didn't appear at all. Tiro assumed the women had kept him in the antechamber outside, where occasional bulletins were issued by the female cohort.

He was making his fourth libation of the night to the lares, the gods of the household, when Britta came to join him. She said nothing, but he knew she was upset. He had never seen her so subdued. When she had also bowed to the gods, he took her cold hand and led her to sit on a couch.

'It'll be fine,' he began. 'The Sisters of Serapis are highly regarded. Lady Julia herself came here to train with them as a young girl, and you know what a fine healer the domina is. She couldn't be in better hands.'

Britta's mouth trembled, and she turned to nestle her head against his shoulder. 'I thought it was bad when she gave birth to Aurelia all those years ago — such a slow, difficult delivery. But this is worse, and she's not young any more. If they can't turn the babe to face right...' She got up slowly, and took herself out of the room — he assumed back to her struggling mistress, to help her fight for her own life and the life of her baby.

With Britta gone, Tiro felt his skin turning clammy despite the warmth from the heated floor. If Julia died, the boss would never be the same man. He would go back to being the damaged soldier Tiro had first met, crushed by guilt and trauma. Only last year, but it seemed so long ago. Quintus might even leave Britannia, abandon his daughter Aurelia, go away as if their whole British adventure had never happened.

Tiro sat, slumped, head in his hands. The room was still and silent. Eventually, he slid into a doze.

A hand laid on his shoulder woke Tiro with sudden dread. It was dawn and Quintus stood in front of him, drawn, with shadows under his eyes.

'Sir — Lady Julia? The baby?'

Quintus thumped down onto Tiro's couch as if his legs had simply given way. Tiro couldn't bear to look at him. They sat side by side, in a terrible quiet that seemed to stretch out beyond measure. At last Tiro forced himself to look at his boss.

THE LOYAL CENTURION

Quintus was weeping. The iron man, the contained Italian patrician who never revealed his feelings, Beneficiarius Quintus Valerius of Rome was crying like a child. Before he could react, Tiro's arm was grabbed and he was dragged to his feet. Quintus pulled his optio into a bear hug. Tiro could feel Quintus's whole body trembling, as he whispered, 'She's alive, Tiro. My magnificent, strong, beautiful Julia. And we have a son. Our son, Flavius. I can't believe it!'

Tiro could only nod, his own fears evaporating into relief as he heard that most welcome of sounds — the strong-lunged squall of a newborn.

The senior wise woman, whose name Tiro never did discover, stalked into the salon a short while later, ushered in by an unusually respectful Britta. Addressing Quintus as if speaking to a recalcitrant schoolboy, she told him he was doubly lucky: to have a son, and still to have a wife.

'Your wife should not have been allowed out in the streets at all, especially not at Saturnalia,' the stern-faced Sister declared. 'You are fortunate, Beneficiarius. Only the timely intervention of the god Serapis, and my own extensive knowledge as his elder priestess has kept Julia alive. The child likewise. Did you know the baby was not due to be birthed for some weeks yet? He's small, of course, but my intervention with our great Serapis, the healer and protector of women, has given you a strong hearty son who sucks already.' She sniffed, her horsey face indicating she was not necessarily in agreement with the god that the Governor's Man deserved such good fortune.

'I am needed elsewhere,' she went on. 'I will leave my acolytes here to assist Lady Julia's recovery for a few days. She has lost blood, and is very tired after her travail. She will need time to rest and heal.' The old woman turned as if to leave, then seemed to see Tiro's grin. It was, he assured Britta later, merely a smile of relief and gratitude; the senior Sister, however, seemed to take umbrage, and snorted at him. She paused to issue final instructions to Quintus.

'Get a wet-nurse immediately, young man. Your son suckles

43

well, but your wife is too fatigued to produce enough milk for a babe born before his time. He will be hungry, day and night. Get a stout wet-nurse, feed her well, keep her inside your walls, and let your wife recover in good time.'

Her parting shot, as her long robe trailed her out of the room, was, 'Look after your wife and son, Quintus Valerius. Be grateful you have them.'

'That's you told, sir,' said Tiro, bursting into laughter. Britta smiled too, but Quintus had grasped his opportunity as soon as the ferocious healer had departed; he was already taking the stairs two at a time, on his way upstairs to meet Flavius Valerius, and to gather Julia into his arms.

Britta turned to Tiro. Her expression was so much softer than he was used to that his willing heart raced into a quicker beat. She opened her mouth to speak as Fronto came into the room, looking harassed. He was ineffectually attempting to maintain his dignity in the face of the craggy soldier accompanying him.

'Optio, here is a messenger from the fortress. I have explained the dominus is not available at the moment, but he wouldn't be denied, and insists on seeing someone in authority.'

Tiro doubted himself to be any kind of authority, but as Britta kept her mouth shut, and the soldier had advanced to stand with legs planted apart on the main mosaic of the salon, he stood to receive the message.

'Legate Marius Crescens, commander of the Sixth Victrix legion and governor of the northern province, requires the urgent attendance of Senior Beneficiarius Quintus Valerius.'

'The beneficiarius is not available —' began Tiro, in what he hoped would pass for a parade-ground subaltern's voice. The soldier ignored the remark, maintaining a martial stance. Tiro decided the man looked ridiculous, and was composing a more suitable retort when Britta broke in.

'Legionary, may I offer you refreshments while the beneficiarius is summoned?' She somehow induced the soldier to follow her out of the room in the direction of the kitchens. Tiro thought grimly it was the unsubtle sashay of her hips that did the trick. Britta had a wealth of such feminine ways at her disposal, which always surprised Tiro, who knew to his cost the rough side of her tongue.

Tiro frowned as he went upstairs to break up the family reunion. A Roman officer was never off duty, it seemed. He did not expect the boss to be happy about this untimely summons.

He was right.

'Tell the legate where to stuff himself,' said Quintus tranquilly. He was sitting on the bed next to Julia, the new baby lying between them. The infant was swaddled and looked milkily content for now. Tiro could never see the allure of newborn babies, all wrinkled red skin and squashed features. But apparently Flavius looked attractive to his parents, judging by their faces.

Quintus glanced at Tiro, adding, 'No doubt Legate Crescens wants us to avenge his wife. Well, she won't be any more dead tomorrow, but *my* wife, if I have anything to do with it, will at least be more comfortable and rested by the morning. I'm staying right here to make sure.'

But Julia, looking pale and crumpled against the linen bolster, said softly to her husband, 'For my friend Placidia. Please, Quintus.'

Quintus took her face in his hands to kiss her. Slowly releasing her, he rose to join his deputy.

'By Mithras, he'd better have a damned good reason to call us now!'

Tiro, relieved he wouldn't have to relay a refusal to the legate's messenger, swallowed his own resentment and followed the Governor's Man downstairs. He flicked a look at Britta, as he straightened his uniform and sheathed his sword. Britta nodded at Tiro, and then, astonishingly, blew him a kiss.

Suddenly this new day felt brighter. Tiro was ready for business again.

Chapter Seven

Eboracum

Legate Marius Crescens stood in the centre of the room, hands on hips, as Quintus, Tiro and Lossio entered his office in the fortress basilica. On the wall behind him was the dramatic image of a pawing bull, symbol of the Sixth Victrix legion. The legate was flanked by six senior officers, among them five tribunes wearing tunics with a narrow purple stripe. Tiro noted the absence of the senior broad-stripe tribune, Gaius Laelianus. His place was taken by Camp Prefect Gargilianus, a large man whose nose had suffered in the past. The older man gave an almost imperceptible nod of recognition to Lossio Veda.

Legate Marius Crescens was a similar age to Quintus, in his early thirties and nearing the peak of his military career as general of the Sixth Victrix legion. There ended any resemblance between the two Roman officers. Set against Quintus's lean wiriness and quiet looks, the legate was beefy, red-faced, and seemed full of himself. Good living and lack of exercise had rounded his belly noticeably. He spoke in an arrogant voice, and as he moved a flop of thick chestnut hair fell over his forehead. Tiro was inclined to dislike the man on sight, and hoped this would be a short meeting. Later he thought he should have been more careful what he wished for.

'Beneficiarius Quintus Valerius,' said Crescens.

'Sir,' acknowledged Quintus. 'This is Lossio Veda, speculator in charge of locus management in Caledonia, who was attached to your predecessor's staff before moving to Britannia Superior. And may I introduce my assistant —'

'Yes, yes,' the legate broke in, glancing at Lossio but not deigning to look at Tiro. 'I summoned you here to demand to know what you're doing about my wife's murder.'

Tiro blinked, taking in the belligerent tone. No grieving widower here. He sneaked a look at Quintus, who was wearing his most rigid expression. The meeting was going swimmingly already.

46

Quintus kept his manners. 'May I offer condolences, sir, both for myself and my wife, Lady Julia Aureliana?'

Some of the arrogant puff may have leaked out of the legate. He looked momentarily ill at ease.

'Lady Julia? Of the Durotriges and the Brigantes?'

'Indeed, sir.' To Tiro's apt ear, Quintus sounded as dry as a mouthful of Arabian sand.

'Ah. Yes, well, I'm sure she has told you how young and naive my wife was. It was foolish of Placidia to venture out unaccompanied at Saturnalia; only to be expected that some slave would attack her. She insisted on wearing her expensive jewellery at all times.'

Quintus made no immediate reply to that. After a moment of apparent consideration, he said in the tone of a junior officer offering a humble view to a superior, 'And yet her jewellery was apparently untouched, sir. When we inspected her body, we found she was wearing bangles of ivory and jet, together with earrings and a gold pendant. What other jewellery might she have been wearing, sir?'

Legate Crescens glared, then blustered, 'I hardly know. I am not my wife's maid! Who, by the way, is still missing. What about that, hey? She must have been in on the plot!'

Tiro now realised the legate was as stupid as he was bullying, and fought to keep back a snigger. Quintus, poker-faced still, answered smoothly, 'Salvia is in my care and helping with our enquiries, sir. It was Salvia who reported to my wife that Placidia Septimia had gone missing last night. I think she would have been unlikely to do so had she been involved in a plot to murder your wife. Salvia was about to return to your household this morning with us, had your command not arrived first.'

Tiro noticed that the legate's piggy eyes were a strange blue, a hot shade shot through with burst blood vessels. Tiro could have sworn they were bulging a little, and hoped the beneficiarius would not allow too much resentment to build up in one who was, unfortunately, their commander in this province.

Quintus bore on unremittingly. 'Which plot do you mean, sir?' The camp prefect, who had stood like stone at the end of the row of flanking officers till now, gave a slight shake of the head. But it was plain to Tiro that his boss had the bit between his teeth. There was to be no shaking him off. 'From the condition of Placidia's body when I saw her first, I believe she was strangled. Her clothing was not disarranged, and as far as we know nothing was stolen. That does not suggest a chance attack by a passerby. Especially as she had removed her Saturnalia mask, and her body was found near the fort. I think it possible she may have known her attacker.'

Crescens opened his mouth, then closed it when the nearest tribune murmured in his ear. Instead he looked around the room, as if seeking inspiration.

'Ha! I knew her to be a little hussy. Never one to do her duty, to provide the heir I married her for. Instead of staying at home like a good wife, weaving my clothes and running a sober modest household, she was out at all hours, dressed like a tart and mixing with the bucks of the city. Well, she got her just desserts, thanks be to Juno. What do you think of that, Beneficiarius?'

Quintus looked frustrated, as well he might. Tiro and he both knew that Placidia mixed in unimpeachable social circles. But they'd also heard from Salvia that Placidia had confessed she was planning to run away with the missing Tribune Gaius Laelianus. She had hardly been dressed like a tart; her bright but elegant festival clothing would have suited the imperial court. Whether or not she had ever found her tribune, it seemed she had left home with the intention of meeting him, and then paid a high price for trying to escape her marriage.

Tiro was not surprised when Quintus asked, 'Could she have been expecting to meet someone outside the fort, Legate?'

The answer was screaming out to be heard, but Crescens seemed reluctant to give it.

'How should I know? I've been away on a tour of the Wall forts.'

'Was there anyone she was close to?' persevered Quintus.

'Apart from your own wife Julia and her louche friends, who I blame for setting a poor example?'

Now the legate was being downright insulting. Tiro stepped forward, ignoring a fierce warning look from the camp prefect.

Quintus whitened, but said evenly, 'Not now, Tiro. I'll overlook the legate's remark, coming as it does from a newly-bereaved man.'

There was a long silence, while the murmuring tribune once more gained his superior's ear.

Crescens nodded, and said stiffly, 'I believe Placidia was seduced by my senior tribune, Gaius Laelianus, who I am told persuaded my wife to run away with him in an act of outrageous disloyalty. Apparently he is nowhere to be found within the fort.'

'And yet as we know, your wife did not leave with the tribune, wherever he went.'

A sly look crossed the legate's face. 'No. He must have changed his mind, or come to his senses. Instead he killed my darling wife, leaving her body where I would know of his cruel infamy!'

It was all the most ridiculous farrago of fantasies, and not at all convincing to Tiro. Quintus shook his head, while Tiro waited for more fairytales from this stupid but dangerous man. Dangerous because he had power, and no regard for the truth.

Quintus cleared his throat. 'There is something more, sir. An incident in Lagentium I feel you should be aware of.'

'Yes?' The legate looked impatient. Quintus glanced at Lossio, inviting him to contribute.

Lossio took a step forward. 'We found the body of a woman I believe to be Pictish, who was murdered recently in circumstances that suggest she had escaped from kidnappers. Coupled with recent reports from my speculatores, it raises suspicions in my mind. We would appreciate your permission to investigate.'

Strictly speaking, there was no formal need for permission. Lossio was no longer on the staff of Britannia Inferior in Eboracum, as he now reported directly to the governor in Londinium, this legate's superior officer. Thus he did not need Crescens' permission to act, whilst Quintus and Tiro had never reported to Crescens or his forerunners. But without the co-operation and resources of the northern governor, they would struggle to carry out effective investigations. They all three knew that; and so did Marius Crescens. The sly look was back on his face. But Tiro, glancing at the solid camp prefect standing to the legate's left, saw that the beaky-nosed man seemed troubled. The legate again leaned over as one of his tribunes whispered. He straightened, and now the slyness had hardened into triumph.

'I see no reason why the death of a native woman, no doubt a working girl of a certain kind, as all these filthy natives tend to be, needs to concern the Roman administration. Let us not be side-tracked from more important matters. I wish you to immediately pursue Tribune Gaius Laelianus and take him into custody for my darling Placidia's murder. You will concentrate on that task, and only that task, if you know what is good for you. You are in my jurisdiction now, Beneficiarius, not that of Governor Rufinus. Remember that.'

Quintus looked wooden. 'Very well, sir. The tribune is clearly not present in the fort. May I begin my enquiries?'

The legate brightened at this. Tiro gave up trying to make sense of what was on the mind of this unpleasant bully, glad to follow the boss and Lossio out, now they had permission to go. Quintus must know what he was doing. Mustn't he?

They retreated through the imposing hall of the principia, passing between huge gritstone pillars on either side. Eight men, forming a smartly-turned out guard at the legion's shrine, clashed spears as they passed. This was the sacred heart of the principia, where the standards of the Sixth Victrix and statues of the three Capitoline gods were reverently housed. It seemed an over-large show of manpower to Tiro, but maybe there was much to protect in the legion's strongroom below stairs. Tiro grinned at the image of generations of Roman legionaries serving in this remote city. They had certainly deserved their pensions.

The risen winter sun was now washing down from the clerestory windows of the hall, high above. Outside they crossed the courtyard towards the tribune's houses lining the main street of the fort. The bulky camp prefect stepped out from a side alley to intercept them. Lossio held out his hand, smiling.

'Antonius Gargilianus! You keep well, I hope?'

The camp prefect's big features brightened. 'Lossio Veda, back from the south. It has been a long time since we served together.'

'Long indeed, my brother. How are matters here?'

The big man looked around.

'Come with me. You will wish to search Tribune Laelianus's house. But we should not be seen together.'

He quickly ushered them inside the young tribune's home, decorated with simple white panels bordered by red and black paint. It didn't take long to look around the house, which bore all the hallmarks of abandonment. Tiro could see nothing incriminating, or indeed useful.

'I was hoping to locate a twisted wire bangle Salvia told us about,' Quintus said to Gargilianus. 'If that love-token of Placidia's is here, then it would seem unlikely that Laelianus planned to kill her and simply abscond. It would be immediately damning, and only a fool would leave it lying around his home.'

Tiro had been thinking about that, too. 'Yes, but sir, if he did kill her, wouldn't he simply take the bangle with him, or throw it away somewhere to make it look like she was robbed by a stranger?'

'Or,' offered Gargilianus, 'it could have been taken by someone else. But I may be able to tell you more of Gaius, to put your mind at rest about his involvement with Placidia Septimia.'

'Right,' said Quintus, sitting down on one of the tribune's camp stools. 'Tell your story, Praefectus.'

Gargilianus settled himself gingerly onto another stool, being a big man easily capable of breaking furniture.

'It's like this. I've had a soft spot for that silly boy from when he first arrived in Eboracum with the new legate's party. He was clearly out of his depth, being the only son of a family with ambition and money, but not much sense. I took him under my wing, so to speak, seeing as how the legate was not going to help the lad along at all. But then he started making sheep's eyes at the domina. He confessed they'd been childhood sweethearts, back in Leptis Magna. I told him plain, it's a fool's errand. You're begging for dismissal at the least; more likely a knife between the ribs from the legate's lackeys.'

Lossio raised his eyebrows. 'You mean the other tribunes?'

'Yes, of course. They're all in it together. The legate brought his own gaggle of courtiers with him from Rome.'

'All in *what* together?' Quintus asked sharply.

The big prefect shrugged his solid shoulders. 'Don't know, Beneficiarius. I've not been able to put my finger on it, but ever since the new legate arrived there's been a crooked feel round here. Not like in our day, Lossio.'

'No, indeed,' said Lossio. 'Our old legate was a principled man. He knew how to keep peace beyond the Wall and protect our little province. Only today I heard that our allies in Lothian, the Votadini, are restless and unhappy. Not sure why, something to do with delayed payments. Another worry.'

Antonius Gargilianus sighed, resting raw hands on his big knees.

'Things are different now, Lossio. And I'd swear by Hercules, something rotten is happening in the Wall forts, too. Trouble is, what with being praefectus castrorum, I rarely get outside the fort. Nor the city, really. All I can tell you are the last words of one soldier, sent badly injured from Vindolanda to our base hospital here in Eboracum a few weeks ago. Some sort of grudge gone bad, I believe. He was knifed in a night attack in the vicus, probably caught out with some local's wife. I went to see him — part of my duties to know all the men on roster, wherever they've come from. He was in a bad way. The wound had festered and the army surgeon told me the miasma was rotting him away. I was at his bedside when the man suddenly came babbling out of his coma. I sat with him for a while, in case there was anything to be learned. There was. He talked about "the barbarians inside the camp", and something about silver being turned into swords. At the end, he seemed to know me. He grabbed my hand, hard, and whispered, "The Sabine women are taken. You must save them. The beehives…" Then he died, still with his fire-hot hand in mine. I asked the resident priest to interpret his words. He couldn't tell me much, but wondered whether the mention of "beehive" was an allusion to the goddess Mellona, who fed Jupiter Best and Greatest on honey. I went to our temple of Jupiter here, and made sacrifice of a fine black cockerel. But I've had no sign from the gods. Until your governor sent you back, Lossio my friend.'

Gargilianus was clearly a devout man. Rightly so, thought Tiro. It was well worthwhile in Tiro's view to stay on the side of the gods. Tiro watched Quintus taking the measure of this experienced soldier, and saw the moment when his expression firmed. Quintus had decided to trust Antonius Gargilianus, as Lossio evidently already did.

Lossio spoke first. 'There may be something in that soldier's words, if we could understand them. We're not here just to butter up your boss, Antonius. For some time I've been collating worrying reports coming out of this province and beyond from my speculator network. Perhaps nothing to do with the death of Placidia Septimia, but your dying soldier's words might have meaning.'

'Well,' said Antonius, adjusting his thick cloak as he stood up, 'There's little enough else I can do to help you. My instincts tell me Gaius is an innocent man being incriminated for a murder he would never have committed. But there's no denying he's scarpered, the gods know where. Set himself up for a manhunt right enough.'

'You don't think he's killed his lover, sir?' asked Tiro.

'Nope.' The big man shook his head decisively. 'He really was besotted with her. Just foolish about trying to win her back. Once her family had promised her to Crescens he had no chance, and so I told him. I warned him, knowing the legate to have a vicious side to him when crossed. Gaius is a good enough lad, but not the sharpest gladius in the rack. Touchingly loyal, though.'

'So,' Quintus mused, 'they could have planned to run away together, as Salvia claims, under cover of the masked street festival. And with the legate away on his tour, it was probably the best possible time.'

Antonius coughed. 'Umm, yes, about that.'

'Well?'

'The legate did go away a couple of weeks ago all right, and apparently came back early today, as you say. I thought it a strange time to go on tour, right in the dead of winter, when he should have been here to lead the cult ceremonies to Saturn. It's expected of the legate, you know. But a message came from him three days ago, telling his pet tribune he was leaving Vercovicium fort to come back home.'

'And?'

'Doesn't take three days to travel from Vercovicium, even at this time of year. It's a good fast road, has to be with all our military traffic. Even with snow, he'd have needed no more than two days at the most. And there's been no snow of late.'

He looked significantly at Quintus. 'Be careful, Beneficiarius. I doubt your enquiries, whether into this, or your dead Lagentium girl or any other business, will prosper. Not without some solid boys to back you up. You can rely on me to send word if I discover anything else.' He saluted, and left Tiro wondering.

As they walked to the main gate, with the smell of a delicious African stew wafting from a nearby barrackroom, one of the tribunes crossed the street to them. He handed Quintus a wooden tablet.

'Orders, Beneficiarius Valerius. From the legate,' he added unnecessarily. 'You're to go to Vindolanda immediately. Reports are coming in — the adulterous murderer Gaius Laelianus has been seen on that road. You're to track him down and arrest him.'

Quintus waited till the man was out of earshot, before saying, 'Right. We need to get back to Julia's house. I suspect Crescens will have eyes and ears on us, so we'll have to leave quickly.'

Lossio opened his mouth, but Quintus added, 'Without you, Lossio. I would have been glad of your guidance and country knowledge, but now I think it imperative we keep someone reliable in Eboracum. You can liaise with Antonius, keep us informed of developments here, and watch over Salvia if you would. And —' Quintus paused, looking awkward, '— I need someone I can trust to protect my home. Crescens wasn't subtle with his threats. He knows where my family lives, and he'll soon hear that Julia can't be moved anytime soon. Would you be willing to take care of our household, Lossio? In my stead?'

Lossio's hazel eyes took on a solemn aspect.

'It would be an honour, Beneficiarius. You have my word; your family will be safe with me. And I'll do my best to keep you informed while you're away.'

He held out his arm, and Quintus grasped it hard. The stern look hadn't left the boss's face, and now Tiro saw worry there as well. Not surprising, really, he thought. This was a right bloody mess they'd got into. Chances of a happy outcome? Not good, he reckoned. He wished Marcellus and the Aquae Sulis boys were with them. *Probably out on patrol right now, looking forward to an evening in the riverside tavern with their paws wrapped round jugs of good Summer Country cider. These spies of Lossio's — how much use are they really? Being scattered all round the empty Caledonian mountains and glens. Not much.*

Tiro shook his head. He followed the Governor's Man and the spy chief out through the south gate of the fortress, turning towards the bridge.

Every vestige of his formerly bright mood had well and truly vanished.

Chapter Eight

Eboracum

Julia woke. The baby was making little sucking noises, but when she opened her eyes to look for the wetnurse, she found Quintus instead. He was holding Flavius, rocking him with his little finger in the sleeping baby's mouth. He smiled when he saw she was looking at him.

'Don't worry, he's been very well fed. I let the wetnurse girl — what's her name? — go to the kitchen for something to eat.'

'Her name is Veloriga, she is a nice clean girl, and has more than enough milk for our greedy son.' Julia was amazed to see her proper Roman husband holding their newborn son so tenderly. He crooned happily at Flavius, seeming completely at ease with the tiny sleeping bundle in his arms.

She sighed with contentment, snuggling back under the bedclothes.

'Julia,' she heard. She forced her eyes open. She really was tired.

'Could we talk later, Quintus? I'm so sleepy just now.'

A look of concern crossed his face. 'Have the healer Sisters gone? Should they not be here still?'

'Don't worry, darling. I'm fine, they were very happy with me. And I have Britta fussing around me plenty, now she's found Veloriga to nurse Flavius. I just need my sleep. What was it you came to tell me? Can it wait till later?'

Quintus sat down on the bed, still holding the baby securely. He really was surprisingly good at this, Julia thought. *What a pity he missed Aurelia as a baby. Never mind, he's here now to enjoy these early days with Flavius —*

'Julia,' said her husband in a tone of voice she recognised and mistrusted. She forced herself onto the alert. She focussed on the abstracted look, knowing he was about to give her some bad news.

'It's Gaius Laelianus. He's disappeared. Word is he's been seen heading west along the Stanegate.'

'Why is this your problem?'

'Because the legate has persuaded himself, against all the

evidence, that it was Gaius Laelianus who murdered Placidia.'

'And?' Julia actually didn't want to hear what she guessed was coming. She watched her husband fixedly. He had the grace to look abashed.

'Legate Crescens has ordered us to Vindolanda in search of Gaius.'

'What if he isn't there? No murder suspect in their right mind would wander into the biggest and best-armed fort on the Aelian Wall.'

'He may not be in his right mind. If he saw or suspected Placidia had been killed, he might have panicked and run away. And from what I've heard, Vindolanda is itself suspicious. Praefectus Gargilianus has warned us that all is not well there.'

Julia surged upright, shedding bedclothes, her fatigue and pain forgotten. 'By the goddess Minerva, you're doing it again, aren't you?' Her raised voice woke Flavius, whose little face quickly turned red as he began the sharp scream of a newborn. His hands emerged like starfish out of his swaddling clothes as he built up his distress levels. 'Now look what you've done!'

Britta came into the room. She seemed to guess Flavius would be better off away. She removed his heir from Quintus, muttering something about the baby needing a change. Julia paused her anger until the door was closed behind Britta, and then launched her weaponry.

'Quintus, you are my husband. I have just given birth to your son and narrowly escaped death, according to the Sisters. You keep saying you love me. Can I not have some time and attention from you, even now? Must your work always come between us?'

Quintus drew his brows together, and rubbed his scarred leg. It was a sign Julia recognised, showing he was both worried and emotional, even as his disciplined face displayed little beyond distraction. She hardened her heart. Too many times Quintus had put his duty before their happiness, or even before his own safety: at Corinium when he'd faced off a legion, insanely offering single combat when he was already wounded; again, when he'd sailed from Massilia into certain danger in Rome, knowing that she was ill and had taken ship in the opposite direction; a third time in the imperial palace itself, attempting to rescue the pathetic boy emperor and keep his promise to Governor Rufinus.

Even Aradius Rufinus comes ahead of me and our children, she thought furiously, goading her own resentment.

'We have to go, Julia. The words of a dying soldier from a Wall fort can't be ignored. Passed on to me today by Praefectus Gargilianus, a decent man and a worried one, I judge. What that sick lad said to him might be key, if I can only understand it. At the least it's more indication, if we need any, that there is trouble beyond the Wall. Crescens has more to hide than his relationship with Placidia. I must go to Vindolanda to uncover what.'

Julia felt sick. She was so weary, her body only beginning to recover from the birth. She desperately wanted Quintus to stay. She knew he wouldn't. Duty always trumped love. He would go; he would be betrayed; he would never come back from that great wilderness north of the Aelian Wall. Suddenly the fight went out of her. She turned her face away, and felt hot tears soaking her pillow. Her hand was taken, pressed hard, kissed passionately. She did not move, would not turn.

'I *do* love you, more than ever, more than anyone, always,' she heard him say softly. 'I will come back to you; to you, Aurelia, and Flavius.'

Julia burst into sobs, not hearing the door open and gently close. Only when Britta came in with a lamp much later did she turn her head, to find the short winter afternoon was over and she had been left in the dark.

Vindolanda

The last fort they had passed — a tiny place whose name Quintus neither noticed nor remembered — was several miles behind them on the Stanegate military road when Tiro nodded ahead.

'That must be Vindolanda, sir. It's certainly white enough.'

The large fort was beautifully sited on a rounded green prominence. In the intermittent sunshine between scudding clouds it gleamed, the whitewash of its rendering reflecting the midday light. A vicus huddled under the pale walls on the west side of the fort. The village was a busy little place full of houses and workshops, a surprising number being armouries. But Vindolanda was a large fort, and possibly provided nearby forts with weaponry, too. They passed a small temple to some local native god, unknown to Quintus. Many of the houses had small gardens attached, with vegetable plots, chicken coops and pig pens. Dark smoke drifted from chimneys and seeped through the roofs of the houses.

'Coal fires. They burn with dark smoke,' said Tiro, surprisingly. Quintus looked at him in enquiry.

'The men in Eboracum told me they burn black rocks in the hearth here instead of wood or charcoal. Like those ashen rocks in the temple of Sulis Minerva, in Aquae Sulis.'

'Been reading, Tiro?'

Tiro looked mock-offended. 'Only what I heard. We don't get burning rocks in Londinium.'

Before passing under the imposing west gateway of the fort, Quintus paused his horse. He needed a moment to mentally prepare before they entered what he feared could be a wolf's den.

It was the fifth day since they'd left Eboracum, and he was no nearer knowing how to proceed with their task. He had several concerns: to their original mission to sniff out the attitudes and intentions of the new northern legate had been added Lossio Veda's uneasy reports of the Painted People, plus the deaths of Sacra and Placidia, which may — or may not, Quintus was willing to concede — be linked. And now Legate Crescens's commands to seek out the fleeing Tribune Laelianus and take him into custody. He glanced along the road they had travelled, seeing nothing.

He continued to sit, gazing at Tiro without seeing him. After a while he became aware that the optio was fidgeting in his saddle, watching him.

'Sir? Something wrong?'

'Apart from everything, you mean?'

Tiro looked concerned. 'I'm sorry you've had to leave Lady Julia and the new baby so soon, but at least there's Britta and Fronto there to manage things. And Lossio Veda and little Nicomedes to keep an eye.'

Quintus looked at Tiro. 'Was it really wise of me to leave Lossio in Eboracum? His skills and languages could be useful here.'

'Someone had to hold Nico down while we left.'

Quintus laughed despite himself. Young Nico had been so determined to come north with them that it had taken firm restraint to deter him. Lossio had taken him in charge, a kindly look on his face as the boy struggled and wept at being left behind.

'That's a very determined boy, despite his withered hand and his limp. And how he got up onto Julia's big hunter with no one seeing, I'll never know. If Fronto hadn't barred the courtyard gate, he'd have been galloping out onto the north road ahead of us!'

Quintus tucked his knees lightly into his horse's sides to walk on.

'Seriously, Tiro, we'll need to tread carefully here. Antonius Gargilianus warned us of trouble at the Wall forts. I keep going back to what he said about silver being turned into swords. What do you suppose that meant?'

'Dunno, sir.' Tiro had a puzzled look on his face. 'Thing is, you can't live in the Summer Country for long — home of Vebriacum silver and all — without realising how rare and precious the stuff is. I never heard of any silver found beyond the Wall. Except what Rome sends, to keep our native allies in the lowlands happy and on-side. I mean the Votadini and the like. Someone at Coria told me their hillfort of Dunpendyrlaw is just stuffed with silver. Those native chieftains do love Roman money.'

'True enough. Anyway, we'll have to make do without Lossio. It seemed to me better to leave him in Eboracum, where he can liaise with Antonius at the fort and get messages to us quickly if there is need. Legate Crescens may not trust us, and we certainly can't trust him, so we need someone on the inside while we're away.'

But Quintus wondered how long it would be before Lossio too fell under suspicion. Whatever his origins north of the Wall, he *was* Governor Rufinus's man, one of his best and most experienced spies, with a useful network of observers in Caledonia. The legate surely knew that by now, and may not want such a man watching him.

His thoughts were broken by a hail from the gatehouse ahead. They gave way to a troop of the Fourth Cohort of Gauls trotting out, intent on an afternoon's hunting to judge by their clothing and the spears they carried. Some also had bows slung across their backs; all were well-bundled up against the chill of the changeable day. No doubt dinner tonight would be enhanced by roast boar or a side of venison.

They entered the fort, passing unusual round stone huts on both sides of the street. Some were apparently in the process of being demolished, looking abandoned and ramshackle. Quintus noticed, though, that the row nearest the barracks had new straw roofs and stout doors, and the stonework looked well-maintained. The sole window in each hut was high up, right under the roofline.

'Pity,' said Tiro, 'the bathhouse is outside the walls, over there.' He pointed to a large bathhouse fit for a sizeable city. 'Still,' he cheered up, 'it might stay dry this afternoon if we get time to wander outside for a bath. And I'll bet they have snacks and beer.'

As it happened, they didn't get to the baths till some time later. The commandant had been forewarned of their arrival, but seemed not to care much. When they went to the fort headquarters to report to him, his clerical officer told them they were expected, but asked them to wait as the prefect was busy. It was a full two hours before they were admitted to his large well-lit office. The prefect was a small mousy man who barely glanced up from his paperwork as they saluted. They waited to be acknowledged. After a few moments, a senior centurion also entered the room. Quintus immediately recognised a fellow beneficiarius, who wore, as Quintus did, a miniature hasta on his baldric. The ceremonial spear badge signified the rank of a senior detached officer on investigative and policing duties.

'Centurion Litorius Pacatianus. He'll assist with your enquiries, and arrange your accommodation.' The prefect did not raise his eyes. He waved dismissively, and turned his attention back to his desk.

Quintus held himself politely erect as they saluted again before leaving the principia, but he could tell Tiro was fuming at their treatment. The two of them were used to being regarded in the south as a senior investigative team, and had been sent here by a superior provincial governor to assist the new legate. Being treated with indifference by a fort commander was not what they expected.

They marched behind the centurion, who also seemed disinclined to acknowledge them or offer any friendly hospitality. He stopped at the doorway to a barracks close to the principia, indicating a suite set aside for visiting officers.

'Your rooms,' Pacatianus said, in a resonant voice. He was older than either of them, probably late thirties. This would make him very experienced, assuming he had joined the army at the normal age of 16 to 18. He was olive-complexioned, with short dark hair shot through with grey threads. His severe face had the strange pallor of those bred in the Mediterranean region who had lived long in the far north. This was relatively unusual, if it was the case. Most beneficiarii were moved from post to post every few years.

Pacatianus was a muscled man, of medium height and build, strong but lacking excess padding. *Probably keeps in shape by boxing or hunting*, thought Quintus, looking him up and down.

'Could you show us where to eat later? Maybe we can buy you a drink, if we're to work with you?' Quintus was making an effort to be polite and friendly. It had struck him they needed an ally in this fort; and who better than a fellow beneficiarius? But there was little response. The centurion seemed unwilling to engage; his brown eyes passed over the two officers quickly before he said, 'Just come to the officers' mess at dusk. We eat then. I'll have your horses taken care of.' He turned abruptly and left them standing outside their rooms.

'Nice bloke,' said Tiro sarcastically.

'Hmm.' Quintus said no more. They dumped their saddle bags on their cots, and finally made their way to the baths. It was only mid-afternoon, but already the air struck chill as the dimming sun lowered itself behind the fort. Some time to wallow in hot water and reflect was much needed before the hard work started, thought Quintus. He doubted Vindolanda would offer much other enjoyment.

THE LOYAL CENTURION

Chapter Nine

Vindolanda

They might not have been accorded the warmest of welcomes, but at least the catering at Vindolanda did the newcomers proud, Tiro was pleased to discover. The fort was big enough to warrant a separate mess hall for officers, who thus did not cook for themselves like their subordinates. Tiro, eagerly sniffing the aroma of hot food, tucked in behind Quintus to enter the well-heated triclinium. The room was a good size, and boasted a barrel ceiling and rich decoration featuring painted panels in pink, grey and pale blue with images of various gods and golden crescent moons, framed in marble-effect decor.

Despite his promotion to the rank of optio, and the imposing bravery phalera glinting on his chest, Tiro felt uneasy at mixing with the fort's upper-class officers. Quintus turned to him with a reassuring smile as they were greeted at the door by a steward, who indicated places for them on a couch set back against a wall, shadowed in the flickering light of the wall-lamps. A few heads turned, and then turned back as they crossed the room. Their couch was already occupied by Beneficiarius Pacatianus. The older officer gave the pair a silent nod, and moved up to allow them room to sit. He beckoned the waiter over. Quintus ordered a Massilian red; Tiro contented himself with local beer. The centurion ordered water. Tiro reclined awkwardly on his left elbow, trying to sip elegantly. His boss, meanwhile, began to engage their curt colleague in conversation.

'I understand you have been in charge of the beneficiariate here at Vindolanda a number of years, Litorius Pacatianus. You must have some interesting experiences to tell of?'

The older beneficiarius's face closed, as if a curtain had dropped.

'Who told you that?'

'I heard from Legate Crescens that you were highly experienced, and that part of your role here is to train officers seconded to the province's policing services.'

Pacatianus merely grunted and applied himself to his water. Tiro felt Quintus stiffening a little. They sat in uncomfortable silence until their food arrived. The smell rising from the tureen placed before them was delicious. It turned out to be neither fresh-killed venison nor boar, but a piquant stew of tiny pork meatballs, soaked in a rich sauce. After waiting impatiently for the two senior officers to serve themselves, Tiro spooned a large portion into his own dish. He could distinguish coriander, leeks, and sweet apples, but there were other mysterious and wonderful flavourings he couldn't tell. Plus honey and vinegar, perhaps, to add a sweet and sour flavour? He was so intent on the food he did not at first notice the slaves refilling their tureen, nor his boss turning politely to try again with the silent Pacatianus.

'Litorius, I was hoping you might be able to give us the lie of the land, here and beyond the Wall. Tiro is a native Briton, but from Londinium. I'm frankly a stranger this far north.'

Litorius stirred, shooting a sharp look at Tiro before allowing his gaze to rest on Quintus. Tiro wondered uneasily what he was looking for. At length the older beneficiarius spoke.

'Yet it is you two, Quintus Valerius, who are renowned for your recent adventures in Britannia. And abroad. There is talk of your part in nullifying the plots of the previous governor of Britannia Superior, Gaius Trebonius, and capturing him for trial. And I hear you prevented an attack on the emperor in his throne room, only last summer.'

Quintus grimaced in acknowledgement, saying, 'I wish we had indeed been able to bring Gaius Trebonius to senate trial in Rome. That justice was denied us. Luckily, Tiro and I were able to protect the young emperor from an associated plot, although we could not save his chief counsellor, Ulpian, alas! It seems nothing works out how one hopes, in the end.'

Now it was Quintus who sat still-faced and silent, while Pacatianus continued to look at him. Around them other officers were deep in conversation at their tables, laughing and drinking. The lamplight was soft in the large room, casting sufficient shadow here on the edge of the room to mask their expressions. Tiro understood when Litorius next spoke, his deep voice lowered, that he had arranged this deliberately. It seemed the severe beneficiarius did not want to be overheard. Tiro's hackles rose in anticipation.

'Given your high-profile previous missions, Quintus Valerius, I wonder why your governor has sent you to us, so far north. What can interest you in our province?'

Quintus also cast a look around at their relaxed fellow diners. Tiro saw they had reached the contented point of filling up the corners: platters of fruit, nuts and sweet cakes had been placed on the low tables, and wine cups and beer tankards refilled. No apparent notice was being taken of the three imperial investigators.

Quintus told their cover story, which had the advantage of being true.

'Ours was a courtesy visit, but after we arrived in Eboracum we were tasked by Legate Crescens with tracking down a tribune who is a suspect in the recent murder of Placidia Septimia, the legate's wife. You'll appreciate the domina's status as a member of the imperial family is of considerable concern.'

Litorius Pacatianus nodded. 'I heard Tribune Gaius Laelianus was seen making for Vindolanda. He has not been seen *in* Vindolanda, however.'

'You are sure?'

The older man frowned. 'I know my job, Quintus Valerius. I have my own sources, as I am sure you have yours.'

Quintus did not immediately reply. Tiro felt his buttock muscles begin to twitch. He was no good at all this subtle nonsense. It was always his instinct to go straight to the point, as he did with his pugio when threatened. He stirred restively, wishing he could stand up. He remained reclining and thought he did a reasonable job of keeping his own voice low. 'Litorius Pacatianus, do you know anything about strangers visiting Vindolanda? Barbarians, as you might say. Maybe trading?'

Quintus flashed a warning look at him, but Tiro was careful not to look at his boss. One of them needed to get somewhere with this man, he felt.

Pacatianus sat slowly upright, apparently considering. He turned to gaze at his colleagues.

'I thank you for your company, gentlemen. We can go over your orders in more detail in the morning. I'll be riding out on my rounds early; you may wish to accompany us, to get a feel for the lie of the land. The earlier the better; the stable boy warns of snow coming in later.'

He said no more, ignoring Tiro's salute as he turned to leave the triclinium. Tiro, watching, saw how scrupulously the other officers avoided looking at Pacatianus as he left, and glanced at Quintus. The boss shrugged.

'Not a popular man. And not a drinker, it seems. But our beneficiarius colleague has more to tell us, in private. He's established our credentials, so he's aware of who we are, and that we are unlikely to be here primarily on a wild goose chase for an innocent man. Yes, I'm certain he knows more, and will tell us in his own way. Be prepared for an early start in the morning, Tiro.'

Tiro grunted and followed his boss out. They too were largely ignored, especially by the braying young gentlemen surrounding the commanding officer at his top table. This was all to the good; the more invisible they remained, the more they could snoop around. Tiro began to look forward to tomorrow. With snooping in mind, he stopped Quintus before they reached the barracks.

'Sir, I'll just look in on our horses, make sure they're sorted.'

'Right. And while you're looking carefully in the stables, do let Nicomedes know that Lady Julia will expect him to take care of her hunter.'

Tiro stopped in astonishment. 'Nico's here, sir?'

'The silly boy has been following us all the way from Eboracum. I am not blind, Tiro, nor deaf. I had hoped he would trust me enough to catch us up, but no matter. Did you not notice I've had quiet words with the inn-keepers along the way? At least he's been fed and watered at each stage, and that fancy horse too.'

Tiro slapped his forehead. 'Well, sir, I have to say you fooled me too. I guessed he would not stay with Lossio and Fronto, no matter how stern you were, but I never spotted him following. How long have you known he was trailing us?'

'Oh, from about noon on the first day. He came too close when we stopped by the roadside for our snack lunch; I thought you might have noticed. Though it is unusual for you to be discreet for so long, I admit. So you didn't see that tall chestnut coming up behind, and then quickly dropping back?'

Tiro blushed, abashed. *Call yourself a horseman, Tiro, and not be able to spot Lady Julia's stallion, whether a mile behind or only a few yards? Shame on you!*

'I can't believe I bollocksed that up, sir. I've been so caught up with this strange country, and so worried about Legate Crescens and his shifty mates back in Eboracum, and what with leaving Lady Julia and Britta there, and little Flavius too...'

Quintus laughed, a welcome relief after the tense evening. 'The family will be fine with Lossio there. But it's time our lad Nico came in from the cold. Make sure he's fed well, and properly bedded down in the warm, will you, Tiro? I'll take more thought for him tomorrow, once we've heard the latest from Beneficiarius Pacatianus.'

Afterwards Tiro realised he had brought it on himself. He hadn't made the time to offer adequate greetings and offerings to the genius loci, the guardian spirit of Vindolanda. He berated himself for his neglect, but by then it was too late. As he rounded a corner making for the stables, the passage ill-lit with a persistent north wind making the nearest wall-flare flicker and blow out, he sensed rather than saw a dark shape coming towards him. A moment later, with the benefit of clouds scudding away to uncover the waxing moon, his night vision kicked in better. A smaller shape next to the large one resolved into Nicomedes, leading the chestnut. A scruffy dog was padding at his heels.

'Nico?' Tiro hissed, nonplussed. The boy paused, but before he could respond two more people approached. Not a lantern-carrying and uniformed watch, as might be expected. These two were wearing dark clothes, clearly making every effort not to be seen. They paused, and Tiro saw the unwelcome glint of moonlight on steel.

This scenario was distressingly familiar to Tiro, reminiscent of the attack at the mansio in Calleva on his first mission with the Governor's Man. Then he ceased to think as he ran forward and his fine-honed pancratium instincts took over. He twisted into a crouch, grabbing the first attacker and throwing him over his shoulder. He heard a clank as the knife flew away, then the sound of a heavy landing, followed by an ominous crack and a piercing shriek. Sounded like the first bloke was now sorted, but Tiro was eager for more. The second attacker was more circumspect in his approach, waving his own dagger around from side to side. Didn't do him much good though -- too damn slow. Tiro slugged him hard, first a lightning punch on the nose, then an uppercut to the jaw that threw the man backwards to slide into an unconscious crumple.

Tiro checked the first man. Ah, that cracking sound had been his arm hitting a mounting block at an awkward angle. Nasty break. The man was crooning in pain, and offered no more resistance. Tiro shrugged and picked up the knife. Unfortunate, but there it was. Shouldn't set just two northerners to attack a London lad. Still, the knife looked a good one, worth keeping.

It seemed the noise of the fracas had not reached beyond the deserted stableyard. The passageway remained empty but for Nico, the horse, and the dog. Nico was holding position despite shivering a little, his good left arm stretched up to calm Lady Julia's Pegasus who was looking sideways at the smell of blood. At Nico's feet was the dog, a rough-haired mongrel of indeterminate breed and age, unhappy but sitting in place. Nico was controlling the animal with a single foot, and although the dog was quivering, she was clearly in thrall to the boy.

Tiro hurried over. Nico pointed towards one of the curious round stone huts flanking their barracks block.

He whispered, 'Sir, my dog smelt someone in that b-beehive hut, and wouldn't leave when we passed. I managed to attract the prisoner's attention, and spoke to her through the window. She's been wrongly locked up and b-badly treated. She needs our help. Please don't be angry, Tiro! We c-can't leave her here. But don't worry — I have a plan worked out with Pegasus.'

Again Tiro shrugged; looked like the genius loci of the place was acting through Nico, and who was he to go against the wishes of the gods? Nico stopped under a small window high up at the back of the hut. He reached his arm up again to the chestnut, pulling its head towards him with affection to whisper softly in the animal's ear. Tiro didn't catch the words, just a soft buzz of communication. He was puzzled to see the horse moving in careful parallel steps to range alongside the hut, stopping with his blanketed back immediately under the window. The moonlight inconveniently faded somewhat as Nico used his good hand to tug the reins out of his clenched right hand. It seemed to Tiro that somehow Nico twisted his left side to lift his other leg over the horse. Pegasus stood stock still, and Tiro thought for a moment the horse was lowering itself slightly, allowing the boy to mount. It seemed an impossible leap for such a small lad onto such a tall horse.

Tiro was still shaking his head in disbelief when the boy tossed a pebble through the little unglazed window. A moment later there was a scuffling noise from inside, and the soft sound of rawhide slippers sliding over stone. By now the moonlight was well dimmed. Tiro moved closer, but all he could discern was a bundle of some kind, not large but solid, tumbling out of the window. It righted itself to land with lithe grace behind Nico, onto Pegasus's broad back. Still the horse remained calm and co-operative. The dog trotted behind as Pegasus moved off under direction from Nico, his left hand wrapped into the mane, the other curled in his lap.

Tiro was too struck by the acrobatics he had just witnessed to say anything. He merely followed silently into the stable, shutting the doors securely behind them. He couldn't wait to see who Nico had just rescued. Although he was already trying not to imagine what the Governor's Man would have to say about the inevitable ensuing complications.

Chapter Ten

Vindolanda

Nico slid down off Pegasus to stroke his dog, but it was the stranger in the stable who attracted Tiro's attention. A young female faced him, dark shoulder-length hair tangled by straw and filth, small strong hands bunched into fists. Around one wrist remained a gnawed loop of fine rope which had left a line of oozing sores like a cruel bracelet. It was obvious her muscular body was on the verge of attack.

Tiro took all this in at a glance, but what stopped him in his tracks were the animals writhing over the girl's skin. Her white arms, as far as he could see in the poor light and the cut of her rough robe, were painted to the shoulder in blue depictions of creatures. The tattoos crowded side by side and above each other: wolf jostled by deer; a serpent wound itself round a bucking horse; an eagle perched above a bull. He wondered whether he might also find the Pictish symbols from Sacra's necklet: the spear, trident, and crescent moon Lossio had told them of in Lagentium. He had bare time to think this before the girl leapt at him, her fists lashing out towards his face.

Only one hand made a brief sliding contact as Tiro reflexively swung aside, causing an eye-watering but not harmful contact on his left cheek-bone. He caught her other fist, noticing the wrist was scarred, and held the girl off as Nico exclaimed, 'No, no, Aila! This is my friend Tiro!'

She seemed disinclined to call off the attack, twisting in an effort to squirm out of Tiro's reach. He was equally determined to keep hold of this wildcat, as he felt sure her nails would be the next weapon to be deployed.

Nico, who still had both his animals under calm control, called again.

'Aila, stop it. Friend!'

Aila was quite small, as short as Nico but sturdier. With eyes now dark-adjusted, Tiro saw a girl in her mid-teens, ferocious of aspect, muscular and as lithe as the female gymnasts he'd seen touring Londinium in travelling shows. She glared at him.

'Who're you looking at? What's your clan?' Her voice was surprisingly strong and commanding, her accent reminding him of the Cambrians he had met in the Summer Country, crossing the Sabrina river from the western country of the Silures.

'Clan? What's she going on about, Nico?' asked Tiro, bewildered.

'You betwattled southern softie! Who's your tribe?'

'I'm from Londinium.'

'Och, betwattled *and* soft in the head. That's a poncy Roman city, nay a clan.'

'My forebears were Cantii,' said Tiro, feeling defensive.

Nico intervened. 'Tiro, this is Aila. Camilla smelt her in that round hut, and we thought — that is Pegasus and I, and Camilla —'

Tiro's wayward interest was distracted. 'You're calling that scruffy mongrel Camilla?'

'*Loyal attendant*? Yes, for so she is.'

Tiro set aside his amusement, knowing what Quintus Valerius would want him to do in this bizarre situation. He said sternly to the girl, 'If I let you go, will you please stop hitting me? I'll leave you to sleep here for a while, but I must take you to my boss before anyone is awake in the morning. You won't be safe for long here. Either of you,' he added, flicking a kinder glance at Nico. 'Yes, he knows you're here, boy.'

Looking around outside for his two damaged victims, he saw that the one with the sideways-smeared nose was still out cold. He was making a bit of an untidy mess in the street. The other had disappeared, presumably to take his broken arm to the fort medicus. Tiro looked carefully at the blood-spattered one for future reference, then shrugged and left. Not his problem any more.

Though he fancied Aila might well become his next problem.

It was a mercy that the winter dawn came so late in these parts. Long before Litorius and his men had roused themselves to begin

71

their morning patrol, Quintus was up and dealing with the unexpected additions to their party. Tiro had told him about Aila. Under cover of an early morning visit to the latrines, the two soldiers made a side-trip. With most of the cohort's horses housed alongside their riders in barracks, there was little traffic before dawn to the separate officers' stables. They encountered no one as they smuggled Aila into their rooms. Nico joined them, leaving his horse and dog to fend for themselves in the stable.

'Well?' Quintus lifted an eyebrow. Aila made a ferocious face at him.

'Another hackit Roman, too feartie to do his own dirty work! Who are you, then?'

Quintus resisted the temptation to rise to the girl's hostility. Under the ferocity, beneath the sinuous painted animals and the dirt, he sensed deep wells of fear and outrage. This young woman would merit careful handling.

'I am Beneficiarius Quintus Valerius, and it may be that I can help you. But you must tell me what has happened to you. How did you come here, to Vindolanda I mean?'

She stared at him, thrusting out a grubby freckled chin. Her answer was hissed.

'The boggin' man my mother was made to marry after they'd killed Fairther — he sold me.'

'Who to?' Quintus kept his voice even. He could see in Aila's dark eyes that she was very close to tipping from anger into panic. He was sure hers was a tale of brutality and trauma, but their need to learn had to take precedence over gentler instincts. As it was, he found it difficult to keep out of his mind another feisty dark-haired girl, his own daughter Aurelia. He must not conjure up the picture of anyone doing to Aurelia what had happened to this girl. He summoned up all his Roman dignitas, and waited.

'That monster, Athair,' she spat. 'His warriors swept into our lands, forced our men young and old to fight, then took everything. Our farms, our fishing runs, our grazing stock, our wealth. They took our leaders, and made them bow the knee. Anyone who refused to be subjugated, they beheaded on the spot. So died my noble fairther; he refused to kneel. They made my mother, my sisters and me kneel by to watch. As my fairther's head was cut off, the hot blood sprayed over my robe. My mother screamed and begged as they dragged her away. They gave her to one of Athair's honoured bodyguard. He took her to his house to despoil her, in front of his other wives. I was offered to another, but I bit him hard in his spear hand before he took me. The hand festered, a right midden it was. They took off the hand to save him. The only family I have left — might have left — are my uncle, my aunt, her sister and my two young cousins. My mother told me she had helped them run away. After that, my mother's man had me sold and sent here. They've been holding me here ever since. These men — the soldiers come at night, and use me when they have no money for the real whores in the vicus.'

As she recounted these horrors, Aila's belligerent attitude softened. Her head began to droop, her voice lowered, and by the end she looked and sounded a subdued and scared girl. As indeed she must be, thought Quintus, again putting images of Aurelia firmly away.

His voice gentle, he asked, 'But why keep you here in Vindolanda, Aila? Surely to make money, the new chieftain — Athair, you called him? — would have you sent to a recognised slave market like the one in Eboracum, or perhaps Pons Aelius or Luguvalio, where you could be sold for decent money?'

She raised her head at this and gave Quintus a penetrating look. He had not seen an expression so scornful since his encounter in Rome with the Augusta Mamaea.

'Athair isn't interested in selling us. He wants only power, and that comes from the land and the people his warriors capture. He wants total dominion. He uses the threat of kidnapping young women to silence his critics, to rid himself of his enemies. You have nay idea what you're getting into here. Get away from this country, before you're eaten up by the wolves. They are tracking you, they circle you, yet you cannot see them. Foolish saft Romans!'

'We —'

Nico made a sharp movement of alarm, signalling silence with his folded-in right hand. He turned his head to listen to a noise outside.

'Get under the cot!' Tiro hissed at Aila. She disappeared instantly, sliding like a serpent into a narrow space under the bunk beds. She was hidden and still long before the door was knocked. At a nod from Quintus, Tiro opened up to reveal one of Pacatianus's men, sheepskin-booted and woollen-cloaked, announcing that the patrol was ready to leave. Quintus remarked casually that their slave boy would stay behind, hoping Nico would have the sense to keep Aila secure and quiet. There would be trouble if not; they had no choice but to keep the escapee hidden as best they could until better plans could be laid.

Outside, the world was wrapped in a chill mist. The temperature had dropped overnight, lending veracity to Pacatianus's warning of snow to come. They left the fort by the east road, soon after breaking away from the Stanegate to cross a small burn which flanked a wood. Beyond, the line of the Aelian Wall reared in the gloom. There was barely light to see the horses around them, as the patrol made its way, two by two, along a rutted trail through dips and hollows towards the trees. Quintus soon realised he could trust his horse not to slip on the frozen trail, as it seemed to know how to cope. It was quiet, the only regular sound being the clink of unshod hooves on icy turfs, and drips off the odd tree branch. Once a jay screeched a harsh call, but Quintus saw no corresponding flash of pink body or blue wings. A flock of redwings harvested berries in scrubby hawthorn trees edging the woodland before fluttering away, scolding each other.

Gradually the mist thinned, and Quintus was able to see their companions in more detail. They were some twenty troopers, well-dressed against the cold, and obviously highly-trained. For the most part they maintained an unbroken silence. Occasionally Litorius Pacatianus, leading, leaned towards his second-in-command in muttered discussion. Once, the young dark-haired optio turned to survey his following colleagues, seeming to be satisfied with his inspection. Under the cover of taller trees the horsemen moved into a single file, picking their way carefully round trunks, hollows, and the odd fallen branch. They were now well inside the wood, screened from both the road and the fort.

Ahead was a clearing, large enough to accommodate the whole troop, where their mounts gathered into a circle. Puzzled, Quintus flicked a glance at Tiro, who shook his hooded head. The other men looked alert, interested and open, rather than puzzled or dismissive as the other soldiers in the fort had been. Quintus wondered about this change of attitude, but on the whole was pleased. Litorius Pacatianus directed his horse to the centre of the circle and paused, pulling his hood back to be heard clearly.

'Men, you will have noticed we have been joined today by two colleagues from the southern province. Quintus Valerius, Tiro, please come forward.'

They did so, flanking the older beneficiarius. Tiro's horse danced a little; he skilfully calmed it. Pacatianus spoke, keeping his voice modulated so it was low but carried well.

'All of us in this troop are hand-picked men, detached from our legions and cohorts to act as investigators, to carry out government missions and investigate crimes. Our duty is to ensure law, order, and justice in our province of Britannia Inferior. As such, we are all sworn to the service of the emperor, under the aegis of our legate as governor and general of the Sixth Victrix legion.

'Quintus Valerius and Tiro are senior investigators sent by Governor Aradius Rufinus in Londinium. They are looking into the murder of a prominent young woman in Eboracum. They have been set on to chase down a tribune from Eboracum, as you may have heard. They are also enquiring about any barbarians seen here at Vindolanda.'

There were definite stirrings among the troop now, heads turning to stare at the two strangers. One or two of the soldiers spoke in subdued tones to his neighbour. Pacatianus, frowning less than Quintus had previously seen, sat quietly until the buzz died down. Puffs of warm breath rose from the horses' noses. A thoughtful silence reigned, disturbed only by a single crow breaking from a nearby tree, cawing loudly and swerving towards the horses before rising away on strongly-beating wings.

Pacatianus spoke again.

'My friends, my brothers, we long ago swore an oath of fealty: to the gods, to our emperor, to our duty; above all, to each other. I ask you now: shall we admit these fellow officers, whose faithful discharge of duty in Britannia and in Rome we have all heard of — shall we admit them into our brotherhood? Shall we share what we know with them?'

His voice rose commandingly, sending a shiver down Quintus's back.

'Shall we join with these, our southern brothers, in the duty to worship Justicia, protect the weak, defend justice, and punish the guilty?'

The silence shattered. With a single voice and movement, the troopers raised their swords and shouted '*Sic erit*! So shall it be!'

Then followed utter stillness, as they watched Quintus and Tiro raising their own swords in salute. It might not be enough to make a difference, but Quintus allowed himself a moment of warmth at the thought that at last, they had allies around them.

For now.

Chapter Eleven

Vindolanda

Over a picnic breakfast of dried meat, bread rolls and soft ewe's cheese, washed down by water and weak beer, the troop rested on branches under ash and elm trees, wrapped in horse blankets, eating and murmuring together. Quintus and Tiro sat with Litorius and his optio, Marcus.

'You were attacked last night, Tiro?' Litorius asked.

'Yes, sir. But one of them got away before I could see his face.'

Marcus spoke up. 'I heard a man reported sick this morning with a smashed elbow. Claimed he'd fallen badly while mounting his horse.'

Tiro laughed. 'Well, he certainly had an accident with a mounting block.'

Litorius narrowed his eyes at that. 'You and your superior seem good at making enemies. As I am myself. That may not matter much now, however. I believe troubles at Vindolanda are coming to a head. Either we will prevail, in which case those injuries are just collateral damage; or our hopes will fail, in which case we won't care. I could not speak openly to you in the mess hall, Quintus Valerius. But now you are joined with us, we can work together.' Marcus nodded in agreement.

'We noticed a constraint between you and the commander's staff,' acknowledged Quintus. He was quickly coming to terms with the change around in their fortunes. 'Do they all mistrust you?'

Litorius did not answer at first. His face was inscrutable. Marcus nodded, saying through a mouthful of cold mutton, 'The centurion and our whole troop were stationed here long before the new legate took over. Soon after Marius Crescens arrived in post at Eboracum, changes began to be made. Not just here in Vindolanda, but all along the Wall. First some of our officers requested new postings, or retired, or were moved on. Then the roundhouses here, which had been partly demolished, were refurbished and made secure as if in readiness for a new wave of prisoners. They had been empty since the wars of Septimius Severus, when Caledonian captives were kept here prior to being sold as slaves in Britannia Superior. They were strong young men, the Caledonians, much in demand as slaves.'

The young optio, brown-eyed and slight of frame, fell silent. His senior officer took up the story. The centurion's features regained the set look of the previous evening. His voice was harsh; his eyes gazed into the distance.

'We soon found out what sort of prisoners were to be housed here. Young girls, all of them, blue-tattooed for the most part. All were from beyond the Wall, speaking several dialects — or so those of our men who were local said. Many came of the Painted People, some from nearer tribes like the Votadini and Venicones. All had been trafficked, to be used as unpaid whores. Never to be sold or freed. To be used, until they died or went mad. It seemed they were sent as some kind of payment. It is said there is a new overlord of the northern tribes, who is determined to control and command all of Caledonia. But I have never heard where the silver has gone, if indeed the girl-trade is paid in silver.'

Quintus nodded and broke in, 'So we were told by our spy chief, Lossio Veda. His reports suggest that the chieftain you refer to is eliminating all possible rivals, within and beyond his own Painted People. We fear he is moving into the fertile lowlands emptied by the recent wars. We have also been told that this man, Athair, is kidnapping young girls to punish any who would defy him. But why are they held here? I don't understand.'

'Neither did I,' said Litorius, looking even grimmer. 'But I was determined to find out. When I discovered these captive girls, I went to the commandant to enquire. He dismissed me, saying they were simply troublemakers or orphans unwanted by their tribes, coming here to fill the need for women at the fort. You must understand, Quintus, there is a permanent shortage of women along the Wall. The country and climate are harsh, it is very remote, and the few professional whores attracted by the soldiers' silver soon become bored and unhappy. They quickly return to the cities and towns of the easier south. In former times, female slaves taken in war and sold to brothel keepers were a solution. But there have been no new slaves since Emperor Caracalla pulled the legions back to the Aelian Wall, at the time of the ceasefire nearly ten years ago.

'Garrisons of young men pinned down on permanent guard duty with few local women can soon become restless and dissatisfied. The commandant made it clear to me I was not to question where these girls had sprung from; I should merely be pleased my men would have female entertainment on tap, inside the fort.'

The young optio broke in. 'Sir, the centurion said you asked about barbarians round here. Strange you should arrive just now to ask that question. Only two days ago, one of our Wall patrols saw a knot of tribesmen emerging from the fort at dusk. They were heading north, and might have been making for either of our mileforts, to cross through into Caledonia. But I think not.'

Quintus cocked his head in enquiry. 'Why not?'

Marcus swallowed. 'Because I saw something odd in Vercovicium myself, a week or so ago. It's our closest sister fort, commanded by an officer who came from Rome on the staff of Legate Crescens. There is a small beneficiariate office there, which like ours dates from before the change of provincial governor. My opposite number and I had been discussing recent reports of unusual movements by tribesmen, parties of Painted People who have rarely been seen this close to the Wall.'

Quintus nodded, remembering Lossio's warnings.

'As we were making our way to the baths, two stable lads went past. I heard one grumble to the other, 'I thought he was staying another day before going to celebrate Saturnalia at Vindolanda. And now we have to get his horses ready to go at the crack of dawn. Another freezing early start.' Shortly after, the legate himself came out of the principia with the commandant. There were two others with them, strangers, and the legate seemed to be bidding them farewell through an interpreter. I didn't see much more, but in the light of a flare carried by the commandant's body slave, I caught a last glimpse. The strangers were not Roman soldiers, I would swear. The taller of the two, the guest of honour, had long loose hair and wore a native plaid cloak. Vercovicium straddles the Aelian Wall, and has a gateway to allow passage north out of the province. I may be wrong, but I would swear the two men left that way. The next morning, the legate and his bodyguard departed east back to Coria.'

Quintus understood. 'And that way leads to the fast road south to Eboracum. We ourselves came that way.'

Litorius sighed. 'Had I known that the legate was not coming here on his Saturnalia tour, as planned, I would have gone myself to Vercovicium. I was already troubled, wondering whether I should report my fears to the legate himself. We of the Wall, we have our own values and our own laws. We do not make needless war on women and children. At this time of peace, the mysterious appearance of shackled young girls makes me very uneasy. From what we can make out, these are not slaves, nor professional women wishing to earn a living. These girls are being wrenched away from their families, or even their husbands, taken for political reasons to browbeat those who would deny the new power rising in the north. I made enquiries at our sister forts; the same stories came back to me. Some of my colleagues elsewhere are as unhappy as I was. Others blessed their good fortune. Some recently posted officers made veiled threats; heated words were exchanged; and gradually my men and I were ostracised. I did not know where to turn, or who could be trusted. Your arrival and your governor's concern are some relief. But I warn you, Quintus, the forces ranged against us are formidable. As yet, I don't see how we are to act.'

Quintus, who had been listening with close attention, shook his head.

'I understand you, Litorius, and I know Tiro and I both agree with your stand. There *are* like-minded others, a few in positions to help us. But I see a bigger, perhaps more complex picture forming, one I dislike very much. As you have found, it's already clear whatever is happening is affecting several of the Wall garrisons, at least. Marcus, did you notice anything else untoward at Vercovicium while you were there?

The young optio thought, then shook his head. 'No, sir, it was just as usual. Very busy with patrols coming and going, masons

80

making wall repairs, the vicus full of industry — I remember wrinkling my nose at the stink of tanners making leather goods, the fires of the smiths, noise of metalworking, and a kiln firing rough pottery for the fort.'

Quintus nodded, turning back to the centurion. 'Litorius, I think you may have had a lucky escape in not meeting the legate at Saturnalia. There are two murdered women to account for, far apart and of very different backgrounds. My fear is they may form part of the same picture, which certainly stretches as far as Eboracum. One of the dead women may not seem at first glance to be connected, and the other, Sacra, was killed many miles south of here. Nevertheless, it was plain from what she told our horse-boy, and evidence we found at the scene, that Sacra too had been stolen from the far north in similar fashion, escaping to what she may have imagined was a place of safety in Lagentium. Poor woman, I fear she was tracked down and killed before she could tell her tale to those in a position to listen and act. I wish —'

He was interrupted by a shout of alarm. A trooper ran across the clearing to Litorius, panting.

'Sir, sir!'

'Slow down, soldier. Make your report properly to the centurion,' said Marcus.

The trooper drew a long breath, facing the centurion more steadily.

'Sir, I went behind some trees to relieve myself, and found — fell over — a body. A stranger, an unknown officer.'

Quintus felt his stomach tumble-turn, and stood quickly. Tiro met his look.

'Sir, could it be—?'

'We'll know soon enough,' Quintus said grimly.

The four officers hurried behind the young trooper as snow began to fall gently out of a heavy steel-grey sky. They were led past men now stirring and alert, on into the shadow of trees where the soft, fat snowflakes were settling on the body of a young tribune. He was lying on his side, almost curled round the bole of a rowan, as if seeking to embrace the spirit of the beautiful tree. Three arrows protruded from his back.

Quintus turned to Litorius.

'Are there archers based at Vindolanda?' he demanded.

'No, but the Wall fort at Magna was long the base of a cohort of Syrian archers. I understand their sons and grandsons have kept the skills alive, and are still operational there. It's a bare dozen miles west along Stanegate.'

'Ah.' Quintus was silent, thinking. He remembered the innkeeper at Lagentium, and his patchy recall of two archers with unusual curly bows.

Marcus broke in. 'Your missing tribune, sir?'

'He may well be. I've never met the unfortunate young man, but he was closely associated with the dead woman in Eboracum, who I was about to tell you of. She was Placidia Septimia, the wife of Legate Crescens. We found her, strangled, at the Eboracum fort. If this is her friend, he may be wearing or carrying something that will identify him.'

Between them, Tiro and Marcus uncoiled the dead man from the rowan and laid him on his side, face turned towards them. His fine purple-fringed cloak, once white, was soiled by bloodstains and mud. The arrows piercing him had caused wounds large enough to glue the cloak to his back with dried blood. He was wearing long breeches tucked into high-quality studded leather boots. His sword was missing, but a silver-embellished belt and baldric still kept his long-sleeved tunic pulled in to his waist. His handsome face, fine-featured and olive-tinted, bore a look of trepidation. He would have been a very frightened young man by the time his enemies caught him up.

They conducted a respectful search, finding little of note until Tiro turned back the dead man's tunic sleeves to reveal a bangle pushed up tight over his elbow. A dainty bangle, made of silver and gold twisted wires, which spoke eloquently of his dead lover's wealth and taste. Tiro exclaimed, sitting back on his heels.

'Well, sir,' he said to Quintus, 'we can safely rule poor Gaius Laelianus out of contention for the death of Placidia Septimia.'

Quintus nodded. 'You're right, Tiro.' He looked down at the dead tribune, wondering. He fingered the shafts of the arrows, noting the arrowheads were trilobate, intended to cause maximum damage to muscles and blood vessels. The drawback of such arrows was that they covered less ground than a lighter bodkin arrow, and would be less effective at piercing armour. They would, however, be perfect for dropping a fleeing target at a close distance, especially if the victim was not wearing armour. Quintus sighed, drawing a hand across his face; he may not have known the young officer, but it was a wasteful and cruel death. At a stroke, too, a witness had been removed from their investigation. He suspected that was the whole point. 'It seems Gaius was being pursued by skilled, ruthless archers, who knew their quarry and were hunting him down like an animal.'

Tiro scratched his chin thoughtfully. Quintus waited.

'Yep,' his optio said suddenly. 'That's it.' He nodded to Quintus. 'I had a good look at one of my attackers, the one I laid out last night. He seemed an ordinary enough sort of bloke. Not like a Syrian, didn't resemble our old friend Tertius at the Vebriacum mines.'

'Well, why would he, even if he was descended from a Syrian archer?' pointed out Quintus reasonably. 'It has been many generations since the Cohort of Archers came here from Syria. Any archers manning the Wall now would have mostly British blood in their veins.'

'That's not it, though,' added Tiro slowly. 'What I did notice, although I reckon I didn't know it at the time, was the calluses. On his hand, I mean.' He paused, and Quintus could almost see the wheels spinning round in Tiro's head.

'What of them?' asked Litorius. 'We all have calluses from arms training. I do myself.' He held out his right hand, showing the build-up of hard skin between his thumb and forefinger. Tiro persevered, colouring a little.

'Yes, sir. But this man had callused fingertips. Especially his right forefinger.'

There was a pregnant silence, until Quintus slapped his colleague on the back.

'By the gods, Tiro, you're right! Litorius has swordplay calluses. *You* were attacked by an archer. No wonder you bettered him in the dark. He certainly wouldn't be as skilled in hand-to-hand combat as you are.'

A gust of cold wind passed between them, bringing with it a whirl of thickening snow. Around them the woods were settling under a white blanket. The clearing was covered more thickly, snow crunching underfoot as the restless horses began to shuffle and stamp in the increasing cold. Marcus signalled to the troop to remount. Litorius turned to Quintus, frowning.

'What should we do with the tribune, Quintus Valerius? Bury him here? Or bring him back to the fort?'

Quintus didn't like the notion of the missing tribune, shot in the back, coming to the attention of the commandant of Vindolanda. He sat still on his horse as he turned options over in his mind.

'I think we should leave him here for now; it is not yet time to reveal this dead man to the fort in general. And, Litorius — there is something else you need to know. My horse-boy Nicomedes has rescued a Pictish girl from one of those roundhouses. We have her hidden for now, but we must get her out of the fort unseen.'

'I see. Well, I agree with you about this dead man. We know there are those hostile to us at Vindolanda. The less they suspect we know, the better. But I fear there is no time to bury the poor soul; the weather is worsening quickly, and we need to move on. I will send a burial party back later. I suppose we must notify his family. Did you say he was from Rome?'

'Africa — Leptis Magna,' said Quintus, absently. He shook his reins in irritation, knowing he was seeing only darkly the outline of connected events, here and in Eboracum.

The troop moved out, their horses' hoofs muffled by the snow. They forced their passage home into a heavy snowstorm, against rising wind and whirling wet flakes. Litorius had allowed the bulk of the party to go ahead of them, led by Marcus, as he and Quintus were still discussing events. Thus it was Marcus, a conscientious and sharp-eyed officer, who spotted the danger first.

He wheeled his surprised horse about, and cantered back to the rear of the little column to reach Litorius.

'Sir! There are archers positioned on the walls, aiming at us. We must get away!'

Litorius drew his cavalry sword, signalling to his men to circle round him.

'It's us two they're after, Litorius,' called Quintus, grimacing. 'You must go on without us. Tell the commandant you came after us, found Gaius, knew us to have killed him to silence him. Tell him you cast about for us, but we had gone. And then the bad weather set in, and you came back to report.'

'Never! We have sworn to support you, to uncover the truth of whatever devilry is going on along the Wall. I will not abandon you. Neither will my men.'

Quintus moved his horse next to the centurion's, grasping Litorius by the arm.

'Listen, brother! If we split up now, we allay any possible suspicion falling on you and your troop. That way you retain freedom of movement, and can help us. We *will* need your help. Do not let me down!'

Litorius nodded, slowly. 'Yes, you are right. We can be safely admitted, I judge, as long as you are not seen. I will defray suspicion as you suggest, and help your horse-boy and the girl join you outside the fort.'

'Right. We'll stay close by till we see Nico and Aila come out.'

'Quintus, if you wish to stop this trade and will take my advice, head north for the old Roman stronghold of Horrea Classis, on the south side of the Tausa estuary. I will furnish you with what directions I can, but I know the speculatores have a man based at Trimontium, on your way. He will help you.'

Quintus waited no more, but clapped his heels into his horse's sides and made straight into the blizzard. Tiro reined his own horse round to follow. He saluted farewell to the troop as the two of them were swallowed up into the storm.

Chapter Twelve

Eboracum

'Mistress? Mistress!'

Julia turned from gazing at her tiny son as Britta came into the bedchamber. She looked away again, not noticing the worry on Britta's face. Julia was too far bound up in her own thoughts to register another's concern.

'It's no good,' she said, holding the little bundle out to her friend in despair. 'Take him away, Britta, back to Veloriga. He just fusses around, turning his head to find milk. Milk I don't have!'

Julia felt tears in her eyes, by no means the first of the day. Truth to tell, she was exhausted with guilt, regret and resentment. Her son loved a stupid milky wetnurse more than his own mother. She couldn't produce enough milk for him, barely any at all; and her attempts to nurse him caused only pain and frustration. Her body was stiff and sore from her labour; her husband had disappeared off on a wild goose chase; and no one seemed to understand that life just wasn't worth living. She sobbed, feeling intensely sorry for herself.

Britta came over, uttering no word of reproach. She took the baby from Julia to lay him carefully in his crib. Then she gathered her mistress into her arms, holding her close while Julia wept.

Some time later a knock came at the open door, and Corellia Velva walked in.

'Julia, my dear! What is all this? I came to congratulate you and to greet your wonderful son, so healthy and strong. I never would have guessed, from the difficulty we had bringing such a tiny chap into the world that he would thrive so only a week or two later. He's growing faster than I have ever seen in a baby.'

She paused, her kind refined face reflecting the sobbing of her friend. Britta nodded a relieved greeting to Corellia. She released Julia, taking Flavius away downstairs with her. Corellia sat until the crying eased a little.

'Julia, my sweet one, Britta came to see me. She's worried about you. She told me you were feeling tired and low. And it's no wonder to me — I was here when Flavius was born. But my dear, now you have a beautiful baby, and so much to look forward to. So I have brought you a visitor, someone who can help you.'

Corellia beckoned to the tiny figure in the doorway. The old woman came in and sat down in a chair next to the bed, reaching for Julia's hand. Corellia smiled fleetingly, and left the room. Julia sobbed herself to an exhausted standstill. The senior Sister of the Serapeum smiled at her, her wise old eyes narrowing as she looked carefully at her former student. She continued to hold Julia's hand, seeming to count carefully. Finally she nodded in apparent satisfaction.

'Well, my dear, perhaps you can tell me what has happened to cause you such distress. I have seen your precious little son, who looks to be prospering splendidly. I can tell that you have no fever, and judging by your ability to weep copiously, also no lack of vital spirit and fluids. That suggests to me that you are gaining strength, and your body is beginning to return to normal. So what is it that ails you?'

Julia was quite shocked. Surely the senior wise woman could tell how desperate she felt, how swollen and leaking her useless breasts were, how empty her life had become? But there the old lady sat, just smiling and holding Julia's hand.

'Oh Mother, everything is dreadful! I cannot feed my son. There is not enough milk, and now he loves the stupid girl my husband hired as nurse more than me, his own mother, who gave him life. And Quintus, he has of course gone away when he is most needed here. He may never come back. Well, he can stay away for ever, as far as I am concerned — I hate him!'

'Do you, my dear? Well, I cannot blame you. He has after all, merely given you two thriving children, and become the great love of your life. How thoughtless of him to go away on his duty as a Roman officer, when I am sure you would admire him much more for turning his back on his mission, his governor and his colleagues.' The clear blue eyes peered into Julia's. 'Or is that wrong?'

Julia pulled herself upright, rubbing her eyes. She stared at the wise woman in resentment.

'Britta said you had come to help me, but all I hear from you is reproach, Mother. I should thank Minerva for my blessings, make offering to Serapis for his care, and welcome the household lares back into my heart — is that it?' She laughed scornfully. The old woman simply nodded.

'Well, my dear, I think you would be sensible to count your blessings. Look about you. You have a comfortable home — actually three, I am told. All here love you. Your husband is doing what he must to protect and safeguard all our people, including you, Aurelia and Flavius. You are beautiful, healthy and young enough to achieve anything more you wish as a healer and leader of your people. Or is that all wrong, too?'

Now Julia saw the crinkles round the wise woman's eyes, and the turned-up corners of her old mouth. She smiled back reluctantly.

'Why then do I feel so overwhelmingly sad and sorry for myself, Mother?'

'Because, my dear, your body shaped itself to bear a great burden, which you have now released into the world as a new person. That has meant changes which you must accept with patience. It takes time to get back into being just Julia, after being Julia-and-Flavius for so many months. The process is hard work, and you must help yourself with that restoration.'

'How?' Now Julia was intrigued, her professional instincts taking over as she saw a path to healing being laid out for her.

'I will prescribe three medicines for you, which taken together will help you recover your strength and spirits more quickly. First, eat fish.'

'Fish? Is there a magic in the spirit of the fish I can absorb?'

'In a manner of speaking. I have often observed in cases like yours that new mothers benefit mightily from eating fish frequently. So ask your housekeeper to order fish, of the sea, mind, and to serve you a portion every day. Secondly, put behind you the thought that only by feeding your son can you be a proper mother. A mother is not merely the one who feeds. She is the one who cares, who holds, who rocks, who sings, who tells her son tales.

Do this for your son, and you will benefit too.'

Julia nodded in understanding. 'And the third thing?'

The old woman rose slowly, shaking out her long robe. 'Go to your goddess, Minerva. Am I not right to think you have neglected her, the wisest of the gods, she of healing and knowledge?'

Julia nodded, her mouth trembling. 'Yes, Mother. You are right. I am ashamed; I have neglected my goddess. I will make amends. Thank you!'

The old woman smiled as she left the room. 'I leave you in the capable hands of Corellia. I hope to see you better, very soon. Bring your son to visit me.'

Corellia came in, carrying Flavius in her arms.

'Such a precious little poppet, Julia! You are a very lucky woman.' Julia, knowing how much her friend had longed for children, burst into tears afresh. This time they were healing tears, tears of empathy for another.

The next day Julia left her bed and her house, for the first time since Flavius had been born. It was a fine winter's day, a still morning of thin sun, clear blue skies, and the faintest of chill breezes. Wrapped up warmly, Julia went with Corellia and Britta to worship at the temple of Minerva, where she unburdened herself to her patron goddess and made a generous sacrifice of chickens and wine. As the priest burned her offering and the delicious aroma rose to the heavens, she felt a weight lifting from her heart. She turned to her companions, clutching Corellia's hand. 'Thank you. You are a wonderful friend to me.'

'You mustn't thank me, my dear, it was Britta who went to beg the senior priestess of Serapis to come to you. I am so glad she did, and just wish I had thought of it myself.'

'Well, I am indebted to both my friends,' said Julia, smiling at Britta. She paused a moment, a cloud crossing her face. 'I just wish Placidia Septimia were here with us. Do you think she sees us, and knows about Flavius?'

'I am sure she does, Julia,' said Britta warmly. 'The gods have her in their kind care now.'

Julia brightened. 'Let's go home to eat honey cakes and drink hot, spiced wine. I want to hear all the news and gossip from you, Corellia!'

As they crossed the forum, a party of decurions decked out in formal purple-striped togas were leaving the curia, where the government of the city was carried out. Corellia whispered, 'Don't look now, but there's our esteemed legate, in company with his cronies.'

Julia paused in thought.

'That reminds me. Let's visit Salvia on our way home.'

Britta knit her brows. 'Yes, Julia, but where is she living now? Surely not with Marius Crescens, after all that's happened! Have you heard where she went, Corellia?'

Corellia paused, too. She said slowly, 'I don't know. But I believe I know someone who will.'

The wine was still warm, and not all the spiced cakes had gone, when Fronto announced Lossio Veda. The tall raw-boned spy chief stalked in, his face breaking into a huge smile to see Julia up and about again. Once he'd been assured all was well in the house, the conversation turned more serious.

Julia explained. 'We're worried about Salvia, Placidia's maid. We've heard nothing of her since she went back to the palace, the day after we found Placidia. We were hoping you might be able to help, Lossio.'

He considered, looking at the three of them in turn before answering. 'Yes, I think it is safe to tell you ladies. You were all good friends of Placidia Septimia, and your husband, Lady Julia, is leading the investigation into her death. Salvia is still in the city, but she's gone into hiding, in a safe house I have found for her. But I think it would do her good to see you; she is alone and fearful with no female company.'

Lossio took them by back streets and alleys on a short but circuitous route downhill towards the river. Behind the city's main bathhouse was a narrow street of modest single-storey houses, the homes of dock workers and bath attendants. Lossio stopped at one of these, looking round carefully before he knocked at the door. It was opened by a burly man, who nodded at Lossio and let them in quickly. They found Salvia seated by a hearth, feeding a small fire. She looked up with surprise, warring expressions of pleasure and apprehension on her little face.

'I beg your pardon, my ladies. I have no suitable wine to offer you. But please do sit down.'

The only other seating was a single rough bench pulled up to the fireside; all three ladies shuffled onto it, rather too close together for comfort. Julia smiled at the nervous girl, saying, 'We are so glad to see you safe and sound, Salvia. Is there anything you need, anything we can get for you?'

'No indeed, Lady Julia. I need very little, and Lossio Veda takes good care of me.' She blushed deeply, and Julia, alerted, looked up at Lossio to see a fond and foolish look cross his face. Julia was about to make some polite acknowledgement when Salvia surprised her. 'But I think there is something I can give *you*, my lady.' She stood, reaching into a cupboard. It was a crude affair of planks fixed across a hole in the wall. She brought out a small letter tablet, wrapped in cloth.

'My lady left this with me for safekeeping, the night she was to meet Gaius...the night she was killed.' Salvia paused, blinking away unshed tears, then went on, 'She said I was to give it only to you, Domina Corellia, or to Lady Julia. She would not trust it to anyone else, so I have not revealed it even to my kind Lossio.' She handed the package to Corellia, who opened it, looking puzzled. She exclaimed, nearly dropping the tablet. Following the flowing words with an unsteady finger, she read silently, holding the wooden cover open on her lap with her other hand. Towards the end of the script, her hand fell away, and she looked up in amazement.

'Do you know what this is, Salvia?'

'No, mistress. I can't read,' Salvia said simply.

Corellia turned to Julia. 'It seems Placidia kept a secret journal, Julia. Written right up to the day she died. In this note she talks obliquely of her journal being a record of her life since she married Legate Crescens. And —' she fell silent a moment. 'Yes, I fear she had discovered that her husband was involved in some kind of conspiracy, one that frightened and alarmed her.' Corellia cleared her throat. 'Placidia writes:

Now I know what Marius is doing, more than ever I must get away. I dare not think how he will act if he finds out what I know. He may already do so. There is no one here I can trust except you, my friends Corellia and Julia, and I would not bring danger to your doors. My only hope is Gaius, who also knows why we must flee. I will run away with him tonight, but in case our plans fail, I leave this note with my trusty Salvia. My journal with full details of all I know is left in the safest possible place. It will come to you, my dearest friends, when it is needed.

I think about the missing girls all the time. I pray to Juno, protector of women, and to Minerva the just, to avenge me should I not survive. Above all, I pray to Serapis, lord of fertility, destiny and fate.

Placidia Septimia

Salvia stared at Julia, a puzzled expression on her narrow face. Britta was frowning, picking at her skirts thoughtfully.

'Well,' said Julia slowly, 'Now we know, at least partly, why poor Placidia was killed and why Gaius has disappeared. It seems they both knew too much. But about what? Who are these girls she mentions? And where is the journal now? I know what Quintus would say if he were here: everything depends on that journal. We must find it. Lossio, any ideas?'

Lossio had been sitting apparently staring at the grubby wall opposite. He turned his hazel eyes to hers.

'Lady Julia, I beg you most earnestly *not* to search for Placidia's journal. Quintus left you in my care because he feared you were being watched. For you to be found looking for evidence of the circumstances of Placidia's death would put you and Domina Corellia in grave danger, I believe. I was struck by one phrase in particular in Placidia's letter: *It will come to you when it is needed.* I think that means Placidia left her journal with someone in a position to watch and intervene at the right time. The book will come to you then. Now I have a difficult choice to make.'

He sat a moment longer in silence, his unfocused eyes drifting back to stare again at the wall. Then he spoke quickly.

'I promised Quintus Valerius I would take care of his family while he was away. But my role is also to act as liaison, and now I have information so sensitive no one else can safely be trusted with it. Give me the letter: it's too revealing to leave here. I will take it myself to Quintus. It may have great bearing on what we suspect is happening all along the Wall, and beyond. I'll call in at Vindolanda, where the beneficiariate base will have the latest intelligence from the locus gatherings. I'm sure to hear more of Quintus and Tiro there.'

Lossio smiled, but Julia thought he looked worried.

'One more thing, Lady Julia. Quintus knew very well he had placed himself beyond the confidence of Legate Crescens, and so he asked me to watch over you and your household, as well as finding Salvia a secure place. I'm unwilling to leave you without protection and a channel of communication while I am gone.' He thought for a moment, then nodded and stood, stretching his tall frame. 'Well, there is someone we can trust — a friend of Tribune Laelianus, someone who has a senior position at the fort and so can watch the comings and goings of the legate's staff. Praefectus Antonius Gargilianus may even know where the tribune has gone. I'll brief him in secret before I leave. And then we must look to the gods to get us all through this mess!'

Chapter Thirteen

Vindolanda

The snow turned out to be quite a blessing, Tiro thought, albeit a very cold one, as he and Quintus circled round Vindolanda to approach the gateway closest to their barracks. They tethered their horses to trees, and crept well out of bow range of the archers posted on the walls. By now the air was so thick with blizzard that any view from the fort would be masked by snow gusting from all directions. Even a master archer like Odysseus would have been hard put to hit anything in this weather. All they could do now was wait for Nicomedes and Aila. Tiro was worried the two young ones would be caught before they had even left the fort.

'It's all up to Litorius now,' Tiro hissed to his boss. 'I just hope he gets those two away without raising a hue and cry!' Quintus nodded.

They had reckoned without the indefatigable Nicomedes. They had barely settled themselves for what Tiro expected would be a freezing wait till sundown, crouched down in the snow to allow it to shroud them, when he heard a faint noise behind. He whirled round in alarm to find Nico right there, finger to lips, swathed in a thick hooded cloak and well-disguised by the snow. The boy crooked his finger, beckoning them to follow. Tiro was already cramped, the cold sunk into his bones, but he and Quintus stretched out their stiff limbs and followed until they had reached well beyond the treeline. In the slight shelter of the trees they found five horses, a shivering dog, and Aila, alert with knife in hand. Tiro was impressed.

They mounted in silence. Nico used a fallen branch as a mounting block; Aila merely leapt onto her horse in her athletic way. Nico, transferring the reins from his strong left into his clenched right hand, apparently knew where he was taking them. In single file they emerged from the woods and made for the Vindolanda milecastle. Tiro had no idea how they were to pass through unchallenged, but Litorius had seen to that. Nico showed

94

a pass to the guard, and he nodded them through the gateway.

Abruptly they were out on the other side, the Aelian Wall behind them. For the first time in Tiro's life he had left the Roman empire, and they were entirely alone in barbarian territory. Tiro shuddered. Even in their worst moments in Rome, he had not felt this insecure. Quintus held his hand up, and they gathered round as he looked at Nico.

'Sir,' said the boy, 'Centurion Pacatianus gave me directions and a map. Also food supplies.' He held out a little wooden tablet. Quintus moved under the shelter of a tree to scan the instructions.

'Excellent! Litorius suggests we pick up Dere Street, but with caution. We'll need to strike across country initially to reach that road. At all costs we must avoid meeting patrols out of the Wall forts between Vindolanda and Coria. We don't know how many have been suborned, but to play safe we must not be seen by any soldier of the Aelian garrisons. Once we're on the fast road running north from Eboracum, we go via the old fort of Trimontium, making for the firth of Bodotria. The Severan fort at Carumabo on Bodotria was abandoned by the army some years ago, but Litorius says there is a sizeable Roman settlement there still, retired soldiers and traders. From there we should be able to take Emperor Caracalla's bridge across Bodotria to get through Fiv, the peninsula country of our allies the Venicones. Litorius believes there to be a good road across Fiv, leading to the fortress of Horrea Classis on the south side of Tausa. That was a mighty stronghold and fortified harbour built by Emperor Septimius Severus. I was stationed there myself, briefly, before we campaigned further north with Caracalla to draw out the Caledonians.'

Quintus sighed, evidently remembering the glory days of the old emperor's final war, when it seemed inevitable that he and his mighty army — 50,000 strong, as Tiro recalled — would quickly quell the ill-equipped, untrained barbarians. Then it had all gone horribly wrong: the boss had seen his beloved younger brother Flavius killed, had his own leg smashed up, and recovered from his near-fatal wound weeks later, only to hear that his emperor was dead. Most of the army — what was left of it — had scuttled back to Rome, never to return.

Tiro shuddered, and spat over his shoulder for luck. Did they really want to venture into this deadly country full of savages, in the midst of the coldest winter he had ever known?

I dunno who the gods are round here, but whoever you are, just tip me the wink and I'll make sure we do the generous by you. Whatever sacrifice or offering you like! Can't promise better than that, hey? Though you might have to wait till we get back home, cos I have no idea where we're going. Or why, come to that.

He gazed at his boss, wondering what he was planning. Quintus looked up from Litorius's tablet and glanced at Tiro, shaking his head. There would be nothing forthcoming from the Governor's Man yet, Tiro knew.

'We'd best not keep the horses standing in this cold,' Quintus said. 'Let's get as far as we can while we have fresh snowfall to cover our tracks. When it gets dark we'll take shelter for the night. I have some rough ideas of how to progress with our investigation, perhaps even a plan. But we'll need to take some thought for Nico and Aila. You two will need warm food and shelter soon. You can't come much further with us.'

Nico opened his mouth to protest, but Aila leaned forward on her horse, saying fiercely, 'Ye'll no get me scuttling awa' like a feartie! Ma hame is ahead, not behind.' She closed her mouth like a trap, refusing to look again at Quintus. He raised an eyebrow but said no more. Camilla the dog was standing alert, tail out, pointing her nose into the northerly breeze. Quintus pulled his hood down and led them onwards into the snowfall.

It was a long cold day. They found no settlement, and were forced to make rough camp in the dark. Fortunately there was plenty of firewood, and Litorius had furnished generous rations, even a cook pot which Nico had slung over the saddle of the packhorse. Once they had eaten, Tiro threw some ox-tail bones to Camilla, who settled near the fire to crunch and splinter her treat before lying down to sleep next to Nico. Aila was wrapped in a large blanket with her moccasin-clad feet tucked inside. Only her dark blue eyes and the red tip of her nose showed, but she was humming to herself. After a while, Tiro asked what she sang.

'Och, it's a wee ditty my mother taught me. It's a song we use to charm the fish to the surface when we go fishing. That's women's work in our tribe, fishing.' She fell silent, and Tiro wanted to hug the girl, knowing it was unlikely she would ever see her mother again. He thought of another pretty-voiced young girl, Vibia in Rome. That memory made it difficult to talk, so he contented himself with saying, 'You have a lovely voice, Aila.'

'You do,' added Nico. 'I know that song, too,' he added, in a low voice.

'How so?' Aila sounded surprised.

Nico looked at her, and Tiro felt for him as he explained.

'I had a dear friend called Sacra, who may have been of your tribe. She told me tales of her home, the open coast looking north over great ceaseless waters. She wore a necklace with signs like your pictures.' He reached for a stick, and drew the crescent moon, the trident and the spear, in the ashes of the fire. Aila looked closer, and said suddenly, 'But I know these signs!'

Quintus had been sitting at a little distance, letting the young people and the dog have access to the fire, but now he moved over to Aila. He pulled Sacra's silver necklet out of his pouch, offering it to her. She took it, holding the glinting amulet towards the firelight to make out the engravings.

'So, my sister, you are found.' Her dark head bowed; she was lost in thought, or sorrow, for a long moment. Tiro wondered what Aila meant. He tried not to intrude on her obvious grief, but after a while he had to shuffle his numb feet. She looked up.

'Tell me of this necklet, how you found it. The bonnie lass who wore this, Aine, was my foster-sister, my best friend. She was amongst the first to be taken when Athair and his men attacked us.'

Tiro reached to grasp her cold hand in comfort; she let him hold it, gazing still at the necklet. It was Quintus who answered.

'We found a dead young woman, your Aine as I fear, a long way south at Lagentium. She was working at a mansio, having escaped traffickers, and she befriended Nicomedes. I am sorry: it seems she was pursued by evil men, who I believe killed her to stop her telling the story of her kidnapping to the Roman magistrates.'

Aila said nothing, but her pinched face drained whiter. She sat in silence, but she was shuddering so hard, Tiro had to tighten his grip to keep her small frozen hand in his. Nico stood awkwardly, and limped round the fire to sit with her, shoulder to shoulder with the shivering girl. Camilla followed, offering warm comfort in her own way.

Quintus said gently, 'I am very sorry to be the one to tell you this, Aila. But I'll say something else: Tiro and I will ensure your foster-sister is avenged. The men who did this to your family and friends will be unmasked, cut down and destroyed. I promise you that. I suspect these same men are also the killers of a Roman woman and her lover, who would have told of what they had discovered. I am convinced this evil has cast its shadow far into our own country.'

Nico stirred at Aila's side. 'Quintus Valerius, sir? You've reminded me of s-something odd I heard, the night we arrived in Eboracum. You remember, you told me to stay behind in Lady Julia's townhouse, while you went in search of her? Well, I did, sir — for a while. But then I thought I would just nip outside, a quick patrol to check the garden terrace and the street. I wandered downhill onto the bridge for a moment, j-just to see the festival and all.' His thin face appealed to the boss not to be angry with him for disobeying, and Quintus nodded, showing quick interest.

'Well sir, I came up behind three men in the street leading up to the fort from the river, and one of them was wearing especially fine robes, all bright green and gold edging. He was masked, like everyone. Another man c-came up and said to the fine man, 'Were the auspices good at the evening sacrifice, sir?' And the first man nodded, saying, 'The auspices are excellent tonight, my friend.' I thought little of it, sir, and soon after went back home to wait for you. But I should have t-told you, because it occurred to me later that the person who conducts the sacrifices and reads the auspices at Saturnalia —'

'— is the senior priest. Who is also the senior civilian and military leader in Eboracum,' Quintus finished for the boy, his face and voice both grim.

'Legate Crescens!' Tiro blurted out. 'Just as Praefectus Gargilianus suspected — he was in Eboracum all along!'

'Yes, it seems the legate's alibi of touring the Wall forts for the whole holiday was a lie. If Nico heard aright, he was really prowling the streets of Eboracum when his wife was strangled. Too many coincidences: Crescens hiding his whereabouts on the night Placidia met her death, and Gaius Laelianus disappearing the same evening,' said Quintus. 'Gaius was still carrying their love token, that bangle, when he was killed here, suggesting he intended to honour his vow to Placidia. I think he went to meet her as planned, and something — or someone — prevented them meeting.'

'Perhaps he did go to meet her, and found her already dead?' Tiro said. 'But no, Placidia's skin felt warm when I picked her up. Surely we, or anyone around the fort at that time, would have seen him?'

'Someone else did see him, I imagine. I don't know who, but the outcome was that Gaius feared, rightly, for his own life too. Hence his desperate flight to Vindolanda. But they caught him all right, the poor young man.' His gaze turned to Aila and Nico, still sitting huddled together, with Camilla curled up between them. 'I am reluctant for either of you to continue any further north in our company. I must go on, and Tiro, I hope, comes with me. But now I think this path is too dangerous for you.'

'But sir,' broke in Nicomedes, leaning forward eagerly, 'why? Nothing has changed since this morning.'

'Yes, it has. We know more since we spoke of this earlier. The scale of this business, whatever its main purpose, has been revealed. Aila has told us that Sacra, or Aine as she knew her, was kidnapped and trafficked from the Pictish lands of the north coast. Despite escaping from her captor, she was ruthlessly tracked and murdered far away in Lagentium. We'd already been warned by Antonius in Eboracum, and Litorius at Vindolanda, that all is not well in the Wall garrisons. Marcus tells of Picts being welcomed through the Wall, crossing in and out of Vercovicium with impunity. And then there are the archers from Magna who attacked you, Tiro.

'Now Nico tells us that the legate lied about his whereabouts at Saturnalia. Together with finding Tribune Laelianus dead at Vindolanda, we cannot escape the conclusion that these deaths are linked. These are markers of a large conspiracy, the sort of treason that Governor Rufinus fears and Speculator Lossio Veda could smell in his espionage reports.'

'But then, sir,' said Nico, 'we are surrounded by enemies! How can I take Aila safely back to Eboracum? Or would you leave us unprotected in some barbarian village?'

Tiro stirred. 'I know you don't like it, sir, but the boy is right. There is nothing we can do now but take them with us, for better or worse.' *And hope that the gods will protect all of us.*

Quintus made no reply. He seemed to be looking inward, and his face was bleak. Tiro thought it was lucky for Legate Crescens that they were now too far away from Eboracum to easily return. He also guessed that whatever trail Quintus was contemplating, he would not turn back, now or ever, until he saw his duty done. Tiro shivered and got up to feed the fire. When he lay down again, he pulled his blanket tight round him.

It would be a long dark night.

THE LOYAL CENTURION

Chapter Fourteen

Trimontium

Quintus had ample opportunity to call down the blessings of Mithras onto the head of Beneficiarius Litorius Pacatianus for his supplies, his travel instructions and his warnings. Roman Dere Street was in reasonable condition, but from the Wall north-west across country to reach it was a slow and tortuous route. They had hills to traverse, and boggy, near-frozen rivers to ford. Frequent dense knots of trees made keeping line of sight tricky. But they also had reason to be thankful for the trees: twice they heard the clear jingle of other horsemen approaching, and each time were able to keep their own horses hidden under the cover of foliage. Nico more than paid his way with an almost magical ability to calm the animals, Pegasus and Camilla included. It seemed he had only to touch or look at the nervous horses or excitable young dog, and they stood till released from his enchantment.

As it was, Quintus reflected, without Litorius's careful directions and generous rations they might have aimlessly wandered the vast landscape till their food ran out. No doubt they could have hunted what little game braved the weather, but that would have delayed them and meant more rough sleeping in bitter conditions. Even so, Quintus was concerned about Nico. The lad was painfully thin and seemed always to be hungry. He never complained, but Quintus made sure he got the lion's share of their rations at mealtimes.

The snowfall ended on the second day before they reached Trimontium, but the air was so cold every touch seared like sparks from a fire. To save the unshod horses' hoofs they kept to the verges wherever they could, muffling the sounds of passage. The skies had cleared, and although Quintus might have preferred their progress to be less perceptible to passersby, he couldn't deny the beauty of the pearlescent northern light filtering through traceries of overhanging branches, and limned with brilliant frozen crystals.

Nevertheless, even the hardy Governor's Man was glad to sight the unmistakeable outline of the three hills above Trimontium. The enormous old fort, built on a mound overlooking a river, had been abandoned in the time of Emperor Marcus Aurelius, but recent building was evident in the surrounding village, which looked trim and prosperous. Quintus looked closer, squinting against the sharp light refracting off the snow till he found what he sought. The fort was unoccupied, it seemed, the walls showing signs of neglect. But there were a good few stout houses and farm buildings, and even a smithy, all tucked inside well-defended annex walls. A few villagers were about in the fading light, attending to animals and heading home.

Quintus pointed. 'Tiro, your luck is in. Lossio was right about Trimontium being a locus meeting point with a marketplace. That must be the old forum. And there, right next to it, I make no doubt, is a mansio.'

Tiro whooped, waving his arm in signal to Nico and Aila who were trailing them down the hill. He tugged on his reins and galloped off in the reckless style of a born horseman. The two youngsters immediately gave chase. Camilla streaked along low and fast beside Nico, her shaggy paws throwing up puffs of snow. Quintus followed more slowly, guiding the packhorse and glad to be arriving somewhere comfortable and safe.

The following morning, after the best night's rest they had enjoyed since Vindolanda, they set off again with a pale sunrise fingering the east. Their way for two full days took them across a greying landscape, with the bright sun of the previous day soon broken up by low clouds pushed along by a steady chill wind. All colour seemed washed away from the grey rock, pale birches, hissing aspens and dark Scots pines as the horses trudged along. They passed between low hills, skirting higher ones to the west, where they saw the grey-silver glint of wide Bodotria ahead, and the faint outline of the marshy Fiv peninsula on the further side.

At Carumabo on the south shore of the wide Bodotria estuary, they entered a large walled settlement surrounding a sizeable fort. The fort itself had been rebuilt by Emperor Septimius Severus and then decommissioned and emptied by his son Caracalla, but evidently people lived on in the village. They walked the horses through melting slush past a small cemetery outside the walls, where Tiro, in his usual fashion, paused to pay his respects at an imposing memorial to a former commander. Quintus held in a smile as Tiro lovingly stroked the stone lioness guarding the grave, portrayed in the act of savaging an unfortunate native prisoner of ancient days.

There was an inn at Carumabo, too — of sorts. No longer containing post horses, of course; they would probably have to take their own horses all the way to Horrea Classis, the old Severan naval supply depot on the shores of mighty Tausa. Quintus discovered this from an old hand, a veteran of the Severan campaigns, who had quixotically taken a fancy to Lothian and settled here with a native wife. He was now the innkeeper at the settlement's only hostelry, as well as being a loyal member of Lossio Veda's scattered spy network. The old man didn't get around much himself any more, being crippled with arthritis. But he had two energetic young sons, and he kept his own ear well to the ground. Thus he was able to file occasional useful reports to Lossio.

It was a quiet evening at the inn, the recent snow making travel difficult. Nico and Aila had been fed to bursting point, then shown the washing facilities, which Nico used happily while Aila watched with suspicion. Both young people were now tucked up in the dormitory which constituted all the available accommodation, under the old mansio's patched roof. The suspicious scuttle of little creatures in the thatch didn't seem to discompose either of them; they immediately fell asleep.

The innkeeper was more than happy to be bought a jar of his own home-brewed once Quintus had mentioned Lossio Veda's name. He settled with his boots up in front of the crackling fire, chatting to the two investigators. The old soldier had keen brown eyes, and Quintus felt his intent gaze as they spoke. Tiro was content to let the two men exchange news, while he gave his attention to the beer.

'Horrea Classis? Well now, sir, that takes me back. A mighty base it was in the old emperor's day. I doubt there's no one there now, although …'

'Yes?'

'Well, you do hear all kinds of rumours and tall tales coming out of the north. Still, for what it's worth — it's said that someone might be using the old fort. Probably just seasonal hunters, passing through and needing shelter every now and again.'

The old man paused, his gaze now shifting down to the fire. 'There's more, sir. The old fort — locals call it by its native name now, Cair Pol, "the fort by the slow burn". The thing is about Cair Pol, it's overlooked by a much older native hillfort, on Castlelaw. That was built long ago, in the dim past. It's been abandoned for more time than a man can reckon, but there are reports that native warriors have recently been seen repairing the walls. I don't know which tribe, but I suppose we can all guess. Castlelaw is a lot smaller than our old fort, but built stoutly with massive double walls, and perched on such a sharp spur there can be no coming at it. From what I'm told, it's the ideal place to watch comings and goings at Cair Pol. It's barely two miles distant, commanding a fine view over the flat fields and copses towards Cair Pol on the riverside. And it watches the old Roman road leading to the fort.'

'A road? Still usable?'

'I believe so, sir, though roads in these parts quickly deteriorate. And there's the fortified harbour. Built by Emperor Septimius Severus, of course. It sheltered plenty of ships, back in the day when the old emperor was campaigning.'

'It's still there, the harbour?'

'Oh, yes, sir. Pity the same can't be said for our own harbour, and the old bridge just west of here. You know, the bridge over to Fiv, the land of the Venicones? It rotted and collapsed some years ago.'

This was a nasty surprise. Quintus had been relying on the bridge to Fiv to save them time, and keep them safely heading north.

Tiro burst out, 'No bridge over Bodotria? But it will take us many days to go all the way east to the nearest passable ford, at the end of the old Earthen Wall of Emperor Antoninus Pius. And who knows what the roads would be like, so close to the heartlands of the Painted People?'

THE LOYAL CENTURION

'And yet we must go north, Tiro.' Quintus spoke sternly, his face half-hidden in the flickering shadows cast by the glow of the peat fire. 'We have many reasons to carry on, including gathering intelligence. If the Picts are massing and have reinvested this Castlelaw hillfort, we must see it for ourselves. We need to send timely and accurate warning of any possible attack south towards the Aelian Wall.'

The innkeeper smiled at Tiro. 'I think I can help with the river crossing at least, Optio. I have many customers who esteem my beer, and among them are several fishermen. They use the beach here to land their catches. I can find a fishing boat to take you across the river and land you on the Fiv side.'

Tiro audibly swallowed, looking stricken. But he said nothing as Quintus thanked their host. The old man stood awkwardly, clutching the side of his chair as he straightened. He saluted them, saying, 'I'll be turning in now, sirs, wishing you a safe journey. Call my sons if you need anything, and be up betimes to sail across the river. The fisherfolk start early, even in winter.'

He paused, considering Quintus. His luminous eyes glinted like dark honey in the dying firelight. 'You may find help where you least expect it, Beneficiarius. We Romans have been here before, many times, stretching back to the days of the god Vespasian. And each time the legions retreat, a few of us stay behind. We somehow fall in love with the land and its people.' He smiled again, and left them to the smouldering turf and the beer.

Before he slept that night, tired though he was, Quintus wrote a report for Lossio. He recounted the disaffection at the garrison of Vindolanda; their rescue of Aila; the tribesmen seen by Marcus at Vercovicium; finding the body of Tribune Gaius Laelianus; and now the news from their host at Carumabo. He added:

Brother, I believe we may soon find evidence of the Picts moving south en masse. It is essential that Tiro and I continue to investigate the extent of the potential threat to our British provinces. Further, I now have witness statements of the criminal trafficking of native girls to the Aelian Wall, including the murdered woman we know as Sacra. Pictish warriors are being allowed in and out of Wall garrisons. In addition, our boy Nico remembers seeing Legate Crescens in Eboracum on the night Placidia Septimia died. All the hallmarks of conspiracy are building. We have a duty to uncover the full extent of these happenings, and to avenge Sacra, Placidia and Gaius by apprehending their killers. Also I have a young trafficked Pictish girl in my care, who wishes to go home to her family.

All these factors require me to continue further north. Your man here in Carumabo has told me where I may find Athair, or at least word of him: at Castlelaw, near Cair Pol (the old Horrea Classis). I will try to parley with him, to discover how we can come to terms without conflict. It is likely we may encounter resistance. In that event I will need your urgent assistance, whatever you can arrange.

Please share this information with Prefect Antonius Gargilianus at the Eboracum fortress, and reassure my beloved wife Julia that Tiro and I are both well and unhurt. We will do our duty by Rome, and for our Governor Aradius Rufinus.

Senior Beneficiarius Consularis Quintus Valerius
Carumabo, Caledonia

Before climbing up to his lumpy bed under the roof, Quintus summoned their host's attendant son. He arranged for his report to be taken urgently to Vindolanda, for Beneficiarius Litorius Pacatianus to forward to Lossio Veda at Eboracum by the official post. Enclosed in the packet was a private note for his wife. Then he tried not to think any more about Julia: the way she moved and spoke, the scent of rose-water on her skin, the warmth of her body. Nor did he dwell on his new son, Flavius, or his precious daughter Aurelia. Time enough for such thoughts when his duty was done.

Instead, he silently commended himself and his friend Tiro into the care of the god of light and love, Mithras. Then he rolled into his blankets, and slept.

They woke in the dark. Aila roused the sleepy Nicomedes, and they ate a quick breakfast of more beer (warmed), dried fish, and fire-baked flat cakes (slightly scorched). Within a few minutes they had left the warmth of the inn for the chilly foreshore, where they dismounted and led their horses onto a pair of large flat-bottomed fishing boats, not unlike Roman river traders. These were made of solid oak planks, with a high prow and a single large sail hauled in tight to allow the east wind to slide off as they made passage across the estuary. Quintus took Aila, their mounts and the packhorse on board the first ship. First to board the second ship was Pegasus, led by Nicomedes. The large horse seemed initially unwilling to move, but Nico said something and the horse soon settled and took his place with docility. Quintus watched Tiro, grimacing and shaking his head, leading his own grey horse up the gangplank onto the second boat. As the light broadened, the two fishing boats were pushed out into the choppy waters of Bodotria by other fishermen on the beach, until the sails took up the work.

Quintus, knowing how much Tiro disliked sailing and the sea, became concerned as he saw the grey horse begin to shift round uneasily on the other boat. Tiro grabbed the reins to steady his gelding, and was thanked by the panicking horse rearing up in alarm, wrenching the reins out of his hand. From across the water and into an increasing wind, Quintus heard the skipper of the other vessel swear at Tiro to control his horse. Quintus shouted to his own captain to close the gap between the two boats, not actually knowing how they could stop the plunging, screaming animal from causing disaster. The waters were choppy and uneven as they neared mid-channel, and the skipper instead allowed their boat to fall behind, increasing the gap. Both ships were pitched and tossed around as the vicious cross-currents of Bodotria caught them up.

Quintus watched helplessly as Tiro's horse kicked out at the side of his boat. The skipper on Tiro's boat grabbed a long oar and approached, clearly intending to incapacitate the maddened horse in an effort to save his ship. Quintus swore as the heavy oar struck out at the horse, missing its head and striking its shoulder instead. The horse swung round, rearing up afresh and trying to reach the man with its bared teeth. Tiro lost grip on the reins as well as his precarious balance on the slippery deck, swayed, fell heavily against the gunwale, and tumbled over the side into the heaving grey waters. He instantly disappeared.

Quintus bellowed to the crew of his own ship, 'Turn the boat!

He can't swim! We must turn around!' They ignored him. There was no sign of Tiro, and every second drew the boat further from where the optio had been lost under the cruel, cold waves. Quintus drew his sword, advancing on the captain with the heavy beat of his own blood racing up into his head. He shouted something in Latin — he had no idea what — which of course the man didn't understand. Despairing, Quintus flung off his cloak, and sat down to strip off his heavy hob-nailed boots as fast as he could. He was a competent rather than keen swimmer, but he knew Tiro was petrified of the sea. He glanced up as a flash of deerskin and blue tattoos passed him. Aila jumped lightly up onto the boat gunwale, pausing fleetingly before diving headfirst into the river. At the same time, Tiro's head popped up from the water. His mouth was open, as if trying to scream, and Quintus went cold with horror as a wave swept across Tiro's head and he went down again.

But Aila had seen him. She swam neatly towards the flailing man, grabbed him under his arms and tipped him onto his back. Quintus couldn't make out her words above the noise of wind and waves, but she had clearly gained Tiro's trust. She swam, towing him on his back, towards the nearer ship where Nico had Pegasus positioned ready with a rope fastened to the horse's saddle. As Aila approached the pitching boat, Nico threw the long end of the rope into the water. Aila caught it gracefully while treading water, and slid the rope round Tiro, fastening it with a non-slipping knot. Nico spoke into the horse's ear. Pegasus took up the rope's slack, backing away smoothly to pull Tiro through the water, up and into the boat. Aila scrambled up too, and knelt over the unconscious Tiro. She tipped his head back, pinching his nose, and appeared to kiss him.

To Quintus's amazed relief, Tiro suddenly sat up, spluttering and then leaned over to vomit water onto the deck. Aila waved at Quintus, a signal of "All's well". He slumped, as exhausted as if it had been he who had saved his optio rather than the two young Britons.

Again, he had much to thank the gods for. But as he shivered with cold and fatigue, he was most grateful of all to hear the sound of shingle grating under the boats, as they beached on the shore of

Fiv.

Chapter Fifteen

Fiv peninsula

Tiro was cold, soaked through, and furious with himself. On top of that, he had to endure the mortification of being forced to strip off his wet clothes in front of Aila and the smirking sailors, while his spare clothing was brought off the boat. Aila was apparently already dry. She turned away, chuckling, to help Nico disembark their horses. Quintus had been busying himself collecting dry driftwood to get a fire going. He sat down on the narrow shingle bank and gave Tiro a consoling pat on the shoulder.

'Cheer up. You're alive, we're on the right side of Bodotria, and even your horse has survived in one piece.'

Tiro tossed his disloyal equine companion a sour look.

'I bloody hate the sea. Every time I go anywhere near it, something dreadful happens. Remember that time with Caesulanus?'

Quintus nodded, as they both reflected on their escaping prisoner in the Summer Country, who had drowned in the shivering sands of the Sabrina estuary, nearly dragging Tiro down with him. Tiro continued to shiver, more with delayed shock than cold. 'There was something funny happened just now, sir. You remember that time by Sabrina, I made an offering to the goddess before we embarked?'

'Yes, what of it?'

'I didn't have the chance to pay respects to any local river gods this time. But as I sank under, in the river — the second time I went down, I mean—' he shuddered uncontrollably, and spat over his shoulder for luck. 'Well, there was this nymph. I'll swear it, sir. A water nymph, all marble-skin and blue veins. As I gave up hope and resigned myself to the gods, she appeared in front of me. She swam right up and smiled into my face. She said something — I don't know what —then I felt her lifting me, and suddenly I was above the water, and I could breathe, sir! I must have passed out then. The next thing I remember is lying on this beach, and

110

you calling my name.'

Quintus smiled broadly, hailing Aila. As she came over, he said, 'Here's your water nymph, Tiro. You have Aila to thank for saving you. She is a remarkable swimmer, and went straight to your rescue when you fell in.'

Aila grinned too. 'Och, it's nay such a braw thing. I spent all my young days swimming, in and out of fishing boats on the Great Waters. In my clan they call me and my friends selkies.'

She shook her head at Tiro's puzzled look. 'A tale to tell another time. Look, the boats are all unloaded, and our fishermen friends are crossing back to Carumabo.'

Quintus stirred, saying, 'Time we were off. We still have a long journey ahead of us.'

Nico was waiting patiently with the horses. He waved happily when he spotted Tiro, and Camilla frisked up to the optio, tail wagging.

'I've spoken to your grey, Tiro. He's very fond of you, just spooked by the b-boats and the waves. He won't let you down again, sir.'

Tiro thanked the boy, ruffling his soft, dark curls. 'Truth to tell, I was spooked myself, Nico. Thanks for helping to save me. The boss told me how you got the horse all set up with the rope, to pull me out of the water. You and Aila — I owe you both my life. I won't forget.'

Nico blushed, a shy smile on his thin face. No more was said, but after that Nico and Camilla kept closer to Tiro as they travelled the soggy old log road, stretching ahead northbound through the marshes and boggy fields of Fiv.

'There's something strange about this country, sir.'

Tiro looked across at Quintus. It was their third day on the road across Fiv. The weather had held cold and dry, and they had all become accustomed to the travelling and camping routine. They'd passed a large loch, and were now enjoying some respite from the bogs as the road rose into low hills on their approach to the river Tausa, where they hoped to find the old Roman fort at Cair Pol. Nico and Aila, in the lead, were laughing at a pair of crows ganging together against a young hawk. Tiro had recovered from his extended river dip, but something about this landscape oppressed his normally sanguine spirits.

'It's very quiet, don't you think? I wonder where the people are. Isn't this the country of Lossio's tribe, the Venicones? I mean, they were our allies, and well-paid by Rome to hold this buffer zone, by all accounts. Why would they give up that rich stream of silver to move away?'

No reply came, but Tiro had caught his own attention. There was something about silver, treasure, the gaining and guarding of treasure… Where had he seen that?

He turned to speak to Quintus and was struck by the beneficiarius's attitude. Quintus appeared lost in thought, gazing ahead between his horse's ears for long moments.

'Sir?'

Eventually Quintus roused himself, shaking his head. His face looked pale under his hood, pulled close against the chilly air.

'The people of this land are here all right. We just can't see them.'

Tiro looked, searching for signs of movement, habitation, anything. He turned a puzzled face to Quintus, who pointed at a series of barrows, both round and square, looming ahead. Between them could be glimpsed a white strand and blue-grey flashes of moving water. *The sea*, thought Tiro. *Thanks be to Mercury, we must be nearing Cair Pol and the fortress. Surely there we'll be safe?*

'Those mounds we've been passing. I think some of the people who lived here are under the mounds. The rest are simply gone, who knows where?' Quintus fell silent, looking grim. Tiro wondered what he could mean: that the Venicones had moved south to be nearer their Roman allies; or that something dreadful and unknowable had happened here, emptying the countryside of the living. He shuddered, and though the sky was still light, and the sun not more than half dropped from the noon, he felt uneasy. The quick banter of the young pair faded away. His back prickled, and he was reminded of the last time he'd had to sleep in the shadow of the old people's mounds, at Priddy on the Mendips. He spat again over his shoulder, crossing his fingers surreptitiously. He promised himself, Mercury, and any other listening gods he would make an appropriate sacrifice once they were safe inside Roman walls again.

Not long after he did see walls, big enough and strong enough to gladden his heart. Cair Pol, Horrea Classis as it had been, was still a magnificent sight. It was a full-sized fortress, built by the men of the Second Augusta and the Sixth Victrix, both legions that knew their business when it came to building for the British climate. As they neared the fort, he made out a double-ditched turf rampart round the stone walls, ragged and overgrown in places where the weather had done its work of nigh on fifteen years, but still imposing. The fortress was set on the riverside, a short way east of the confluence of the wide Tausa with a smaller tributary running down from the hills to the south. Tiro's eye tracked beyond the little river, noting the nearby hillfort the innkeeper at Carumabo had told them of.

The thick hillfort walls seemed carved out of the heart of a menacing crag, a bare couple of miles southwest of Cair Pol and the coast. Tiro's heart sank. Every movement they made, every twitch, every sigh, would be visible from that eyrie if anyone was there, watching. He devoutly hoped it was deserted, abandoned back to the ancients who had built it so long ago. Then he shuddered again at the thought of a castle patrolled only by ghosts. He shook himself. *Tiro, pull yourself together! You're turning into an old woman, what with selkies, ancients in barrows, and now invisible warriors with ghostly spears.*

Quintus glanced at him quizzically. 'This is our home for tonight and the future, till our mission here is achieved. It looks a stout enough hostelry, if rather lacking in staff. None of our compatriots are left to stoke the hypocaust, bake the evening bread or man the lookout towers, but we should find the roof still intact. With any luck there will be firewood enough to warm a room in the praetorium. I'll wager this is the first time you've been a guest in a commandant's palace, eh Tiro?' Tiro tried not to look downhearted at the prospect. He caught up with Aila and Nicomedes, who were clearly excited to enter the fort.

'Look, Tiro!' the lad called eagerly. 'Look at those towers! And how big is that palace? Did the emperor live here?'

Tiro was about to demur, thinking of the only emperor he had actually met, young Alexander Severus in Rome. Then he remembered that the old emperor Septimius Severus almost certainly spent time here at Cair Pol while on campaign. It was he who had commanded this vast place to be built, complete with fortified harbour to protect the constant stream of supplies, weapons, horses and all manner of stores shipped from Arbeia to support the crushing Severan campaigns. Or if not the old man, perhaps his martial son, later Emperor Caracalla, had been a resident?

They trotted their horses through the open gates of the main riverside entrance, flanked by sculptured and inscribed panels hailing the emperor. As Caracalla had served as co-emperor alongside his father while Septimius was alive, that seemed to settle matters. Caracalla it was who had lived here as sole emperor, albeit briefly. But not in the winter, as they were to do. Tiro's face fell as he wondered how long Quintus expected them to stay here. The fortress might be full of familiar Roman features like stone walls and towers, a central headquarters building, a huge buttressed granary to one side. Three plaster figures of the goddess Victory greeted them in the main courtyard. But what was missing made all the difference: no soldiers drilling, no slaves bustling to and fro, no smells of supper cooking, no plumes of welcome steam from the bathhouse. This place was dead.

And worse, he thought, the fort might be haunted, too. It was the last fading vestige of Roman might in this hostile land, probably filled with the restless shades of those who had died here. And, he thought with bitterness, there was likely to be a keen-eyed enemy leaning over nearby ramparts, watching this foolhardy pair of Roman soldiers with their pitiful companions, a little horse boy and a snatched Pictish girl.

They made the best camp they could, after feeding and stabling the horses. The praetorium was indeed the cosiest place to make a fire, having an intact roof and reasonable-sized rooms in good condition. There were even hearths in a few of the smaller rooms which hadn't benefited from the now defunct underfloor heating. They set up a combined sitting and sleeping chamber in one of these. With four of them to tend the fire and share the cooking rota, it should be fairly snug. The smoke from the fire drew, for the most part, out through the roof. With mosaics, plain but neat, and walls painted with panels and fading colours, they were able to feel a little at home. Even Aila settled once the notion of painted walls had been explained to her.

'Ye Romans, with your snootie ideas, ye'll fail and die out long before we hardy Picts. Ye mark ma words!'

This trenchant view was rather spoilt by Nico's snort of laughter. 'Rome will last for ever, Aila. It's the eternal city, empire without end. I t-tell you what, when we get back to Eboracum, I'll ask Lady Julia to show you her books, written by the poets and authors of Rome. You'll learn how mighty Rome is.'

She looked horrified, whether at the notion of books and reading, or perhaps at heading back south to the effete Roman city. But Tiro noticed she didn't immediately insist on travelling onward to her own country. He wondered if she had realised how unlikely it was she'd find any of her family alive.

Both the young people were tired, and soon settled on one side of the fire, rolled into their blankets. Once they were asleep — Nico neat and motionless, Aila restless, stretching her tattooed arms above her head to sleep like that, with the blue lines catching the firelight, coiling and circling in mysterious patterns from wrist to shoulder — Tiro took the chance of a quiet chat with the boss.

'Sir?'

'Mmm?' Quintus was seated in a folding campaign chair, the leather old and cracked but still sound. He had closed his eyes, but Tiro could tell by the occasional slow rub along his scarred leg that his boss was awake.

'About our plans now, sir. I was wondering how we're going to make contact with the Pictish chief. Now we've arrived on their doorstep, I mean. If, as we've been told, there are Pictish warriors in the old hillfort up yonder.'

'It's pretty straightforward, Tiro. I shall do exactly as I said I would. I am now the representative of both British provincial governors, for different reasons. Aradius Rufinus has tasked me with negotiating with the king of the Painted People, to stymie the attacks and bloodshed of previous generations. Obviously we do not come here at the head of 50,000 men, as Emperor Septimius Severus did before us, so my approach must be diplomatic. As for Legate Marius Crescens — we are no longer obliged to arrest Tribune Laelianus, the poor young man. And we're no nearer understanding why Placidia Septimia was killed, although we now know her husband had the opportunity, at least, if not the motive. But I need to find out about the movement of Pictish warriors through our great Wall. Such security breaches have apparently escaped the notice of the legate, which concerns me.'

There was a long pause, during which Tiro felt glad that Quintus acknowledged their lack of an accompanying Roman army. Such considerations had not always stopped him when faced with desperate odds, such as at the Battle of Corinium against the rebellious Second Augusta legion; or indeed in the imperial palace on the Palatine in Rome, when he and Quintus had taken on the Praetorian Guard to protect Emperor Alexander Severus. True enough, they'd lived to tell the tale, both times. But never had they been this remote, this far from any possible help. Which reminded him …

'Sir, about Nicomedes and Aila?'

Quintus turned to Tiro, considering. His face, normally a healthy olive tone even in winter, looked pale. He frowned.

'I want to keep them out of this, Tiro. Aila has her own plans, and we owe her whatever help we can give. Although finding her path back home seems dark and dangerous. Nico? I wish I had sent him back to Eboracum when I could. I will consider what we can do to help him get back to Julia safely. He deserves a good life, and I know she would ensure that for him.'

To Tiro it sounded as though the Governor's Man was quickly sinking into one of his dark moods. These were inevitably dangerous, leading as they often did to the sort of behaviour Lady Julia would call reckless. Tiro shrugged. He knew the boss was never more menacing to enemies than when his dander was up.

Just a question of backing him up when that happened. He sat upright, squaring his shoulders. He'd do whatever he could to support the boss. Simple.

Quintus was deep in thought, staring into the fire as he so often did when thinking things through.

'I keep coming back to what Marcus, Litorius's optio, told us at Vindolanda. If the warriors he saw at Vercovicium really were Picts being accompanied by the legate's senior officers through the Aelian Wall, then that alone changes the nature of our mission. Such cosy relations fly in the face of Lossio's reports. Add to that the words of Antonius's dying soldier. His ramblings about "Sabine women" and "beehives" I think I now understand: he meant girls like Aila being kidnapped to be traded as comfort women. Like the myth of the early Romans stealing the Sabine women as wives, back in the day. "Barbarians inside the camp" would be Marcus's Pictish warriors again. But the soldier's comment about silver turning into swords? That has me flummoxed.'

'Swords, yes,' said Tiro. He pulled out his own dagger, running his thumb along its edge critically. 'That reminds me. Let me have your gladius, sir. I'll sharpen both our weapons in the morning. At least we can have good edges to our blades before we go looking for trouble.' As he spoke, Tiro felt his blood stirring in anticipation. By Mars, he did love a good dust-up!

Quintus lifted his head suddenly, his grey eyes alert as if he had spotted something hitherto hidden.

'Tiro,' he said slowly, 'when we arrived in Vindolanda, I was surprised at how much smoke was coming from the armourers' workshops. Do you remember, Marcus said he'd noticed the smiths at Vercovicium were very busy. There was no obvious need for that. What if they were making weapons for someone else?'

Tiro scratched his chin, thinking. 'You're right, sir, they were very busy. But there's been no action along the Wall since the days of the old emperor. Are you thinking those weapons are being made to be sold? Who to, and why? Why would the legate allow Roman weapons to be traded away? Unless perhaps he doesn't know. And even if the Picts or another tribe wanted them, how would they pay? It's well known there are no silver mines in Caledonia. Gold neither. No wonder we gave up invading the place, it's worthless. Why on earth would anyone, Crescens or his cronies, want to trade weapons to these barbarians?'

Quintus lifted his head, sighing. 'You're right, Tiro. There's no reason why Crescens would conduct or allow such a trade. As always, though, I return in my thoughts to Cicero: *Cui bono?* Who benefits from the crime? Answer that, and we find our criminal. Suspicions aren't enough — we need proof. That's why I must speak to Athair.'

In silence, the two soldiers and the dog sat side by side in the old fort, as the embers of the fire sank, guttered and went out, leaving them to the black chill of this unknowable country.

Chapter Sixteen

Cair Pol

Quintus woke, cold and cramped. He had dozed off by the dead fire with Camilla asleep on his lap. Her body was the only warmth he could feel. He glanced round the room. Tiro was asleep and frankly snoring, lying on his back on the dirty, paved floor. There was no sign of either Aila or Nico, but before he could begin to worry, they both came into the room.

'Just been checking the horses, sir,' said Nico. 'Pegasus was happy to see me, of course, and the others are all f-fine.' He looked cheerful, and was carrying the pack with their rations, including the stirabout that now featured as breakfast on a daily basis. Aila had brought water in a wooden pail, and the two busied themselves rebuilding the fire and getting the breakfast cooked. Quintus disliked this local oatmeal dish, finding it bland. He sighed. It did stick to the ribs, he supposed, but what wouldn't he give for some slices of ham, a pot of honey, and a fresh loaf of bread?

'Have you found a well, Aila, or is there a spring inside the walls? I hope you didn't go outside to fetch that water?'

'Nay, dinnae fret. I found a well right enough, by the stables. I found summat else, too. Footsteps. You'll want to look yoursen'.'

There was perturbation on her freckled face. His heart sank. They were not alone in the fort. Quintus remembered the comment by the innkeeper at Carumabo that signs of life here had recently been reported. Waking Tiro and taking his sword, he followed Aila through the courtyard, down a barracks row, and round a corner under the high crest of the east wall. On the far side of the well, in a muddy pool of shade where the low winter sun never reached, he found several footsteps. Much the same size as his own, and judging from the gaps between, made by a man of similar height to himself. Whoever it was wore native footwear, though. No sign of nail marks, as were universal on the outdoor boots worn by Romans. Quintus pointed the marks out to Tiro, and finger raised to lips, summoned Aila. She understood immediately, lifting one

119

of her soft deerskin boots to show him the sole. There was no doubt about it; their unknown visitor was a native. Given the lack of Venicones left in the region, this could only mean one thing: a Pict was inside the fort.

Moving as silently as they could, the three retreated carefully, casting about for more footprints. They found nothing, but as they returned to the praetorium, Quintus heard the unmistakeable voice of Nicomedes in conversation. The porridge in his belly turned to stone. He signalled to the others to stay outside, and hurried in. The faint hope that Nico was merely playing with his dog faded immediately, as Quintus entered the room. A slim muscular young man was standing by the fire, facing an eager Nico. He was dressed in native leather breeches, with a tunic of the same hide, finely tanned, falling to his thighs. A pointed hood, clasped under the chin and woven of material to match the leather, trimmed with long fine tassels along the bottom edge, had been pulled away from his head. He had long dark hair, tied back by a leather thong, and his eyes too were dark. He was bearded, but had made some effort to trim the beard to a point just below his chin.

As Quintus moved in, gladius raised, the stranger spun round to face him. He made no attempt to attack, but spoke with painful effort.

'No weapon. I am a friend.' To Quintus's astonishment, it was a form of Latin — clumsy and old-fashioned, but recognisably a forefather of Quintus's own tongue.

Nico limped towards Quintus. 'S-sir, he *is* a friend. He is staying here. He saw us arrive last night, but waited till daylight to come to us. Please, sir, let him explain.' While the boy spoke, the young man had turned towards the light falling from the high windows in the room. Quintus saw flecks of russet flashing in his dark hair. His face, lifted now to the morning sun, hadn't the whiteness he had come to associate with Caledonians; it was more like a subdued tone of his own colouring, had Quintus but known it. Quintus lowered his sword, keeping it to hand.

'Sit,' he indicated one of the camp seats. 'Who are you?' He took the other seat, and was rewarded with a lessening of the wary look in the man's dark eyes. They watched each other for a silent moment until the native spoke.

'I called Kian. Kian mac Dougal. I come from west, lands near setting sun, sea and many islands.'

Quintus took this to mean Kian had travelled from the lands of the Gael, a country the Romans had never yet marched over. Why then did he know some Latin? Before trying to convey this question, he signalled to Kian to remain seated. Quintus looked outside to fetch in Tiro and Aila. He needed interpreters.

They soon discovered that while Aila struggled with Kian's dialect, between them she and Tiro could supplement whatever Kian couldn't express in Latin. He, in turn, seemed to grasp much of their Latin. He was quite willing to tell them where he came from: the island-studded west coastal region of Dál Riata, where incomers from Hibernia had settled, intermingling with the original Caledonian tribes. He talked about his journey to Fiv, saying the journey east was a rite of passage for the young men of his tribe. He intended to stay here for some time, they gathered. But how he knew his strange old Latin, and why he had taken up residence in the abandoned fort, they could not get out of him. His answers turned evasive, and he seemed not to understand their questions.

In turn, he asked why they had come to Cair Pol. 'Nothing here for you. Only bad people,' he said. 'Keep away from hillfort. Very wicked man there, the king of the Picts. I have seen this man and his warriors.'

Quintus looked at Tiro, who shrugged. So now they knew their enemy was indeed here at Castlelaw.

Kian moved closer to Quintus, intent on being understood. 'You are leader? Your soldiers nearby?'

Quintus had to shake his head.

'You see the only soldier I have with me — my optio Tiro. I am here to open peace talks with the king of the Picts, not to fight.'

Kian looked at Tiro, then at Aila and Nico, frowning.

'Then you will die,' he said simply. He reached out to touch the hasta brooch on Quintus's baldric. As they were travelling beyond the boundaries of the empire, Quintus had thought it wise to travel

121

incognito, apart from this small badge of office. Kian looked at Quintus in mute enquiry.

'I am a beneficiarius consularis, an imperial investigator representing Governor Aradius Rufinus of southern Britannia. He has sent me beyond the great Wall of Hadrian to negotiate with the king of the Picts, Athair. We wish to prevent the bloodshed that so often results when Romans encounter the warriors of Caledonia.'

Quintus decided not to mention the murders they were investigating — Sacra (or Aine, as he should now call her), Placidia Septimia, and Tribune Gaius Laelianus. Nor, yet, the kidnapped girls. Kian might be the sort of ally the old soldier at Carumabo had meant, when he talked of finding help where least expected. Or he might not. It was just as likely he was a spy for the Pictish leader, keeping watch on the Roman fort and any who entered it. Until he was sure about the snaking connections between all their lines of enquiry, Quintus could only persist with his original peacekeeping mission. However deluded the effort might turn out to be, he thought grimly.

Later he found Tiro emptying saddlebags, frowning over their provisions. Nico was attending to the horses, taking Camilla with him. Aila had gone off with Kian to fetch firewood, and to search the mouldering buildings of the fort for anything that might be useful.

'How long do you reckon we'll be here, sir?' Tiro asked bluntly. He looked upset, his yellow hair standing up in disorder where he'd run his hands repeatedly through it. He seemed reluctant to make eye contact with his superior, which Quintus knew with resignation meant his optio was not a happy man.

'Out with it, Tiro. What's on your mind?'

Tiro did not answer immediately, continuing to stare sullenly into the food bag.

'That's an order!'

Quintus sounded sharper than he intended to. He knew very well he wouldn't last long without his British colleague. But he wasn't sure himself what he hoped to achieve here, at the most remote end of the world, with not even a small troop at his command.

THE LOYAL CENTURION

They were running out of food, and possibly at the mercy of barbarians who at any moment might discover their presence in the deserted Roman fort. And now they had been joined by an unknown native, who spoke some of their language and looked less British than Mediterranean, but refused to tell them anything meaningful about himself.

'It's that Kian!' Tiro burst out. 'We know nothing about him, he could be from the enemy, infiltrating the fort to spy on us. And you let him have the run of the place, even agree to him strolling off with Aila! It's not right, sir.'

He paused, face scarlet with unspoken concerns. Quintus waited.

'I mean to say,' Tiro went on, evidently making an effort to control his outburst, 'I know it's not my place to ask, but I can't make head nor tail of what we're doing here. I know you have your duty — don't we all? — but there's duty, and then there's meaningless sacrifice. I never thought I'd feel I didn't want to follow you into anything, but … this time, sir, I think you're wrong. We have civilians with us, young vulnerable ones, barely more than children. They shouldn't be here, Nico and Aila. And we shouldn't be here either.'

Tiro stopped, looking confused and resentful. Quintus could see why, but suddenly he didn't care.

'So you want to go, Tiro? Go running home, back to Vindolanda, or Eboracum? Or even Londinium? Yes, why don't you do that? Just go, take Nicomedes and Aila with you; tell Governor Rufinus that you left me here alone to try to overcome the Pictish hordes and their cruel leader. Tell him you turned a blind eye to three innocents killed, countless girls trafficked, maybe for weaponry that no doubt will be used to kill our own people, our soldiers, our townsfolk when this war comes! For come it will, Tiro, no matter how far you run!'

The wave of anger that had been rising in him for weeks, crushed down again and again as they travelled towards danger and evil in this inhospitable dark land, now rose and overwhelmed Quintus. A drumbeat sounded in his chest, loud in his inner ear. He crushed his eyes closed, seeing bright spots pass rapidly in the dark. This anger was an old and bad friend, one he had long since believed under control. Forcing his eyes open, he turned away from Tiro. He strode over to the back wall of their dirty little room. His gladius was somehow in his hand, and he raised it, to stab — who? Or what? In disgust he dropped the sword, letting it spin onto the floor, the clang of steel on tile ringing in his ears.

He recognised the anger. It was for those pitiful victims they already knew of: Gaius, Aine and Placidia; for Litorius and his spurned comrades, objects of derision and disdain to the corrupt officials brought to power by the new legate; anger for the other victims they didn't know: all the peaceful people of Caledonia, subjected to genocide by the Romans over the centuries, then trafficked, murdered, deposed, and disinherited by a brutal Pictish warlord.

And, if he was honest — and he *must* be honest with himself, or his whole life was in vain — he was angry for himself. Angry at not being with Julia and his new son; angry for his son's namesake, his younger brother Flavius, slain in battle right here; for his noble father Senator Bassianus Valerius, brought to suicide in Rome by political intrigue; Tertius, the brave whistleblower in the Summer Country... Yes, by Mithras! He was angry at all the injustices and wickedness in the world. What could one man do? What could he, Quintus Valerius, do?

He could not bring himself to speak, knowing how words would spill from him, hot and thoughtless and full of revenge. Long moments passed while he leaned his forehead against the cool damp wall, controlling his emotions using the Eastern slow-breathing technique. Gradually his thudding heart slowed, he felt his breathing calming, and he turned back to apologise to Tiro.

Four people stared wide-eyed at him. While he had inwardly raged, they had come back, the three younger ones. They now stood still on the threshold. Tiro, his faithful friend Tiro, was still there, his fixed face burning. They were all looking at him, the Governor's Man. He sat down heavily, resting his elbows on his knees, his face lowered into his hands.

A wet tongue licked his face, and he started. Camilla was at his feet, tail wagging. The wave of emotion finally broke over him, shattered, subsided, and withdrew.

Nico limped over, his left hand held out. He spoke shyly.

'Sir? We found something. Aila and Kian did. Look, sir. It's the k-key to the fort strongroom. Kian wants you to come with us, to see what is inside. That's why he's come here, to Cair Pol. There is something wonderful here.'

Chapter Seventeen

Cair Pol

They had not previously noticed the strongroom in the headquarters building because it was underground, reached down steps obscured by a pedestal and a fallen statue. The statue's head was missing, but Quintus guessed from the club the figure still bore, and the lion skin that composed its sole clothing, that it was Hercules. He was very popular amongst soldiers of the northern provinces.

Quintus had given the key back to Kian, and was surprised at how easily the lock opened. They all filed into a small dark room. Tiro had brought a torch, and Quintus waited for his eyes to adjust as Tiro carefully swept the flame around to search the walls.

'There!'

Kian pointed to a wooden paychest, sitting solidly on the opus signinum floor next to the niche where the legionary standards would once have been stowed. He glanced at Quintus, ceding the honour to the older man. Quintus knelt before lifting the lid. The box was unlocked. He supposed there would have been no need for another lock, given the strong door and permanent guard that would have been in place in former times. There would certainly be no money left in this chest now.

He was right. There was no money. There was something else though. Quintus beckoned Tiro to move closer with the torch. Kian came too, and all three men stared into the chest at the strange object.

It was quite large, wider than it was tall, lumpen in its fraying wrapping. Quintus nodded to Kian, who reached with trembling hands to lift it out. He exhaled sharply — the thing was obviously heavy for its size. As he lifted it, the rotting fabric tore apart. The lamplight glinted onto bright yellow metal. Kian cradled the thing in his arms, lifting it clear of the box. Quintus shut the heavy wooden lid, and all three gazed with deep emotion at what Kian now rested on the lid, peeling away the remnants of the wrapper.

Tiro groaned. 'No. It's — but it can't be... can it, sir? Can that be what I think?'

Quintus discovered he had been holding his breath for too long. He let it go, sighing deeply. He reached out to touch the cold bright metal, his fingers tracing the edge of one raised wing, moving down to slide along the sharp aquiline beak. The bird stared haughtily at him, its proud feathered head looking at the first Roman soldier to see it for generations.

Eventually, Kian said, 'This is god of my people. I have come to worship, and keep it safe. Always the eldest son in each generation, he makes this pilgrimage.'

Quintus looked at the Gael, considering. Then he turned to Tiro.

'Yes, Tiro, I believe this *is* what you think. This is an eagle, the solid gold standard of a Roman legion.'

'But ...how? We know Cair Pol was built by the Sixth Victrix, and visited by the Second Augusta. Their eagles are not lost. We both saw the eagle of the Second with our own eyes, at Corinium last year. And the eagle of the Sixth is safe in Eboracum, or we'd know all about it.'

He was correct. The loss of an eagle was the greatest possible dishonour that could occur to a legion, and would never be covered up.

Quintus said, slowly, 'Yet this *is* a Roman eagle. There can be no doubt of that. Kian, tell us: you just said this is the god of your people. What do you mean? Why would you keep your god so far away from your homelands?'

Kian thought, then shrugged. 'I will trust you, Roman soldiers. This is your story too. Yet if any discover I have revealed where our god lives to strangers, I am punished with death. This my duty as son of son of son of son of Loyal Centurion. Each son, when he becomes a man, he goes to where the god is hidden, to worship the eagle. We polish the god, take him into sun for a single day to stretch his wings and glow in light. Then we place new wrappings around the eagle, and replace him in box. Here he will be safe for another generation, here in the strong stone castle of the Romans. No other knows the eagle god is here. It is our greatest secret, the burden and honour of my family.'

'Your family? Who is your family, Kian?' asked Quintus, already guessing the truth.

The young man drew himself up proudly. 'I am Kian son of Dougal, son four times over of the Loyal Centurion. He it was that saved the eagle god from a great battle long ago, a battle no other Roman survived. None remember that day when the legion died. Only we, his sons and aftersons. So I have another secret name, the same name as my ancestor. I am also Lucius Saturninus.'

Tiro looked dumbfounded. He shook his head, saying, 'This is crazy. There are no missing eagles, surely?' He reached over to stroke the eagle, wonderingly. 'But here it is, a legionary eagle where none should be. Do you understand this, sir?'

Quintus smiled crookedly. 'This is more your history than mine, Tiro. But I will tell you what I know, from my studies as a young boy in Rome. The historian Tacitus, son-in-law of the great general Agricola, wrote of the four legions that invaded Britannia and won the province for Emperor Claudius. One of those legions was the Ninth Hispana. After the conquest, the Ninth stayed in Britannia as part of the island's garrison. It was stationed at various forts round the country, ending up at Eboracum.'

'Of course! I've seen inscriptions from the Ninth recording its rebuilding work at Eboracum.'

'Yes, and the legion is recorded as building the fort at Lindum. They fought here too in Caledonia, under Agricola. And then a generation later, the legion disappeared.'

'Disappeared? How could that be? What happened?'

'I don't know. My teachers certainly didn't know either. All I can tell you is that when the Aelian Wall was built a century ago, and Emperor Hadrian came himself to supervise the construction, he brought the Sixth Victrix legion with him. They became the new garrison at Eboracum. I've never been told how the Ninth were lost, but it's my belief that Hadrian had to bring a new legion to put down conflict north of his Wall. Because the Ninth had marched away into Caledonia and never come back.'

Kian stood silent while Quintus spoke; now he said simply, 'I do not know this tale of the legion you speak of. We do not write, we of the Dál Riata, nor the old people who lived before us in our country. I know only that my ancestor Lucius Saturninus was the survivor of a terrible battle. That he saved his army's god, and swore to keep it safe forever. He escaped to the west lands, married a woman of our tribe, farmed and had children. When his eldest son was grown into a man, he told him of the god. He made him promise to revere the eagle and continue to hide it somewhere no one would ever find it. He swore his son to secrecy, and put on him the solemn duty to teach his own son the Latin, and pass this burden and joy down each generation. And so my family has done, up to my time.

Tiro broke in, puzzled. 'But why then is the eagle here? Why hide it in a strange land where it might be found by another tribe?'

'It was my grandfather who moved it, when the Dál Riata first came from over the sea to merge with the old people. He judged the god should not be exposed to the risk of being found by the newcomers, who were then strangers to him. It was taken to a new hiding place, I know not where. Then one day, during my father's young days, a merchant travelling into our lands told us of this mighty new fortress, built by the people of the eagle here at Cair Pol. Father knew this was the best possible home for our god. As soon as the Red Crests had departed, when I was a lad, he brought me here, and showed me the key and how to hide the eagle. It has been here ever since.'

'What brings you back, then, if Cair Pol is deemed such a good home?'

'It is no longer safe,' Kian answered simply. 'The Great Pict has ravaged his way south, and even the mighty stone walls of Cair Pol are not enough. I come to take the god away, to find him a new hiding place elsewhere.'

There was much to consider. Quintus was more determined than ever to prevent the war he and his governor both feared, a war that might burst through the border of the Aelian Wall into Britannia. Clearly the crooked relationship, whatever it was, between the leaders of the Painted People and the government of Britannia Inferior had become a menace to the safety of the Roman populace. But Quintus could not attack the hillfort, or offer open battle to force Athair away, without a sizeable Roman troop at his back. And yet, he must do something. He could feel anger and frustration rising again, and pushed them away. He stood, beckoning to Tiro. Nico followed them.

'Come on, let's walk. We need to think, and decide what to do.'

It was a rare day of bright winter sun. On the south side of the fortress the walls had slightly warmed. They did not dare pass through the main gate and risk being seen by the watchers Kian assured them had invested Castlelaw. Instead they walked to and fro in the frosty courtyard of the principia, cloaks wrapped tight round them, warmed breath rising as they spoke. Kian and Aila, who had been fetching water and firewood, soon came into the courtyard, heads close together as they exchanged rapid chat in their own tongues.

'First things first,' Quintus said to Kian. 'Is there any chance we can drive Athair and his warriors away?'

Kian shook his head. 'I watch for many days. The Great Pict has gathered together the tribes of the north and mountains. There are as many as he can cram into the hillfort, and many more on the way.'

Aila broke in. 'They have stripped my north country of fodder and food. Athair's army has come to take the fertile lowlands of Fiv and the south of Caledonia, and they will not be driven back while he holds sway.'

Quintus looked thoughtful. 'While he holds sway? Is there anyone you know of, Aila, who might try to undermine Athair? I am sure he made himself very unpopular in some quarters. Your family and the leaders of your people, for instance?'

'Och, aye,' Aila burst out, scowling fiercely. 'There were plenty who resisted, at first. They were punished by death for themselves, and their womenfolk carried away into foul servitude. Like ma own fairther, and me! Athair keeps power through fear, and punishes his enemies at the same time, the scabby monster!'

'How did he rise to such power in the first place?' asked Tiro. 'I mean, was he the son of a tribal leader, or do the Picts hold elections, like us Romans?'

Kian gave a questioning look, and Tiro repeated his question in

Brythonic. The young man laughed, a short unhappy sound.

'No, Tiro, he took power by the sword. That is why he kills the royal families, the traditional tribal leaders. Like the friend of Aila, Aine, whose family were good chieftains for long years till Athair had them executed.'

'And now he will get a supply of superior Roman weapons, to shore up his power indefinitely,' said Tiro, shaking his head.

'This is true?'

Quintus nodded. 'We fear so. But I need to intercept some of these weapons as proof. Only then can I take action to stop the trade. That would be a step towards undermining Athair and whoever may be trading the weapons clandestinely.'

'Perhaps.' Kian wrinkled his brow, his dark eyes narrowed. 'But unless the gods help us, we have no way to overthrow the tyrant.'

Quintus was thoughtful. 'Does the Great Pict have sons, or appointed heirs?'

Kian nodded again. 'There is a grown nephew at his side, his sister's son Bedwyr. Heritage comes through the women in Pictish royalty. Bedwyr is a quiet one. I do not know whether he holds with his uncle's ways. He says little, but obeys.'

Quintus made up his mind.

'Right, I think we now know as much as we can. Today is a clear bright day, a blessing from the gods, and I will take this as a good omen. We will make sacrifice to Mercury, that he may lend me his powers of eloquence and communication, and then I will go in embassy to the hillfort. Kian, you may accompany me if you will, to help interpret my parley with the Great Pict. We will go unarmed, to present no appearance of threat to the Picts.'

Quintus did not see the need to mention to the Caledonians that Mercury was also the god of trickery and thieves. He foresaw he might have to call on all these powers; he hoped he would live long enough to put into play any help Mercury, and his own special god Mithras, chose to send him.

Kian straightened his shoulders, lifting his head proudly. The other two voiced loud objections. Why would Quintus go with only a single companion, and worse, unarmed? Why such a useless sacrifice? They were incredulous: Tiro deeply troubled, Aila

131

almost screeching her defiance.

'To be admitted to Athair's presence by his guards, I must appear both respectful and non-threatening,' the Governor's Man explained evenly. 'Tiro, your presence would be disastrous. They must not know you are here, or have the chance to take you prisoner. If anything happens to me, it is you who must report back to the Roman authorities. Julia will have need of you, and Governor Rufinus relies on our reports.'

Tiro remained stubbornly unconvinced. 'I am your right-hand man, sir,' he reminded his boss. 'We've been everywhere together. This is easily the most dangerous position you've put yourself in yet. And you're not going in there without me at your side! Lady Julia — what would she think if I cowered here while you walk into that stronghold of barbarians? What would Aurelia think, or Britta?'

Quintus smiled faintly at the reference to Britta, but shook his head.

'I cannot take more than one other, for fear of looking either overbearing or afraid for my own life. Besides, I need an interpreter who speaks both our tongues. And I rely on you to take charge here.' Tiro subsided, mumbling and shaking his head in frustration.

Aila was not so easy to placate. Her face was blotchy, and her voice rose steadily as she reiterated the many reasons why she should go too. Most of them revolved around how she would take her revenge on the hackit boggin' Picts for her family and herself.

'That is exactly why you cannot come, Aila,' Quintus said gently. 'Fear not, you will get your chance to help. I do not go to lightly yield myself to the enemy. I need you, and Nicomedes, to work with Tiro behind the scenes to make sure our mission is successful. You may have a role to play yet.' He glanced at the swirling blue designs on her arms; she had rolled up her sleeves while fetching water, and the animals leapt about with animation in the bright sunlight as she moved in protest. She looked at Kian with a suddenly moistened gaze, and Quintus noted the slight smile in return. Neither spoke.

To Nico, who was looking quietly unhappy, he said, 'Can I ask you to look after our precious horses, Nico? We may need them in a hurry, and there is no one they trust like you.' Nico looked mollified, nodding vigorously.

Quintus left to compose himself. He walked to the foreshore of Tausa, and stood for some time looking across the heavy white-tipped waves, and at the northern snow-capped mountains beyond. After a while he noticed he was shivering, and went back inside to dress for his mission. He was wondering where best to stow his beloved gladius when Tiro came looking for him, breathless in his haste.

'What's up?'

'It's Aila! She's sneaked off on horseback, and Nico says he thinks Kian has gone after her!'

Chapter Eighteen

Eboracum

Julia turned as Britta entered the room, carrying letters. Julia's status as the wife of a high-ranking army officer meant she received a priority postal service. Her position as heiress to her wealthy and celebrated Brigantian aunt also helped, she supposed. It wasn't what you knew in Eboracum, but who you knew.

Britta lingered. 'I see that one's from Bo Gwelt, my lady.'

Julia smiled. 'Sit down, Britta. Let me run my eye over it first, then I'll hand it over. I know you'll want all the gossip from home.' She broke open the seal, unrolling Aurelia's letter to scan it. 'Well, here's good news! The foal has been born.'

Britta shook her head, none the wiser.

'You know, the first foal of Aurelia's breeding programme with Drusus at Bawdrip. He's a stout little fellow, out of Aurelia's mare, by Agrippa Sorio's best stallion. Drusus and she are delighted. There's quite a bit more about the horses. Mmm...'

'Please do scan down as fast as you like, Julia. You know how fond I am of horses.'

Julia laughed; Britta was renowned in their household for being that rare Briton, not a lover of horses nor riding. Although she had recently learned to do so at the behest of Tiro, as payment for teaching him to read. Julia skimmed through the rest of the letter. Bits of household news, a report from Demetrios on finances. Local news: apparently Centurion Marcellus Crispus, Quintus's deputy at the Aquae Sulis beneficiariate station, had gone on business for Governor Rufinus in Londinium. But all was quiet in Aquae Sulis and the neighbouring Summer Country, and Marcellus's own second-in-command was holding the fort. Towards the end of the letter there was a request from Enica, Bo Gwelt's much-esteemed little cook, to pass on her best wishes to Tiro.

Britta tapped her fingers on a side table.

'Enica, indeed. What about your news?' she said. 'What does Aurelia say about Flavius, and Quintus?'

Julia looked up. 'She says she's thrilled to be a big sister, after having to wait long enough to be Flavius's mother herself. I think that means she's pleased. She says nothing about Quintus going north, except "Father knows what he is doing. Anyway, he has Tiro with him, so everything will be all right. I expect they will be back before you get this letter."'

Julia's mouth quivered, and Britta got up quickly to hug her. The two women clung together for a minute.

Britta rubbed her eyes, saying quickly, 'And the other letter?'

Julia reached for the letter knife to open the wax seal on the tablet.

'Ah, it's from Quintus, sent on from Vindolanda! Forwarded from somewhere called Carumabo. Never heard of it.' She held the tablet out so they could read it together.

Greetings to my dearest wife, Julia.

I write in haste to tell you both Tiro and I are well. We have reached the Bodotria estuary, which we will cross tomorrow to travel through Fiv to our destination, Horrea Classis (Cair Pol) on the Tausa. We have another travelling companion, a Pictish girl, Aila, whom we saved from captivity in Vindolanda. I will explain when I return, but finding her has confirmed our fears that the kidnapping of Sacra was part of a large-scale criminal trafficking of Pictish girls to Roman garrisons. As we were told, there is disaffection and corruption along the Wall.

Sad news: we found the body of Tribune Gaius Laelianus outside Vindolanda. Also Nico reports hearing Legate Crescens in the streets of Eboracum during Saturnalia. You will know what that may mean. I have sent a more detailed report to Praefectus Antonius Gargilianus, who will share it with you. When I arrive at Cair Pol, my plan is to negotiate under a white flag with Athair to stop the clandestine Wall crossings, and forestall any attacks south by his warriors.

Stay safe, and take great care of yourself, our new son, and our household. Tiro sends his greetings to Britta.

Your loving husband embraces you.

Quintus Valerius

Carumabo on Bodotria

Britta thumped her generous bottom down into a basket chair, wailing.

'My dear, what is it?' said Julia, mystified.

'I let him go without telling him…' Britta sniffed loudly, and blew her nose on a piece of rag. 'And now that silly little Enica thinks she can get him. Well, just because I said Tiro wasn't my idea of husband material doesn't mean anyone else can have him!'

'Oh, Britta, you are impossible. Amidst all the shocking news today, what you care about most is poor little Enica? Come on, I know what we both need. Let's get our cloaks and walk over to the fort. With any luck we'll find Antonius off-duty, and hear more from him.'

With a brisk easterly wind to hasten their steps, they made quick work of getting to the fortress. They were greeted politely by Antonius's slave, a worried man, who said his master hadn't yet returned from a hunting expedition.

'Hunting? That's odd. We were told he rarely leaves the fort, even in his spare time.'

The slave, a whippet-thin man of middle years, nodded unhappily.

'You were told true, Domina. I don't understand it. I went out this morning to fetch fresh bread and buy provisions for dinner, and came back to empty quarters and a note telling me he was gone hunting all day.'

He held out a tablet.

'Is that your master's hand?' Julia asked quickly.

'I'm…I'm not sure, Domina. I don't think so. And now he has been gone many hours, and I don't know —' He broke off as a commotion came from the main gate. Through it passed a cortege of soldiers, dressed for the hunt with bows slung over their shoulders, carrying a limp body. Julia walked over quickly.

'I am an army-trained healer,' she said. 'Let me through. I may be able to help your comrade.' As she spoke she was shocked to recognise the face turned to one side, eyes shut. It was Antonius Gargilianus. She recoiled, immediately halting the little procession. But the big man's pulse was still, and when she lifted open an eyelid, there was no reflex shrinking of the pupils.

'He's dead,' she said sadly to Britta, who had now caught her up.

The lead soldier spoke. 'That's right, Domina. Nothing more to do here. We'll take him to his quarters, and report to the officer of the watch.'

'How did it happen?'

'Nasty fall from his horse. Broke his neck. Could happen to anyone. Poor old Antonius. Still, his burial club payments will see him off fine, nice little monument too, I'll be bound.'

Julia stiffened at his somewhat jaunty tone, making no reply. She and Britta followed into Antonius's house, where the distressed slave broke into lamentations. Under cover of helping the slave, Julia and Britta lingered till the soldiers had deposited Antonius on his cot and departed. Then Julia carried out a fuller examination. Not for a second did she believe the tale they'd just heard.

'Well, Britta, his neck is broken all right. But that wasn't what killed him. Look.'

With some effort, for he was a heavily muscled man in the prime of life, she lifted up Antonius's left arm. 'As I thought. He was stabbed here, with a knife long enough to sever a major artery. He would have been unconscious in moments, and dead within a minute. Someone has washed him very carefully, as I found only a small trace of blood. Even in a few seconds, a wound like that would cause heavy bleeding. I suspect he was laid down in running water, a river or stream, to wash away the blood.'

'But his clothes, mistress? There are no blood stains,' said Britta.

'No, but look, Britta, where the shoulder seam has torn. I would wager my Eboracum inheritance this is not the prefect's own tunic.'

Julia thought for a moment, then called the slave over. 'Where would your master keep his papers? Correspondence, and so on?'

The slave, clearly in shock, stared at her dumbly.

'Quick, man,' she said impatiently. 'There are confidential reports here, sent by my husband. We must find them.'

But there was no sign of any written material at all. A cupboard that should have contained Antonius's papers was emptied, the door carefully closed so a casual glance would find no change since the prefect left. Julia compressed her lips. She turned back to the slave, telling him he should leave. 'Just forget what you may have heard, for your own sake,' she said. 'It is not safe to stay here. Leave everything, and go away immediately.'

'But where can I go, Domina? I am a slave. If I'm found without my master, they'll think I am a runaway.'

'Very well, you must come with us.' Holding her finger to her lips, and shaking her head when he opened his mouth in alarm, she moved quietly to the door of the prefect's quarters. 'Coast is clear, Britta. We must go, quickly. Now!'

All three left the prefect's home as discreetly as they could, and were fortunate to be able to merge with a large party exiting the fort. They hurried towards home, Julia wondering what on Earth to do now. Before they had gone very far, she stopped. She said to the trailing slave who was still shivering, more with distress than cold under his thick birrus, 'What's your name?'

'Sextus, Domina.'

'Sextus, I am Lady Julia Aureliana. I'm going to call in to see a friend on my way back. You head straight home. Tell my man Fronto I sent you, and you are to be given a bed and a hot meal.' She gave him directions to her house. He bowed and hurried off, the long coat flapping round his skinny legs.

Britta raised an eyebrow. 'To Corellia's?'

'Absolutely. We might be getting into deep water, Britta. We need a wise friend to listen and advise.'

Corellia welcomed them warmly. Britta opened her eyes at the opulent furnishings and large well-heated rooms of the plush mansion, clearly the home of a very wealthy couple.

'You may not be so glad to see us when you hear what I have to say,' warned Julia.

'Never mind. Come into the salon,' Corellia urged them, sending a slave for snacks and spiced wine. 'It's a shame Aurelius is away on business today. He has a cool experienced head. But tell me your news.'

Julia drew breath, composing her thoughts. She told her friend of the letter from Quintus and the longer report about trafficking and collusion with enemy natives he had reportedly sent to Antonius; how he had found the dead tribune Gaius Laelianus; that

138

THE LOYAL CENTURION

Legate Marius Crescens had not in fact gone away over Saturnalia, but had been witnessed roaming the streets in disguise the very night Placidia was killed; and now the shocking death of Prefect Gargilianus. As she spoke, Julia found to her annoyance that her hands were shaking. She folded them together tightly. Corellia noticed, and called sharply for the slave to be quick with the refreshments. There was a pause while Corellia urged the two women to eat and drink. She sat in silence, apparently turning over in her mind what Julia had reported.

'Well,' she said at length, 'I think the killing of Antonius Gargilianus could turn out to be a real mistake, if it was Crescens who ordered it. Antonius was a long-serving and highly regarded officer within the legion, and across the city. His loss may have repercussions the legate doesn't expect. There are other matters we need to consider, too. First, Salvia remains safe and secret. She sent me a message this morning to say Lossio had changed his mind, and is heading back to Eboracum instead of trying to follow the beneficiarius.' She raised a hand, as Julia opened her mouth in protest at this. 'I don't know why, and of course this morning Salvia had no especial reason to think this a significant change of plans. I assume we still don't know where Placidia's journal went?'

'No,' Julia said, wishing Lossio had not advised them so strongly against searching for the book. In her heart Julia was convinced Placidia had uncovered something critical, something so dangerous she was prepared to flee. She pictured the gently born and carefully brought up young woman trying to deal with a deadly secret alone, and shook her head, troubled. She owed it to their vulnerable young friend to uncover the plot that had taken her so brutally from them. Poor Placidia deserved to rest in peace; it was all they could do for her now.

But who was the secret holder of Placidia's writings? Someone she trusted, and knew well, clearly. Who in the city was strong enough, senior enough, so well-placed that they would never be questioned, even if they were known to have spent time with Placidia? Who in Eboracum would be above all suspicion?

Julia began to wonder...

Corellia broke into her thoughts. She smoothed back her dark hair, reaching to pour more wine as she said, 'There is something else Salvia told me. It seems Placidia, who like me had prayed devoutly to Serapis for a child, may have got her wish.'

There was silence while Julia and Britta absorbed this.

'You mean, she told Salvia she was pregnant?' asked Britta. 'I suppose her body slave was bound to know. But why would Placidia's own husband murder her, when he was so determined to get an heir? Perhaps he wasn't her killer after all?'

'But remember, Britta, that both Crescens' previous wives had apparently been unable to successfully bear a child. What if it was the legate who was infertile, not our friend?'

Julia shook her head in sorrow. 'Ah, poor Placidia! If he knew, or suspected he was to blame for their childlessness, Placidia was in jeopardy from the moment he thought she might be pregnant. And Gaius too.'

'Indeed. If the legate was beginning to mistrust her, or he simply wanted to dispose of her and gain another richer wife, then her life was truly forfeit. After all, you don't lightly divorce a member of the imperial family, do you?'

After this revelation, there seemed little left to say and much need to ponder. Julia and Britta left for home, Julia so sunk in reflection that it wasn't till Britta ran ahead, crying out, 'Julia, come quick!' that she looked up to notice something amiss. Her household was milling around in the courtyard. The front door had panels smashed in and was hanging off its stout hinges. On the threshold lay an elderly man, still and white. Julia's maid, a quick-thinking lass, was kneeling on the ground and holding a cold compress gently to the man's forehead. Sextus was encouraging the other servants to get back inside, and looked relieved when Julia and Britta arrived.

'Thank the gods you're here, Domina!'

Julia groaned inwardly, and went to crouch next to yet another victim, her loyal old steward Fronto.

Chapter Nineteen

Castlelaw hillfort

Quintus muttered curses under his breath as they neared the Pictish hillfort. Aila's impetuous actions could spell disaster. At the foot of the crag he recognised two of their horses, tied to a discreet picket line between birches in a dense copse. He paused, issuing instructions to Tiro.

'Move the horses further back, and hide yourself too. We'll certainly need the horses, whatever happens; you may have to take them back to Cair Pol without me.'

Tiro opened his mouth, protest on his face, but Quintus cut him short. 'No time, Tiro. We must get our young people out before Athair realises who he's trapped. They are my responsibility. I need you to stay within reach till they come out. Just get them back to the fort. Remember, we have sent reports to Litorius and Antonius, who will share them with Lossio. We can expect reinforcements, but I need you there to coordinate them. If Aila and Kian don't come out by dusk, go back to the fort anyway. But be ready to help them.' Quintus reached out to grasp Tiro's shoulder. 'So much is riding on what happens here, my friend. I need your support and trust. Do I have it?'

Tiro nodded with a wavering grin, and headed into the copse.

Quintus had left his sword, but brought with him a small buckler shield. As he left the shelter of the trees he raised the shield above his head in the time-honoured Roman signal of parley. He had no idea whether this token would be recognised or honoured by the Picts, but what else could he do? At the bottom of the rocky spur, he called out to the guards around the palisades, standing shoulder height above the fort's thick stone walls.

'Parley! I come in peace, and beg speech with the Great Pict!'

He called this out a couple of times while the guards stared down, their conical iron-tipped spears kept at alert. He had no idea whether he was understood, but did his best to portray a man sure

141

of his welcome as an ambassador. There was a protracted silence, during which neither side moved. Then came a small stir. Two guards stepped aside, heads briefly bowed and spears moved to the at-ease position. A young dark-haired man, tall, of medium build, came to the palisade and addressed Quintus in surprisingly accurate, if heavily-accented, Latin.

'Who are you, who dares to invade the lands of the Painted People? My uncle, Athair the Great Pict, will tolerate no outsiders in his country.'

Quintus guessed this was Bedwyr. He gave his name and rank, replying that he had come in peaceful embassy from the Roman provinces, and wished to conduct talks with the Great Pict to discuss terms of respect for each other's peoples and frontiers. The spearmen openly laughed, banging down the butts of their ash spears so the noise rang out along the stone-paved walkway. But Quintus noted a thoughtful look in the young man's blue eyes. He said something to a shorter warrior beside him, who turned to run lightly along the battlements before disappearing into the fort.

Time passed, while Quintus tried not to look impatient or cold. Bedwyr went away, while the short man leaned over the palisade to hail Quintus, instructing him to come up. Successive flights of steps were accessed by gatehouses, the largest one leading into the fort. It was an imposing set of defences which would not have shamed a small Roman fort. Except for one thing, Quintus thought: while the towering walls of the fort were made of stone — double-walled and vitrified, according to Kian — the gatehouses, as well as the palisades, were all wooden. He walked carefully through a spread of knee-high sharp stones set upright in the ground, clearly defence obstacles.

The gates were open by the time he had scrambled, panting, up the final stretch of the boulder-strewn slope. He needed both hands to climb the sheer scree. He swung his buckler over his shoulder, reckoning it had played its part. Bedwyr met him at the top, saying curtly, 'Follow me. My lord would greet you in front of his warriors. We hide nothing from our people.'

Quintus followed him through the gates, along a short stone path leading to a good-sized open space. The fort was roughly oblong in shape, taking advantage of the natural promontory. There were signs of recent refurbishment: raw wooden palings, pale new stone strengthening the thick walls and ramparts, a small group of sturdy wooden buildings, all round, with newly thatched roofs.

In front of the largest roundhouse stood a giant of a man, some years older than Quintus. He wore a rough-woven tunic over wool breeches, with a bright chequered plaid wrapped over a shoulder and round his torso. His clothing did nothing to disguise the sheer scale of his build. He was huge and well-muscled. Tawny hair flowed down his back. Across his face coiled blue tattoos. A red-flecked beard reached his chest.

Quintus did not need to be told that this was Athair, the Great Pict. No one else north of the Aelian Wall, thought Quintus with sinking heart, would have such an implacable expression of hatred on his harsh-featured face. Nor was it likely that any other leader could arouse such trepidation in those around him. None of his warriors, strong and seasoned men though they looked, raised his eyes to his lord's face. The few women emerging from the stockade's houses stepped hastily back inside, with their silenced children quickly gathered into their skirts. Quintus was reminded of a statue he had once seen, of a cruel-eyed eagle stooping to attack a lion. He hoped the young lion, Bedwyr, would display as the rightful king of the animals if the need arose.

Further opportunity for thought fled, as Athair, mouth twisted, paced forward to stand in front of Quintus. He looked long at the Roman, jutting his powerful jaw out. His whole posture was of threat. Quintus fought to retain a sense of dignity. He doubted there would be much parley. What chance would he have to rescue Aila and Kian?

'I have prayed to the gods for this day.' Athair spoke in a harsh voice, which carried across the circle in the practised manner of one who is never disobeyed. Bedwyr, standing tall and self-possessed, translated his uncle's abrupt words. 'For twenty years, I have prayed for and prepared for this day, the day I begin my revenge on the hated Red Crests who took my youth. It would be a great gift from the gods to have any Roman soldier in my power. But I never expected such a magnificent gift. The gods have truly blessed me, sending me one who fought against us in battle, and then razed our homes, our farms, our people from the rich earth. One who colluded with our treasonous neighbours to the south, who received Roman silver in exchange for our freedoms.'

Athair gave a great laugh, a chilling sound.

'Well, we have taken back what was ours, Roman! Now I have you as my god-given gift, I will consider what fitting punishment to make.'

Quintus was distracted as a girl, small and lithe, came out of the roundhouse behind Athair. He was astonished to recognise Aila. She looked at him scornfully, flicking her dark hair back from her forehead with one hand. There was no sign of Kian.

Athair glanced at Quintus. 'Ah, I see you know my new companion. She has turned out to be a doughty warrior despite her traitorous family background. Aila has come back to her true lord, bringing quite a treasure: that disgusting hybrid, who speaks our tongue and also your Latin, calling himself Kian mac Dougal. Now I have him, I will soon force out of him the weaknesses of his tribe, the people of Dál Riata. Their turn will come. But first I have you to consider, Roman, the other prize my Aila has coaxed here. Pah!'

Athair spat at Quintus, catching him full in the face. The gob of spittle rolled down over one eyelid, forcing Quintus to blink in disgust and wipe it away. Athair laughed again, and this time his warriors joined in, bellowing with their chief. Abruptly Athair stopped laughing. His face turned cold.

'Take him. Bind him, and hold him under guard with his mongrel.'

'Wait!' Quintus forced his voice to sound assured. 'I come under sign of parley, to negotiate with you, Athair, the leader of the Painted People. I am sent by the governor of Britannia Superior, who wishes understanding and good relations with mighty Athair. If you have reason to mistrust, or bear a grudge against the legate of Britannia Inferior, I am empowered to listen, make redress, and reach a treaty with the Great Pict. There is no need for hostility between our peoples. Let us talk, and overcome whatever difficulties lie between us.'

THE LOYAL CENTURION

A frozen silence fell over the gathered crowd of Athair's men. All now gazed down at their feet. Athair motioned to his nephew, who was standing slightly behind. Bedwyr went at once into the large roundhouse, and returned quickly with a long iron sword. He knelt and gave it to his uncle. The big man lifted the heavy sword. He swung it in a mighty circle about his head. The swish of its passing through the air was electrifying, and Quintus knew his words had failed.

Athair lowered the sword to shoulder height, holding it out at arm's length as he moved in towards Quintus. The bulging muscles in his blue-painted arms cracked as he moved forward, until he was holding the sharp tip at the base of Quintus's throat. He pushed the sword a little inwards, till Quintus flinched as the iron tip bit through his scarf and pressed into the tender skin at his throat. There the Pict held it steady for a long moment. Quintus had to concede that it was an impressive display of strength. Altogether intimidating.

Athair lowered the sword. 'Your blood is mine, Roman. As is that of your greedy legate, when I will it. But I alone will choose the time for my sword to drink your blood.'

He turned, his plaid sweeping in a great arc as he stalked away into the roundhouse. Quintus caught a last glimpse of Aila, head held high, following Athair. She turned at the door to give Quintus an inscrutable look.

Then he was grasped by many hands, bound and taken through a low door into a cold little cell carved from the inside of the great double-layered wall. On the stone-flagged floor lay a young man with red-flecked hair, dark eyes opening as Quintus was pushed inside. The cell had a low ceiling with wooden beams slung under the stone roof above. It was quite dingy despite the bright sun outside. Only meagre light filtered between the wooden slats of the outer wall, but gradually Quintus could make out his companion's features as he sat up: Kian. The Gael's face was sullen with despondency.

'She has betrayed us. Aila. Little bitch! Soon enough the Great Pict will know about Tiro and Nico. All hopes will end.'

'Do not speak so!' Anger was rising in Quintus. Maybe at being

145

played for a fool by a cruel barbarian; maybe at himself, for being both proud and naive; maybe at Kian for making foolish assumptions. He chose the latter, and could hear the stern tone in his own voice.

'Do not malign that girl until you are sure of the truth. She deserves our trust yet. I believe she could be the most courageous person I have ever met.' *Apart from a certain little Syrian accountant and spy, in Vebriacum, who died to save me, and Julia and Tiro — in fact, to save an entire province.*

Kian looked startled, and then his head drooped as he subsided onto the floor. Eventually he lay down, turning his face away from Quintus.

After many hours — Quintus could not tell how long but his feet had gone numb — the door opened and a rough meal of dried meat and bread, not too stale, was pushed in, together with a jar of water. Also an empty pail.

'Well, they don't intend us to die in here yet,' he said in a falsely cheerful voice to Kian. The young man was slumped on the floor, wrapped in his plaid, neither moving nor speaking. Once Quintus had made an initial check of their cell, establishing that there was no window nor any hole they could work at to escape, he sat down next to Kian. He might as well conserve his energies, and there was no furniture of any kind to sit on. It was cold, so he was glad that at least their cloaks had been left to them. He also had the buckler, his sign of truce, still slung on his back. This had apparently been overlooked when they were searched fruitlessly for weapons; or perhaps it was thought of no concern.

Kian looked up. His face was grey. 'You think so, because you do not know what the Picts do to their enemies,' he said, between gritted teeth.

'Well, you'd better warn me. If it is as bad as your face tells, I'd like to know in advance and pray to Lord Mithras for succour.' Kian shook his head in weary dejection.

Another untold passage of time later — perhaps the next day, judging by the splinters of light now penetrating the wood-planked front wall — the door opened. Expecting more food, and hoping for the removal of the foul slops pail, Quintus was surprised when Bedwyr entered with a guard. The door was closed behind them, and the guard carried a drawn sword at his side. Quintus thought wearily, for the night had been both cold and hard, and allowed him little sleep, that the sword was unnecessary.

Bedwyr glanced at his companion, the shorter warrior who had flanked him on the battlements.

'I come to warn you of your likely fate.' He paused, apparently expecting protest or anger. Both prisoners kept their peace, Quintus by design, and Kian possibly in despair.

Bedwyr said a little testily, 'Is it really necessary for them to sit on the cold floor?'

'The lord's standing orders for prisoners, sir.'

'*I* am not a prisoner, though. I will sit while I hold speech with the Romans.'

'Yes, sir.'

'And bring a bench for them too. I will not speak with a crooked neck!'

The shorter man hurried away. The door was bolted anew from the outside.

Bedwyr suddenly changed attitude, and began speaking rapidly. 'We don't have much time. I am my uncle's faithful man, but I have a greater duty even than that loyalty. One day, mine will be the responsibility to keep my people secure and prosperous. Listen to me carefully; there is something you need to understand. My uncle is so bitter against you because as a young man he fought against your old king. Athair was captured and imprisoned in a beehive in one of your great forts, near the mighty wall of stone.'

This was recognisably Vindolanda, and Quintus's heart raced. Whatever Bedwyr told them might just provide an edge, a chink in the Great Pict's armour they could chisel through.

'He was sold as a slave, and on account of his great strength was sent to labour on a farm. It was many weeks' journey south and east, where the lands are flat, the fields are vast and golden with grain, and one can hear the sea.'

Quintus recognised the description; no doubt Athair had laboured on one of the great imperial latifundia in the old tribal lands of the Iceni.

'He killed his overseer, a bad man with a whip, with his bare hands, even though he was shackled. He escaped. It was a terrible journey home to our lands in the far north, but he survived and became our leader. With his strength of body and mind, he gathered together the tribes of the north into one, and began his campaign of revenge against the Romans and their allies. He has sucked your corrupt legate into his net. He has no regard for your weak leaders, and neither do I. But I don't believe our people will prosper if we challenge the might of your Roman armies again. Neither do I believe we should threaten your Wall. In that I differ from Athair. I was a small child when your king Severus wiped the old Caledonian alliance from the soil of the lowlands. I was told the tale by my wise old grandfather. I do not wish the same to happen again, and I doubt, as my uncle does not, that we can defeat your legions in open combat in the rich south lands. I was so determined, I even learned your tongue from a Roman prisoner of war before my uncle had him killed.'

Despite the chill of this last comment, Quintus saw Mercury's blessed hand at work and grasped his opportunity. 'Bedwyr, what would you have us do? I will work with you to save your people if I can. That indeed was the task I came here to accomplish. But first, tell me about the girl, Aila. How did she come to join with your uncle, surely her enemy of old?'

It was too late. The door opened and the short man, together with another, heaved in two benches.

'You are slow, brother,' Bedwyr said to the men. 'I am finished here for today. But leave the benches, in case my lord wishes me to have further speech with the prisoners.'

As he turned to leave, he nodded slightly at Quintus. The door was pulled shut and bolted behind, with a grating that sounded horribly final.

What had Bedwyr meant? Would he come back? Or was this just another form of torment from the great Pict, keeping them in hope to later smash them onto the rocks of despair? But Quintus had again seen the intelligence in Bedwyr's measured expression. It was possible this young man did indeed perceive danger in his uncle's policies. Bedwyr would save his people, if he could. Now Quintus had to work out how to save Kian and himself. And decide what to do about the enigma that Aila had suddenly become.

He felt in great need of rest. In spite of the cold and uncertainty, he stretched out on one of the benches, placed his future in the hands of the Lord of Light, and fell instantly asleep.

Chapter Twenty

Cair Pol

At dusk Tiro untied the horses from their pickets, turning for home alone with a heavy heart. He stayed under the shelter of the trees until he had emerged into the dusk of the riverside meadows. He'd waited all that short bright day, getting gradually colder and hungrier. Quintus had not returned from the hill fort, and there was no sign of either Kian or Aila. He felt downhearted, sure that all three of them had come to grief inside that Pictish snakepit. Would he ever see the boss again, or their two young Caledonian friends? Then he remembered Nicomedes. The poor lad had been left alone many hours, without news or adult company. Tiro twitched his horse's reins and made all speed. He entered the fort from the riverside gate, halting in alarm when he saw a strange horse. As he wondered, Nico appeared, clearly coming to see to his new equine friend. The boy broke into a clumsy run when he saw the optio.

'Tiro! You're back!'

He hurled himself at Tiro, almost in tears.

'I'm sorry I had to leave you so long, Nico,' said Tiro, both guilty and relieved, hugging the boy. 'But whose horse is that?'

Nico dragged a grubby hand across his face, leaving a trail of snot and tears.

'It's Centurion Litorius. He's c-come all the way from Vindolanda. He's inside, cooking a big stew and he's lit a huge fire, sir. I hope that's all right?'

Nico looked white and anxious, and Tiro ruffled his dark hair.

'Of course it's all right! Get yourself inside and warmed up. I'll see to the horses. Let the centurion know I'm here, would you?'

Tiro had turned the horses out into the stalls, fed and watered them all, including Litorius's rough-haired black, and was hanging up the saddles and tackle when a familiar resonant voice spoke behind him.

'Good to see you, Optio. I hear from your estimable horse-boy

that whilst four of you left for the hillfort this morning, you alone
have come back.'

Tiro turned. Litorius Pacatianus looked travel-weary and
worried, but his tone was considerably warmer than when they had
first met in the refectory at Vindolanda.

'I'm glad to see you too, sir. Let's exchange news over a bowl
of your stew, shall we?'

Tiro began with recounting their meeting with Kian mac Dougal
at Cair Pol, and the uncovering of the eagle of the Ninth. Litorius
looked startled, but was content to keep the precious bird in its
hiding place till matters at Castlelaw had been resolved. Tiro then
explained how Aila had secretly gone to the hillfort with Kian.
How Quintus and he had found their horses at the foot of the hill,
and Quintus had insisted he would go inside too, leaving Tiro on
watch.

He finished unhappily, saying, 'The boss ordered me to stay at
the bottom of the crag, out of sight. He was sure he could get the
two of them freed in exchange for himself. I was to bring them
back here. But that hasn't happened, and now it's just me and
Nico, and I dunno what he thinks he can do alone up there
surrounded by painted barbarians!'

'But I'm here now, and Marcus and my men will soon join us.
We will devise a plan, never fear.' The centurion's expression
remained reserved, but Tiro fancied his eyes brightened as he said
this. 'When I got the letter from Quintus Valerius, I sent my whole
beneficiariate out on patrol to the locus meeting centres, to gather
information from our old allies. They have orders to bring word to
me here, I hope within a few days.'

Litorius, severe of haircut, dress and bearing, looked so much
the traditional Roman officer that Tiro felt more confident.
Though there remained a set look on the centurion's face,
suggestive of weighty burdens carried in secret.

Litorius reached into his saddle bag to pull out a small message
tablet. 'I brought something for your superior, but as his deputy, I
think you should have sight of it too. You can read?'

Tiro nodded awkwardly; his reading and writing skills were

rough and ready, but he would not tell this proper officer so.

'Good. This is a letter left by the lady Placidia Septimia of Eboracum, in the care of her confidential maid, Salvia. I had it from Speculator Lossio Veda, who came to Vindolanda by express, looking for Quintus Valerius. However, when I told him what had transpired at Vindolanda — the death of Tribune Gaius Laelianus, and the attack on you, as well as my optio Marcus's reports of Picts being given free passage through the Wall at Magna and Vercovicium — he became concerned for the safety of Salvia. She is the key witness in unravelling her mistress's death. I understand from Lossio that Lady Julia and her friend Corellia Velva are also known to have been close to Placidia. That friendship might put them at risk, too, so Lossio was eager to return to Eboracum. Also, his speculatores report to him there, with what may be vital intelligence. So here I am in his stead, and I hope I will prove a satisfactory substitute.'

His set mouth lifted into a sudden warm smile, and Tiro wondered anew about the troubles that so often kept his face stern. It was not Tiro's place to ask, though.

Tiro itched to thrash out a rescue plan for Quintus straightaway, and found it challenging to channel his energies elsewhere. But even he could see the sense in waiting till at least some of Litorius's promised men had arrived. He fretted constantly, though, as the days passed. He slept little at night, despite busying himself with collecting firewood and water, helping Nico with the horses, and extending his cooking skills.

One morning he woke to find the world swaddled in dense fog. It was heaviest over the river Tausa, but even inside Cair Pol the fog was so thick Tiro couldn't see more than an arm's length beyond the entrance to the praetorium. It was impossible to tell how far advanced the day was, but Tiro reckoned by the pressure on his bladder it was later than he usually woke. He swathed himself in his birrus, pulling the woollen hood well down over his head, and stepped out cautiously in the direction of the latrine. The air was intensely cold, and soggy to breathe. It felt as if a wet blanket was covering him, stretching and moving in company with him as he stepped along. The mists parted sluggishly as he walked cautiously along the barrack rows, closing behind him almost immediately. He stubbed a toe on the corner of a building when memory tricked him once and he turned too soon.

After a while he noticed that the fog seemed a little lighter ahead. *I must be facing east,* he figured. Sol was up above, trying to pierce the thick wet layers. He now had his bearings a little better. But the silence was oppressive. He felt as if he was the only living being in Cair Pol. That thought unnerved him. Had he actually seen either of his companions when he woke? He tried to remember. Surely Litorius had been rolled up in his blanket on the floor? But Nico — had he seen the boy yet this morning?

Tiro fought his way to and from the latrine, then stopped at what he thought must be the end of the commandant's stables where they kept their own horses. He found the stable doors after some stumbling along the wall, and went inside. There was no Nico, and no Pegasus. Neither was there the inevitable wet-nosed greeting from Camilla. He tried calling the boy but his voice was swallowed up, sounding flat in his own ears. *Curses, where is the lad? Perhaps we passed each other on parallel streets. He's bound to be back in the praetorium by now.*

Tiro returned in what he hoped was the right direction. A tall horse loomed up through the mist, stopping suddenly at the urging of a small hand. The dog trotting at the horse's heels was also silent, until she launched herself ecstatically at Tiro, barking and nearly knocking him over.

Nico explained when they were safely inside, and once Tiro had seen that Litorius was indeed present, still rolled in his blanket. The boy looked nervous, as well he might.

'I woke in the night, and seeing it was so foggy outside, I thought it would be a g-good chance to scout out the hillfort. I wanted to find out where all the entrances and gateways are, without being seen.'

He swallowed, looking with pleading eyes at his mentor. Tiro sighed. There was no point in getting angry at the lad — he had come home safe, after all.

'I know you were trying to be helpful, Nico. But what if the horse tossed you, or hit a tree in the fog, or something?'

Nico was shocked. 'Oh, no, Pegasus w-wouldn't throw me. He's my friend. Anyway, he and C-Camilla both know their way in the fog. And the dark,' he added reflectively. 'And guess what, Tiro? Guess who I saw?'

'Pictish guards?'

'No. I don't think they were expecting anyone to c-come up the hill on such a night.'

Tiro reckoned this was right. Only a madman or a very talented horse-boy would attempt that.

'No, it was Aila! I saw her, and spoke to her.'

Tiro was confused. 'How did she see you in such fog?'

'The top of the c-crag was above the fog. It was clear at the fort. Aila says she comes out every night to look out for me. She knew I would c-come.' A note of smugness had crept into the boy's voice. 'She told me lots.'

'Wait,' commanded Tiro. 'Litorius needs to hear this.' He bent to gently shake the sleeping centurion awake. 'Right, Nico, go ahead and tell us what Aila said.'

'She is very c-clever, Aila,' said Nico with admiration. 'She has made friends with the Great Pict. She even lives in his roundhouse.'

Tiro was taken aback; better than Nico, he guessed how Aila had "made friends" with Athair.

'Go on,' he urged.

'Well, she says K-Kian is being held prisoner, in a cell with Quintus. But Athair says he will send Kian north to the C-Cave of the Dead. I don't know what that is, but Aila is very frightened for him. She says b-bad things happen in the cave; some of her family were taken there.'

Nico stopped; his mouth wobbled. Tiro sat the boy down, saying, 'You need some breakfast. Here —' he poked around in his saddlebag, retrieving a pair of dried peppered meat sticks, one of which he handed to Nico. The boy immediately began to chew, while Tiro gave the other meat stick to Litorius. For himself, he was too anxious to eat, even if he liked the meat sticks. Which he didn't, not much.

It was Litorius who spoke first.

'Did Aila know when Kian was to be taken away? And what about Quintus? Does she know what is planned for him?'

Nico shook his head. 'She said she would try to find out if I c-can come back. I did discover that behind the chief's roundhouse is a bit of wall that is less watched than the rest.'

'Why?' asked Tiro, immediately suspicious of any all-too-convenient oversight.

'Because it's impossible to climb, it's so steep on that side,' Nico said simply.

'What use is that, then?' Tiro exploded. Nico stepped back, mouth wobbling even more.

Litorius spoke soothingly, saying, 'Don't get upset, lad. Tiro is naturally worried about Quintus Valerius, and concerned about how to rescue our friends.'

Tiro nodded, feeling ashamed. 'I'm sorry, Nico. Litorius is right — I am a bit worried.'

'I know you are, sir. Me t-too,' Nico said. 'But I meant, too steep for a man to walk up.'

'How does that help us, lad?' Litorius asked gently.

'Well, sir, it's not too steep for me and Pegasus. You know Lady Julia bought him from a breeder who brings in stallions from Iberia?'

Tiro nodded; he did know that, and was envious of Julia for having such a fine horse. 'So, he can get up that slope,' Nico went on.

'How can you be sure? It would be a disaster to try, and have Pegasus refuse.'

'Oh, I know because we've done it.'

Tiro shook his head again, grinning in bemused admiration. Nicomedes was an amazing youngster.

'I thought all along we might need to get into the hillfort in secret, so I spent a little time teaching Pegasus to climb. But it turns out he already knew it. His Hispanic background, I suppose.'

Litorius looked intrigued, but when Tiro asked him what was on his mind, he simply shook his head. However, that evening when

Nico was asleep, arms wrapped round his warm dog, Tiro caught a look of deep sadness on the centurion's face.

'Everything all right, sir?'

'How can it be, with our people imprisoned by the Great Pict? And that boy — Nicomedes. He reminds me of someone I once knew.'

'I meant all right with you, sir.'

Tiro expected to be immediately rebuffed. Litorius was not one to share confidences. So he was surprised to get a different response.

'That person I remember, a girl who had some of his courage and a great heart — she is gone, and can never come back. Younger even than Nicomedes, my...the girl I knew.' Litorius drew a deep breath. 'This situation can't be allowed to continue. It's no good hoping Aila can save them all. That's my job, and by Hercules I will act as befits a Roman officer.'

Tiro didn't like the grim edge to Litorius's deep voice. He fell asleep wondering about the taciturn centurion and his past. He supposed he would never know.

THE LOYAL CENTURION

Chapter Twenty-one

Castlelaw hillfort

Quintus woke from a dream he had thought long gone. He was an eager Praetorian junior officer, fighting with the emperor's vast army in the glens of Caledonia. In his dream he was trying to catch up with a younger legionary, one he knew so well. Flavius, his brother, was once more about to die in front of him. Now Quintus knew he was dreaming, but could not wake. He lay in sweat-soaked stillness despite the cold, forced to watch in horror and dread as the long-haired Caledonian warrior thrust his spear into Flavius. It never got any easier to watch. He saw afresh the look on Flavius's dying face — accusation, or was it forgiveness?

Around him the noise of battle escalated, until slowly he woke to the realisation that there was an actual din taking place in the courtyard of the hillfort. Kian was already wide awake, crouched on the floor with his head pressed to a crack between the boards of their prison cell.

'Hush!' Kian held a finger to his lips, whispering, 'Another Roman! They have another prisoner.'

As he spoke, the door to their cell creaked open. Bedwyr came in quickly, a warning shake of his head to Quintus before he and Kian were both dragged out into the pewter-coloured dawn. Held between two tartan-cloaked Picts was an upright figure Quintus knew: the dour Centurion Litorius Pacatianus. The older beneficiarius stood erect and still. He made no acknowledgement of Quintus, whilst looking right at him. Quintus shot a glance at Kian, and held himself in readiness. The door to the chief's roundhouse was abruptly pushed open, and Athair strode out. A pace behind came Aila, her plaid shawl slipping off one naked shoulder, her hair tousled. The shock on her face told Quintus this development was none of her doing; not that he had thought it so. He was convinced Aila was acting a clever and very dangerous part, whatever Kian might believe.

Athair looked long at Litorius. With a peremptory wave he

summoned Bedwyr and two others of his closest bodyguard, clearly the warriors he most trusted. They held a muttered conversation for several minutes. Aila moved discreetly till she was in line of sight of Quintus. The puzzlement on her face was signal enough. Quintus held his gaze on Aila. Like Bedwyr, he moved his head slightly side to side. She seemed to understand, and kept her peace.

But Kian heeded nothing of this silent byplay. He said fiercely to Quintus in his accented Latin, 'Another comes to be sacrificed! What do you say now, Quintus? Another betrayal?'

Bedwyr looked up quickly, his face inscrutable. He glanced at Aila, then said something in a low voice to the Pictish king. Athair scowled, but fell silent. He seemed to be considering what Bedwyr had said. He approached his new prisoner, his plaid swinging as he moved. He spoke, loudly and at length. The harshness of his gaunt features intensified. Whatever he was saying, Quintus judged it would not be comforting. As he ceased speaking, Athair spat with full force at Litorius's feet, catching his boot. The centurion gave a faint smile.

Quintus recognised that smile, so weary, so disdainful. It was from another time, long ago. Perhaps they had coincided at the Castra Peregrina, in Rome? They might have met as two younger detached officers in the Roman secret service, between missions. As he pondered, Bedwyr turned the Great Pict's words into Latin, speaking first to Litorius.

'My uncle says he is grateful for your offer. The gods of the Dead will accept you, doubtless, being a seasoned warrior full of honours. But he has also promised them the young mongrel here, Kian mac Dougal. They might be offended to lose a sacrifice already pledged. Athair will consider carefully, and consult our priests. Perhaps it will be best to send both the old warrior and the young together to the gods? As for you, Roman,' — Bedwyr held his voice steady, but Quintus felt the extent of the young Pict's self-control as he turned towards him — 'there will be no quick honourable death for you. You will endure long until an ignoble ending. Athair the Great Pict says the beginning of your death of many cuts will take place when our chief priest arrives from our northern fastness. On the third day from now, at dawn, your suffering will begin. You may choose yourself which finger is taken off first.'

Bedwyr turned away as Quintus, Kian and Litorius were grabbed and pushed back into the cell. Not before Quintus had seen the regret on the young man's face.

Now it was here, the certain prospect of his impending death, Quintus felt strangely calm. There were things he would have wished to witness, of course: his children growing up to be happy and successful, both Roman and British, loved by and protecting their people of the Durotriges. He would miss the green hills and grey-blue waters of the Summer Country when he woke in the next world. He regretted already the adventures, friendship and achievement of working with Tiro, with Marcellus and the Aquae Sulis cohort, and with their governor, a truly great Roman.

He did not worry about Julia, for he knew they were destined to meet and love again in the afterlife. Mithras, Lord of Light, promised his followers life eternal. And Pluto, mighty god of the underworld, would ensure they would be together. Pluto himself had been shot with Cupid's arrow when he saw his own wife, Persephone. He would understand the great love that would never die between Quintus and his Julia. No, Quintus was not afraid of losing Julia.

He noticed that Litorius had seated himself next to Kian on one of their benches, and was talking quietly to him. The young man was in distress, his hands shaking and his face as pale as the winter birches in the Caledonian hills. Quintus had turned in time to hear the end of their conversation.

Litorius said, gently but firmly, 'All of us are in the hands of the gods. But I am sure you will not be sent north. Mine will be this destiny, and I tell you now, I welcome it gladly.'

Kian looked at the centurion, sitting so assured by his side, and said, 'No. I know these cruel people. I have heard of those taken in punishment by the Pict. I know of the bones found in caves, scattered so their souls can never be whole again, even in the afterlife. The Great Pict will take the chance to send a dreadful warning to my own people, the Dál Riata. He will squeeze out of me whatever he can learn to their disadvantage, and then he will have me killed too. But I thank you for your fortitude, Centurion. You remind me of my duty to my people, all of them. I am a proud Gael, and a proud Roman both. I feel less afraid now.'

His hands settled and the colour returned to Kian's face as he stood, stretching his legs to take a few turns in their small stone prison.

Now the time dragged slowly. The cold was constant, and might have prevented them from sleeping. But perhaps surprisingly, both Litorius and Kian slept for long periods. Quintus alone held vigil, unable to rest beyond snatches as his mind kept turning over endless ephemeral plans. His own fate was settled, but he could not shake a sense of responsibility for his companions. They were both here because of their loyalty to him. Kian was so young, so proud of his dual heritage. He and his forebears had kept faith with their god, the eagle of the Ninth Hispana legion. Quintus was as convinced as Kian was about the battered bird's origins. He had seen legionary eagles before, and there was something about that imperial figure that made the hairs stand up on his arms. Surely the goddess Fortuna would intervene to save both the eagle and its carer? Quintus recalled Kian revealing the bird to them in the strongroom at Cair Pol, and felt anew the wonder and awe of that discovery.

There was also Aila to think of. Quintus did not consider himself sentimental in the least, and he acknowledged that for many years others would have described him as cold and unfeeling. But since he had returned to Britannia and found Julia again, and discovered the great joy of his unknown daughter, Aurelia, he had changed. Part of that change was noticing what was happening between other people around him. So he knew that Britta's refusal of Tiro's proposal of marriage after the battle of Corinium had deeply hurt his optio. And now he had become aware that matters between Kian mac Dougal and Aila were not straightforward. The closeness developing between them had not gone unnoticed by him.

THE LOYAL CENTURION

As much as he wanted to save Kian for a full life, even more he longed to restore the feisty Pictish girl to stability, status and a happy family. All these had been stripped from her in the cruellest fashion by Athair and his acolytes. What she had endured, both in her own country, and since then as a soldier's plaything shackled at Vindolanda, was too awful to dwell on. The worst of it was that in her efforts to help Quintus, she had fallen out of Kian's regard and put herself back into the hands of her worst enemy, the Great Pict. This brave-hearted girl warranted all his efforts; she deserved much better from life.

And then there was Litorius. Quintus looked at the centurion, his grave face softened now by sleep. There was something familiar about Litorius. Quintus was reminded of Licinius Pomponius, commandant of the Castra Peregrina secret service in Rome. Licinius had been his senior officer during Quintus's years as a frumentarius, when he had travelled the eastern provinces; now he was his comrade and friend. But although this officer was also strong and steeped in service, it was not perhaps Licinius he recognised in Litorius. He shook his head, and an image of returning from his own final mission in Palaestina came to him. He saw himself walking up the Quirinal Hill in Rome, entering his abandoned house to be given divorce papers from his former wife Calpurnia, along with a vicious note about the child that wasn't his. He saw that man, himself as he had been, and now he recognised something in Litorius too. It was pain and shame, a burden of guilt so heavy it could not be shed.

In his own case it had not been the failed marriage — he had never loved Calpurnia, nor she him. It had been his father's forced suicide, engineered by one who had ultimately deceived and killed his mother too. It had been seeing his younger brother die in front of him, and being so badly wounded he had been helpless to prevent it. It had been losing Julia, as he then believed, and leaving Britannia as a failure, sailing back to a Rome that did not want him.

What, he wondered, was the burden Litorius carried? He looked again at the sleeping man, to find him awake and looking steadily back at him.

It had happened many years ago, before the disastrous regime of Crescens and his toadies had begun. In those days Litorius was already the troop commander of the beneficiariate at Vindolanda, a talented young officer heading for high rank. He worked hard, he played hard, and he was highly regarded by both his seniors and his men. He was a happy, lucky man. His Brigantian wife had married him for love, and had quickly borne him a daughter.

'Her name was Stella, and she was the brightest star in my heavens. My pride and joy; she was so sparky, so energetic, such fun to be with. She told me over and over how proud she was of her father, the best soldier along the Wall. It never mattered to me that there were no more children. Stella was all I wanted. I spent as much time as I could with her. It was too little, as it turned out.

'I said I played hard. Every night after my duty was over, I went to the taverns in the vicus, relaxing and drinking with my men. We were a tight-knit warm community, the best Wall station of the lot. Everyone loved the camaraderie of our drinking parties. But gradually the wine and beer became more important to me than the warmth and friendship, more important than my loving family. In my arrogance I did not see I was ruining it all. I began to make mistakes, to forget things, struggled to perform at my best. My optio, Marcus, once suggested I leave the tavern, saying I must be tired. I was harsh with him, told him it wasn't his place to criticise his commander. My wife begged me to stay at home more, and I spurned her too.

'One night I came home, drunk again. Stella was waiting at the door, waiting for her daddy to say goodnight. I…I did not see her. I thrust the door open, stumbling across the threshold. My wife called out to me, I thought in anger at my late homecoming. She was actually warning Stella to move away, but she was too late. Stella was right there, in my path, and I — hit out at her, not seeing my adored little girl, only something, someone, in my way. I knocked her down. She tripped and fell, hitting her head hard on the hearth.'

It had been Marcus, his optio, who had saved him. He came knocking at the door the following morning, wondering why the centurion had not come to take the morning parade and duty roster. He found Litorius sitting with the dead Stella in his lap. Together they buried her — illicitly, under the floor of the centurion's quarters. Litorius's wife had already left. Later he heard she had moved back to her Brigantian family in Isurium. From that day, Litorius never took another drink. But he was a man alone, with only his fiercely loyal troop as companions.

'So you see, Quintus Valerius, I really have nothing to lose. I am already dead. My only remaining hope is to receive the blessing of Mithras, our Lord of Light. I pray he will allow me to atone, in this world or the next. Mine must be the sacrifice, in whichever way will gain the safety of your two young native charges, and you too.'

Chapter Twenty-two

Cair Pol

Tiro had felt more confident with Litorius there to rely on. Now that the stern centurion had also disappeared into the maw of the Pictish fort, he was constantly edgy. That made him short-tempered and impatient, even with Nico. But the boy was remarkably calm, which had the effect of making Tiro even more twitchy. Two days after Litorius had given himself up, on a murky morning of dripping damp, Tiro fell over a pail of water Nico had left in the courtyard.

'Dammit, by Hercules!' Tiro cursed aloud, making Nico turn in confusion.

'I'm s-sorry, sir, I just put it down a moment to rest my arm.' He looked red-faced, and Tiro felt a rush of compassion mixed with shame.

'My fault, young man. Should look better where I'm going. Sorry I was sharp. I just — I just wonder how much longer we have to wait for the Vindolanda boys to get here. I can't bear thinking about the boss, and Kian and Aila, and now Centurion Pacatianus, all in that dreadful place at the mercy of blue-painted barbarians!'

'I hope it w-won't be long now, sir,' said Nico, looking so despondent Tiro immediately picked up the bucket, slopping cold water into his boots and saying with forced cheerfulness, 'Now then, where are we taking this water?'

As it happened, they did not have much longer to wait. The first to arrive was Marcus, the slight, dark-haired optio to Litorius Pacatianus. He came in so silently that afternoon that Tiro almost jumped when the man and his walking horse emerged from the river mist.

Over the next day or two, a dozen or so troopers arrived from different locus meeting places, in varying stages of exhaustion and mud. Fortunately they came well-prepared with rations, even bringing their own fodder for the horses. Tiro showed them to the nearest barracks block, making sure they knew where to fetch water and firewood, and firing up the bread oven. The old fort seemed to come alive with the noise of soldiers clattering about. Nico was in his element, helping the troopers with their mounts while Camilla frisked at his heels. Marcus set them to work improving the defences and renewing the old wooden gates.

'Best to be ahead of ourselves, should things go wrong up at the hill,' he said, jerking a thumb at the hillfort looming over them.

Later over a bowl of stew, with Nico safely tucked up in his blankets, Tiro was able to brief the young officer more fully. He explained that Aila had smuggled herself into the good graces of the great chief inside the fort, and how she had established communications with Nico. He told how Litorius had come in several days ago, and also gone to Castlelaw.

'He had some idea he should offer himself in a prisoner swap for Quintus Valerius. I don't see how that was going to work. He's just one more hostage for the barbarian. He didn't even tell me he was going. Just upped and went early one morning.'

'That's certainly bad news,' said Marcus, frowning, 'but not really a surprise. This day was bound to come.'

'What do you mean?'

Marcus shook his head, looking uncertain. Then his face cleared as he arrived at a decision. 'It's not my story to tell, but what I can say is that the centurion has carried a terrible burden for a very long time. He did something — an accident, mind — but it ruined his life. He has longed to atone ever since, merely awaiting the right opportunity. It may be that Janus, god of beginnings and endings, has finally offered Litorius Pacatianus what he has sought so long.'

Marcus said no more. His dark brown eyes looked moist, and his face was flushed in the firelight. Tiro reached over to grasp the young officer's shoulder in a gesture of compassion and solidarity, then left him alone to the fire and his thoughts. When he returned, it was to find Marcus in conversation with three of his troopers. They reported that there had been unusual numbers gathered at the locus meetings, many of them young men. When the men of Vindolanda told of the danger approaching from Pictland, the young natives were eager to join the beneficiariate at Cair Pol.

'And I saw something odd, sir,' said one of the men. 'At my meeting, one or two of these boys got quite excited, started waving their swords around and cheering when I asked for volunteers to follow me to the old fort.'

'That's certainly encouraging,' said Marcus, 'but it's hard to see how a few Caledonian farmers can be effective against the warriors Athair leads.'

'Well, sir, it was the swords themselves I thought looked funny. I could have sworn they were old-fashioned gladiuses — you know, short and pointed for close-range stabbing. Not like our army spathas.'

Tiro pulled Quintus's sword out of the straw he had hidden it in to keep Nico's curiosity away from the deadly sharp weapon.

'Like this one?'

The others gathered round to look. 'Beautiful ivory pommel,' said Marcus, admiringly. 'Good steel, too, I warrant.'

'Yes, but I wish it was with Quintus Valerius in Castlelaw, not here with me,' said Tiro. 'But what does that mean, them having old-style swords?'

'I'm not sure,' said Marcus. 'But anyway, we have some forces here now, and more joining us. So let's work out how to rescue our people.'

Tiro turned his mouth down; he'd seen for himself how impregnable the hillfort was. There may not be many warriors there, but there were enough to defend against any attack the few Romans could make.

'Without artillery, I don't think there's any way we can storm Castlelaw. And even onagers and ballistas would struggle, given the steepness of the crag the fort sits on.'

Marcus sat in thought, rapidly tapping one hand on his bony knee. 'From what Aila has told you about the Great Pict's intentions, there is very little time left for us to act before our three men are killed, or worse. Regardless of when our locus allies arrive, we must act within two days if we are to save Quintus Valerius and Centurion Pacatianus. Would it be possible for your horse-boy to meet the Pictish girl again, and get more information?'

It was indeed possible, and Nico was keen to go. But Tiro was reluctant to send the boy alone. At dusk, therefore, he too rode across the river meadows on his grey, keeping Pegasus company until they reached the foot of Castlelaw crag. Tiro's horse wanted to follow Pegasus, but Tiro hesitated.

'It's fine, sir. Your horse trusts you, and I have brought him up here before to teach him the way, and build his confidence.'

Again Nicomedes was right; Tiro marvelled at the boy's ability to align himself, despite his physical limitations, with animals. Camilla was an inevitable shadow the whole way, silent and watchful for Nico's signals. Tiro thought about Aurelia, her horses and her dog, Cerberus. *Maybe there would be a place for Nico at Bo Gwelt? I just need to keep the boy safe through all this, and get him back to the Summer Country. Not much to ask.*

And then his mind reverted to the job in hand. They had a short wait at the top till Aila responded to a prearranged whistle signal. Her head appeared over the palisade.

Nico said, 'I've brought Tiro.'

'Good,' said the girl. She was shivering, and her hands where she clutched a large plaid shawl around her shoulders were white-knuckled.

'Tiro, it's nay sich good news. Messengers have come in: there's a mighty army afoot, heading south from Pictland, not far away now. Ahead of it are coming three druids, priests who Athair has called to do his bidding. They'll get here in two days. And, worst of a' — Centurion Pacatianus has been taen awa'.'

'Taken? Taken where?'

'I dinnae ken. But he put himself as sacrifice, in place of Kian. Athair, that hackit animal, was thrilled to have two real Roman officers: one to send tae the gods, and the other to punish. I fear they've sent the centurion north to the Cave of the Dead already. There's no way to chase them down. They know a' the secret paths. He's gone, that brave man.'

Her voice quavered, but Tiro had to know more.

'What about these druids? Why have they come?'

'Och, Tiro, it's…it's a terrible thing: the death of many cuts. The druids have very sharp knives. The dawn after they get here, they'll bring Quintus out into the courtyard, and cut off perhaps a finger, or an ear, to begin with. They bind up the wound to stop the bleeding. The next dawn, another bit cut off, and so every day till the poor man is deid. And a' the time suffering such agonies, and that man makin' Quintus choose which part next!'

Tiro was horror struck. He could not imagine a worse torture Anger rose in him like a red wave, and he set a foot to the palisade scrabbling for purchase, desperate to scramble up and — do what?

'Whisht!' Aila called out in fright; at the same time, Nico said 'No, sir! If they find you, they'll kill Aila too. We need a better plan.'

The girl looked round, but apparently no one had heard anything Tiro was ashamed that the two youngsters could keep their heads while he raged and nearly ruined all.

Aila said, 'I've found a way to pass a wee weapon to the beneficiarius without the Picts knowing. If I can do that, maybe he can get Kian out safely. Nico, can you help if Kian gets over the wall?'

'Yes, we can,' replied Tiro. 'You must come with him, Aila. Tiro had got himself back under control, and his voice was low but firm. 'Give the boss a weapon, and help him bring Kian out to the palisade here by dusk tomorrow. We'll do the rest, won't we Nico?'

Even in the faint evening light, Tiro saw Nico's eyes shining and heard the eagerness in his voice as he answered, 'Yes, we will, sir Tomorrow night then, Aila.'

'Haste ye back!' She turned and went, leaving a dark space where she had stood. They lingered to make sure she was no accosted, but all remained quiet. At length, reluctantly, Tiro led his grey down the path Nico had picked out and they retreated to Cair Pol in deepening gloom.

Back at base, Marcus had taken charge of new arrivals. A steady trickle of natives, on horseback and bearing a random assortmen of weapons old and new, was arriving from all over the southern part of Caledonia. None from the central valley and beyond, but as Marcus explained to Tiro, this was not surprising.

'The thing is, Tiro, it was our own emperor who ordered the extermination of the people in the great valley, when the Maeatae rose again in rebellion. He was dying, in great pain, and so angered at their refusal to accept Roman terms that he told his vast army to kill anyone they found beyond the Tausa. Man, woman or child. From what I've heard, no one lives in those glens and mountains now. You can travel for many days through a desolate country, and not find a soul until you reach Pictland.'

'Yes, the boss told me about the great killing. But our allies, the Venicones and Votadini? Why have none of them come to help?'

'I don't know.' Marcus looked perturbed. 'It may be they were so intimidated by news of Athair that they've moved further south. Don't forget the Votadini have strongholds and large territories south of the Aelian Wall, where they would feel safer. Your friend Lossio and his speculatores may know more, but...'

'What?'

'Well, I have heard that the payments Rome made to our allies for generations have ceased in recent times. Maybe without the sweetener of Roman silver, their chieftains feel less motivated to stand between Rome and the Picts.'

Tiro's mouth tightened. He thought back to the heavy guard he'd seen outside the Sixth Victrix legionary strongroom. He was pretty sure he knew where that silver was now. He grasped Marcus by the shoulder, saying, 'My friend, you may be right. There's not much we can do here and now, but by Jupiter there will be a reckoning when I get back to Eboracum! Let's greet these newcomers, shall we, and see what kind of force we might put into the field, when and if Athair comes down from his dunghill.'

Tiro said nothing of it yet to Marcus, but Aila's news of a large Pictish army heading south had him deeply troubled. He knew Quintus had sent regular reports to Lossio at Eboracum, but had he requested backup? And even if he had, Eboracum was a long way south, many weeks' march away. He groaned inwardly. Any mobilisation from Eboracum would of necessity involve the Sixth Victrix legion. And the general of the Sixth Victrix legion was none other than Legate Marius Crescens. He was hardly going to get out of bed and put his greaves on to save Quintus.

In the barracks they found a cheerful chatter of men of all tribes and homelands, speaking various British dialects. The odd rusty Latin phrase was being pressed into service to help with communication. They were seated in groups, comparing weapons. In one corner a smith from Marcus's cohort was displaying a device he had made, a hook of some kind. Tiro watched carefully, thinking of the rope that had saved him from drowning in the river Bodotria, now coiled and tucked away somewhere. Might come in handy, if it was long enough.

Marcus clapped his hands to draw attention, and the hubbub ceased as curious eyes turned to the two Roman officers. Tiro studied the group. He saw a couple of dozen strangers, all quite young. Most had the dark hair and blue eyes common among Caledonians, but some had brown eyes and darker complexions than was usual among the northern tribes. He spotted some old gladiuses, the odd legionary helmet, and even a complete cuirass, battered and bent, but whole. He thought back to Trimontium. What had their wise old host said as they parted company? *You may find help where you least expect it. We Romans have been here before. And each time the legions retreat, a few of us stay behind.* That might be truer than the old man knew. These men looked to be rough and ready tribesmen, but perhaps they carried some of the heritage of Rome in their blood, too?

Marcus cleared his throat, saying, 'Welcome! You are all most welcome. Do you know why my men asked you to join us here?'

'Aye!' One man, tall, rangy, with dark auburn hair and a proudly-wielded antique sword, stood. 'Tae beat back that scum frae the north, those scabby Picts. All of us are here because we have a Roman soldier somewhere in our ancestry. And we're the sons and grandsons of braw Caledonian warriors, too. They'll no drive awa' me and my kin!'

Marcus nodded, and gestured to Tiro. 'This is my colleague, Optio Tiro. He and Beneficiarius Quintus Valerius were sent by the Roman governor in Londinium to prevent the deadly war

170

between Britannia and Caledonia that Athair has sworn to bring about. The beneficiarius went in good faith, unarmed and under a flag of truce, to negotiate with the Great Pict in the hillfort yonder. But Athair has him imprisoned, together with two youngsters in his company. Since then, my own commanding officer, Litorius Pacatianus, went to give himself up in their place. We don't know what has become of him, but we know the others are still locked up, threatened with imminent torture and cruel death. But that's not all. Everyone, any tribe, that stands in the way of the Pictish sweep south, is in danger. They destroy or capture anyone in their path, and take all. We must work together to protect our lands and our tribes, and send this beast back north.

'We are not many, but if we can lure the Pict out into battle quickly we have a good chance of prevailing to free our comrades. Athair has as yet only his bodyguard with him. Will you help save our noble Roman comrades, and stop this traitor taking your lands, your womenfolk, from launching a terrible war?'

There was a single shouted answer: 'Aye!' It was echoed by the men of Vindolanda.

Marcus looked at Tiro. 'Right, my friend. Let's hear your plan.'

Tiro swallowed, knowing his plan relied on a vulnerable Pictish lass, and an even younger boy with a limp, a horse, and a dog.

Chapter Twenty-three

Eboracum

Julia had to concede that Fronto was a tough old man. She treated the impressive goose egg swelling on his forehead. Having examined him carefully to rule out a fracture of the skull, she applied a compress soaked in cool water. She would have preferred a vinegar compress; vinegar stank, but it was effective. But as the skin on Fronto's head was grazed, Julia did not subject him to the sting. Instead she applied a salve of comfrey.

Soon the old man was able to sit up and talk coherently. Disappointingly, there was little he could tell them. He had answered the door to an imperative summons, and immediately been hit with something hard. He never saw his attackers. They had stormed the house, terrifying the slaves and turning the place upside down. Clearly they were looking for something. Whether they found what they sought, Julia couldn't tell. Britta led a search: nothing seemed missing, and the only real impact, apart from Julia's outrage, was the confusion and scattering of belongings. And Fronto's injury.

Julia left Fronto with an infusion of camomile, with instructions to drink it all and rest till she allowed him up. Meanwhile Corellia had been questioning the household. All anyone could tell her was that four soldiers had rampaged through the house. They were assumed to be from the fortress, but no one had actually identified any insignia, or could even give a description except to say they were armed and uniformed.

Julia was left exasperated and unsettled. Her first thought had been for Flavius, and she ran straight upstairs after attending to Fronto. Thanks to Minerva and Juno, her son was safe. She found the wet nurse, Veloriga, in her suite at the top of the house, calm and immersed as always in her own milky world, with Flavius held securely in her arms.

Downstairs, Sextus put himself to immediate use, taking over Fronto's responsibilities and generally proving to be an essential addition to the household. Julia was both grateful and touched. She said as much to Corellia, when the two of them paused to sit down with honeyed wine in the salon.

'But I don't feel very safe now in this house, Corellia.'

Sextus respectfully interrupted his new mistress, coming in to announce a visitor.

'Really, Sextus, now is not the time —' began Julia.

'Nonsense, Julia.' A tiny figure entered, and Julia was so pleased to see the senior wise woman of Serapis that she forgot protocol, jumping up to hug the surprised old woman and nearly knocking off her headdress.

'Mother, you are just the person we need here!'

The old woman smiled, and seated herself regally. 'I hope you are going to offer me some of your excellent hot wine, Julia. It's as cold as Hades out there, and I came quickly when I heard of the attack on your home. Unfortunately, I left my thickest wrap back at the temple in my hurry.'

Sextus quickly poured wine for the priestess, who drank with surprising assiduity for such a little lady.

'Your substitute major domo here tells me Fronto is only slightly injured, and that nothing of any moment seems to be missing. Intrusion by armed soldiers, dear me!'

Julia opened her mouth to ask how the priestess knew all this, then shut it. The senior Sister of the Eboracum Serapeum knew everything, and everyone. The old lady seemed to guess what was passing through her former acolyte's mind. She said, eyes twinkling, 'Well, that isn't the only reason I have come. I have a gift for you. It came to me under conditions of sacred secrecy. But this break-in at your home, as well as what I hear around the city, decided me that the moment had come to pass it on to you.' She reached under her palla, and brought out something hidden in cloth, unwrapping it to reveal a scroll of vellum.

Corellia gasped, as Julia extended a suddenly shaking hand to take the scroll.

'Is this what I think it is, Mother?'

'I have no idea, my child. The great god Serapis has not yet endowed me with mind-reading, so I do not know what you think.

I have not read it. I promised as much to Placidia Septimia when she gave this journal into my safekeeping, the very day she died.'

The priestess looked sharply at Julia, and seemed to draw herself up into a taller, more stately frame. 'I must tell you, Julia, I disapprove of much that has recently happened in this city. I have already taken steps. While I am the senior wise woman in Eboracum, my pupils, their families and their friends will not be attacked with impunity. I can assure you, no such further incidents will take place.'

She stood, and despite her diminutive stature, the regal impression persisted while Sextus hastened to help her wrap herself in the enveloping yellow mantle.

'Good day, my dears,' she said and was gone, leaving a faint trace of incense in her wake.

'Have you read the whole journal?'

Julia nodded. She had spent the afternoon reading Placidia's journal, taking time out only to briefly play with her baby and check Fronto was recovering satisfactorily. Corellia had gone away to dine early with her husband, Aurelius Mercurialis, but had come back with a slave bearing gifts of Hispanic wine, and dried dates and figs just shipped in from Syria.

'Yes. Placidia thought she had uncovered the reasons for at least some of her husband's criminality. It seems he had left Rome under a heavy burden of debt. No doubt he thought to plunder this province during his term here, as so many governors do. But Britannia Inferior is a drain on imperial resource rather than being a stream of wealth, being expensively militarised and with a poorer climate and fewer mineral resources than other provinces. He must soon have realised that he would not make his fortune here, not in the accepted way. On top of that, Placidia was not quite the catch he thought. He assumed that as a member of the imperial house she would be wealthy in her own right. But her father had many sons to provide for, and little sympathy from the Augusta. Placidia brought Marius a reasonable dowry, but not enough to placate his creditors. So he came up with a new scheme, a despicable one.

'She writes how he placed his own men in places of power, especially as commandants of the Wall forts. She did not see how this would benefit Marius, until one day she overheard a meeting with a senior officer from one of the forts, Magna or perhaps Vercovicium. They were discussing sending wagonloads of weapons — newly-forged, top-quality, mind — through the frontier. Well, there's only one frontier that matters here, the Aelian Wall itself. She did not understand why he would do that, and could learn no more. I imagine he was more cautious after that about holding meetings in his own house.

'But then, a few days before she fled, Placidia witnessed another key meeting. Returning quietly into the house, she passed by the legate's office where he was sitting with an accountant, of all people. Not just any old accountant. This was the chief civil servant of the procurator, and he was conveying news of the arrival of a large shipment of silver coins for storage in the fort strongroom. He was saying it was to be kept separate from the normal payroll chest. But I am puzzled by this passage, Corellia. Surely any incoming shipments of denarii would be the salary of the soldiers of the Sixth Victrix, or be due to be sent on to the Wall forts?'

Corellia grimaced. 'Ah, you forget our allies north of the Wall. I will admit to you, Julia, when Salvia told me what Placidia had overheard, at first I too could not see what this meant. I said so to my dearest Aurelius, who as you know is a clever merchant with a sharp eye for money. He saw it straight away. We think this may be the regular payment Rome has been sending to our allies in Caledonia for generations. This new source of money for the legate is perhaps the silver that should have gone over the Wall as payment to the Votadini and Venicones, who keep safe the lowlands between our province and the Picts. Aurelius suspects Marius has been diverting this silver into his own coffers.'

Britta interrupted. 'But, Domina Corellia, if the silver is being waylaid by the legate, what has happened to our alliances?'

Now it was Corellia's turn to look troubled. 'I very much fear they have already been driven out of their lands by the Picts; at least the Venicones have. Salvia told me Lossio had heard complaints from the Votadini, who are a stronger tribe, and placed further south. Their northern border is the river Bodotria, so they don't adjoin Pictish territory. But Lossio says reports of the silver going astray are fragmentary, and denied by our officials here. They shrugged it off, suggesting the Votadini are simply being greedy.'

Julia went on, 'There's worse. As we know, Placidia discovered she had married a cold, selfish man. She soon despaired of her marriage, and being young and thoughtless she took comfort in her old friendship with Tribune Gaius Laelianus. She had put that relationship behind her when she married, but when Gaius followed her to Eboracum, and she discovered that her husband valued only her money and connections, she turned back to her old love. The unfortunate girl! She fell into the tribune's arms so thoroughly, so reckless of consequence, that of course the inevitable happened. It's no surprise she found she was pregnant in late autumn. That was why she insisted on accompanying us to the Serapeum. She hoped the god would heed her prayers for a way out of her predicament.

'Gaius was all for doing the honourable thing, but she was too afraid of Marius to ask for a divorce. She had good reason to fear him. He might present a potent masculine front to the world, and especially to his men; but the slaves guessed otherwise. One of them told Salvia he had paid off a former wife, and the other wife had died mysteriously. It may be he took steps to prevent her talking about his impotence.

'Salvia knew Placidia was pregnant, of course, but she swears she told no one. In the journal Placidia writes how Marius, who had begun to hit her on a regular basis, came home drunk one night and taunted her with being no sort of Roman wife. Apparently he said he might have overlooked her barrenness, had she endowed him with a fortune as he supposed she would. She was as useless as his previous wives, and he would be rid of her, he said. He added, most cruelly, that his next wife would be both rich and fruitful. Placidia, goaded beyond bearing, asked if he was sure it was she who was infertile, as she knew better. I can see the provocation, but oh, Placidia, how foolish that was! Of course he began to suspect. He probably had her followed to her trysts with Gaius; easily done when they were both living inside the cramped fortress.

'Quintus always quotes Cicero when he's formulating conclusions about suspects: *Cui bono?* Who profits? And clearly, if Marius thought Placidia was about to cause a scandal by running off with one of his own officers, flaunting her pregnancy and perhaps revealing to the world his own infertility, that would make him a laughing stock. His place as legate, the leader of over 5,000 men and governor of a province, would be insupportable. Plus, if she had found out about his plots to send Roman weapons to the enemy, and to steal money intended to keep the peace, he would be in real trouble with Rome. On top of that, whatever money she did have would leave with her if she divorced him. Whereas, were she to die, he would inherit her estate.

Julia paused, then held up a hand, fingers folded under. She lifted her fingers as she ticked off points. 'Let's add to Cicero's adage: did Marius have the motive, means, and opportunity to murder his wife? I look at it this way: his motive would be to silence Placidia and maintain his status as legate, and widower of an imperial family member. Means? She was easy to kill, that little girl. Such a slender neck. Unlikely to put up much resistance, especially if surprised in the dark. And opportunity? Quintus has blown Marius's alibi wide open. He wrote to tell me that Marius was not, as he had claimed, away touring the Aelian forts during Saturnalia. He was identified right here in Eboracum, masked and out on the streets the night Placidia died.'

Corellia gasped, but Britta already knew this. Julia held three fingers up. 'Motive, means, and opportunity.'

Corellia pushed a frond of dark hair behind one ear, concentrating intently.

'But what about the other girl? The one killed in Lagentium — what was her name? Was she anything to do with all this?'

Julia grimaced. 'I'm not sure. Quintus has a witness who knew her, and says she was a Pictish victim of trafficking, part of a supply chain of native girls kept imprisoned and used as unpaid prostitutes in the Wall forts. I can't see how, but he clearly thinks there is a link. He suspects Sacra escaped her captivity, but was followed and killed to stop her talking about that trade.'

'But what is the connection between kidnapping Pictish girls, and Placidia's death?' asked Britta.

Julia's blue eyes narrowed in thought. 'I have to admit, I'm not sure. Placidia knew that Marius had been sending envoys through the Wall. He may have struck some kind of underhand bargain with the Pictish overlord — the Great Pict, she calls him — which would allow Marius to end the payment of silver to our Caledonian allies. He would still receive the silver from Rome, of course, but divert it into his own coffers. Rome would not know, unless someone independent of Marius — someone like Quintus — found out. Rome is a long way from Eboracum, and even further from Caledonia. Quintus told me in his latest letter that he had sent a more detailed report from Carumabo to Antonius Gargilianus at the fort, who would give a copy to Lossio, and also show it to me. But Lossio is not here, and now Antonius is dead and his quarters have been stripped of all letters and reports. I don't even know if Quintus has arrived at this Cair Pol place he was heading for. In fact,' she said, a frown creasing her brows, 'it may be that the only people in Eboracum who know or guess about Marius are we three.' And, she thought, we might be the only people who know where Quintus and Tiro were heading for.

These were chilling thoughts. Julia felt suddenly vulnerable. With a new baby and a large household to consider, she could only bar up her battered doors, get some hefty replacements in for Fronto, and hope the high priestess's vague "steps" would be quickly effective. She said as much to Corellia.

'What, Julia, do you think I would stand by while you are threatened and your home ransacked? Aurelius has already chosen a squad of hand-picked men to guard your house till Quintus comes home. Don't worry, they are all ex-soldiers and retired gladiators, entirely loyal to us. You will be in safe hands till your husband returns, my dear! In the meantime, perhaps you should let our senior wise woman know your suspicions? I have heard she has contacts in useful places.'

Julia was grateful. It was some reassurance to have Corellia, with her wealth and influence, on her side. But she knew she would remain in a state of anxiety until her Governor's Man was back from wherever it was he had gone.

She tried not to think about where he might be now, and what danger he might be in.

JACQUIE ROGERS

Chapter Twenty-four

Castlelaw hillfort

It was morning, again. A grey dim morning that barely pierced the slats of their cell. It was the day before the Pictish druids would arrive, armed with their cruel little knives. Quintus awoke to find he had changed. Overnight, he had unconsciously moved from a position of acceptance of his lot, to a growing measure of apprehension. As the day wore on, he felt himself become more and more fearful. It wasn't that he had never felt fear before: he had, plenty of it. Fear of failing in his duty to emperor, legion, family. Fear of not recovering the use of his right leg, being invalided out of the Praetorian Guard. Fear had been his companion all those pain-filled months in the base hospital in Eboracum, his first time in the northern city so many years ago. Then he had met Julia. Julia at sixteen: freckles scattered over pale skin, tall, golden-haired, full of joy and trust in their mutual passion. All too soon there had been a new desolating fear: that of losing Julia forever, as he turned away from her to set out on the long sea voyage back to Rome. But now, with Julia as she had become — beautiful, talented and strong — even now, he did not fear losing her again.

The fear that woke him from his carefully cultivated calm this morning was different from anything he had ever experienced. It was a pernicious, creeping infiltration that spread cold tentacles through his body. He woke to the blighting knowledge that he was about to be mutilated.

When Bedwyr told him what fate awaited him, the death of many cuts ordained by Athair, Quintus had not at first thought about the means of his end, only that his end had arrived. He had contemplated his death on many occasions, and never found the prospect daunting. Somehow he had always believed he did not deserve to live, and so had felt there was nothing to fear in death. Even when his life had changed, and suddenly he had a world full of potential losses: his wife and a growing family; his beautiful old

180

home at Bo Gwelt in the Summer Country; the trust and affection of a governor he truly respected; and of course his friend and partner, Tiro, who had turned his career around with an insouciant wholehearted British love of soldiering — even then, the prospect of it all ending held no dread for him.

But now he knew he was really afraid of what awaited him when the druids arrived. He would lose, by increments, all that made him a soldier and a man. It was not the pain or the ignominy he dreaded, as body parts were publicly sliced off him. It was the gradual diminution of his power to act. The essential element of Quintus's being was agency, and his will and ability to do what was right. All this would be taken away by a sadistic savage, tomorrow.

He realised he was watching his own breathing, seeing in his mind the counted breaths come and go. Time had nearly run out for Quintus. Now there was just this young man, his companion and fellow prisoner. He wondered what he could do for Kian, while they still had each other. That reminded him that there was also Aila: incomparable, indefatigable, almost incomprehensible Aila. He smiled at her image, and Kian, who had been looking at him curiously, seemed to relax.

'I've been watching you, sir, and worrying about you.'

'I saw. But there is no need to worry about me. I don't worry about you. You have your god, the golden eagle; your tribe; and your honour. I know you will always obey the dictates of your honour. And you *will* see and hold your god again, Kian mac Dougal. This I promise you.'

Kian nodded, for a brief moment looking very young.

Quintus went on. 'We need not fear for each other. But there is one we should still be concerned for. I mean Aila.' He stopped to allow Kian to vent any remaining invective. It was clear to Quintus that Kian believed, on some level, the front Aila had so skilfully put up: that she had sold herself to the devil by siding with Athair, her Pictish lord. Worse, that she was using the ultimate female guile to keep herself alive — sleeping with the enemy. So Quintus waited.

It was a long wait. Kian said nothing as his face grew troubled.

Even when the usual guard came in with their poor breakfast and took away the slop bucket, Kian stayed silent. Quintus let him be. This was his last chance to convince Kian, and allowing him to perceive for himself the nonsense of his delusions was, he hoped, the way to do it. Quintus was sure that Kian's rejection of Aila was driven more by jealousy than reality. Kian, whether he acknowledged it or not, was in love with Aila. To see her as the plaything of a powerful older man was excruciating to the young Gael. He needed to appreciate this for himself. Eventually, Kian began to talk with head hung, looking down at his scuffed rawhide boots.

'Perhaps I have wronged Aila. When I saw her coming out of Athair's roundhouse, I was so…so angry, I couldn't see beyond the betrayal. I was sure she had saved herself at our cost. But now I see there may be another explanation. I…we need to speak again to her. Perhaps this time I can listen with more understanding.'

He looked up, and Quintus saw self-doubt and remorse on his face. What he had said was more gratifying than surprising to Quintus. It reinforced everything he had come to know about this young man, scion of two great races. So Quintus left matters there, laying a hand on Kian's shoulder for a moment before sharing out their food.

Once they had eaten, there was nothing to do but sleep. But Quintus lay awake while Kian snored gently, hoping it would be Aila who would bring the evening meal at dusk, as usual. If she did, she might be able to pass on news that would help them. If she did not, he must resign himself to the worst. But even as he concluded this, he found himself dwelling on Tiro and Nicomedes, and wondering whether Antonius or Lossio had seen his reports. Even if they had, there would be no help coming from Eboracum, not from Legate Crescens.

Maybe Tiro was working on a rescue plan? Perhaps one to get Kian out. That was all he needed, mused Quintus. Some ruse that might free Kian, while Quintus created a diversion at this end. That might work, mightn't it? Or was it possible that with Litorius here, his men would also be on their way from Vindolanda? But what if the commandant there had stopped them leaving, allowing

Litorius, unpopular Litorius, to sacrifice himself alone?

Thus Quintus: lying awake most of the afternoon, generating and discarding plan after desperate plan, scheme after hopeless scheme. Knowing that it was all self-deception. The Great Pict, that huge man so damaged by Rome, had them all entirely at his mercy. And when he had toyed enough with Quintus and Kian to satisfy his bitter cruelty, he would turn his attention to the crumbling Roman fort. Then Tiro, together with their little friend the horse-boy, and anyone else who might have made their way to Cair Pol, would be the next target.

When the evening came, it did bring Aila, together with the bad-tempered guard Quintus had seen with Bedwyr. Aila carried in a small pail of thin stew, mere morsels of stringy chicken floating in a watery soup. The guard waited outside while she poured the soup into rough wooden bowls. She glanced once through the door, where the guard was close enough to see her, but not within earshot. Her fine dark hair was pinned up on her head by a long white hairpin. Ivory, Quintus guessed, a very fine pin. As she leaned over to serve the soup, the ivory hairpin somehow slipped from her head, falling to the floor. Kian picked it up, saying in a low voice, 'That is a handsome pin. A gift from your lord?' The unhappy expression had returned. Quintus sighed, holding his hand out. Kian reluctantly handed the slender implement over to him.

'Thank you, Aila,' Quintus mouthed to her, turning the ivory over in his hand, testing the sharpened point. 'Ivory is stronger than bronze, thinner than a steel knife, and utterly deadly in the right hands.'

She flashed a quick look of gratitude at him, before hissing less happily at Kian, 'This gift was dearly bought. Ye have nay notion how high a price I paid for it! But I don't betray ma friends!' He had the grace to look abashed, but she had no more time for him. 'Listen, Quintus. You must trick the guard to come inside, and then overpower him. At the back of the roundhouse is a snicket little passage, right tight next to the wall. It's never guarded. That's how you two will get awa', over the palisade.'

'What about you, Aila?' Kian had apparently forgotten his resentment, and seemed really concerned. 'I'm not going without you!' She looked pleased.

'Whisht! I can make some excuse tae get away another time. When he's asleep, perhaps.' Her mouth twisted, and a wash of red swept up Kian's face.

At that moment the guard pushed into the cell, saying with suspicion, 'What's taking so long in here, girl?' Coming in from the relatively bright outside, he would have seen only dim figures — the girl, and one of the prisoners, who had jumped behind her with his arm held tight across her neck.

'I'll kill the bitch,' Kian hissed. 'Come any closer, and I'll break her treacherous little neck!'

That was just the invitation the truculent guard had been waiting for. He stepped in, stooping through the low doorway. Quintus had already hoisted himself up onto the gathered benches, and jumped up to reach the ceiling timbers. He caught hold of a beam with both hands, lifting his feet up high. With the man directly under him, he dropped heavily, knocking the stocky guard to the floor to land on his back. Before the man could cry out, he grabbed his hair, yanked his head sideways, and stabbed the hairpin into his eye, thrusting it deep into his brain. It was an instant death, with very little blood. The tribesman lay still with face turned on the pavement, an almost comical look of surprise on his dead face.

'Quick, Aila, Kian, help me strip these clothes off.'

While they swapped Kian's clothes for the native's distinctive Pictish tartan, Aila told them of an additional step she had taken.

'I know how superstitious these Picts are,' she said, with supreme disregard for her own beliefs. 'I've been dropping hints that the old fort is aye full of dead Romans, since long ago. That the Ban Sith moved in, and can be heard a-wailing around the ramparts if snoopers get too close. These tribesmen know what that means.' She closed her mouth with a satisfied air. Kian looked much struck. Quintus merely felt puzzled, and it must have shown. Aila clucked, 'Surely now, even you Romans know of the Ban Sith? The spirits who wail at night, to warn the unwary away with threats of a death soon to smite their ain kin? Nay? Och, weel…ye are Roman after a'.'

Shortly after, three people emerged from the cell. Aila was in the lead, insufferable pride on her face, followed by a Pictish guard, who was heavily swathed in plaid and leading a forlorn Roman prisoner not long for this world. They shut the cell door firmly, leaving the dead guard hidden behind the stacked wooden benches.

They nearly got away with it. No one thought to accost them as they walked across the courtyard towards the big roundhouse. At the last moment, Aila glanced around, then swerved away left to lead them into the narrow passage behind the chief's house. Quintus could see the glint of a grappling iron in the fading light, snugly hitched over the palisade.

He could also see a startled kitchen slave, breeches round his ankles, who had snuck around there to urinate, not wanting the bother of going to the latrines. He was so intent on stuffing himself back into his trews at the sight of the girl, he forgot at first to draw breath to shout. So as Quintus drew out the hairpin and stabbed through his skinny neck into his carotid artery, his cry was just a strangled croak. Quintus pulled out the hairpin, hastening the unfortunate slave's death considerably. It had been a useful weapon.

Kian was already over the wall, abseiling. Once he was away, Quintus lifted Aila over, instructing her fiercely to get swarming down. 'Follow Kian — I'll come next!'

He had time to see her obey, making her way down the rope, hand over hand like a gymnast. He cast one last glance over the side. Both had reached the bottom safely, and were already mounting the horses Nico had brought with him. Quintus turned and stopped, frozen.

It seemed the kitchen boy's stifled cry had been enough to attract the attention of a warrior heading for his dinner at Athair's house. He was accompanied by two bodyguards, but he silenced them with an imperative gesture. Thus when the warrior stepped into the narrow gap between the wall and the back of the house, he found only Quintus. They looked at each other with quick recognition,

185

despite the rapidly encroaching dark. The warrior set the tip of his longsword in the ground, and leaned on it slightly.

'Well, Governor's Man, it seems you are at *my* mercy, now,' said Bedwyr, wryly.

THE LOYAL CENTURION

Chapter Twenty-five

Eboracum

Britta insisted on going alone.

'Julia, be sensible! You're certainly being watched, along with this house, and Corellia is too well-known in Eboracum. But me? I'm just the housekeeper, legitimately going to market. I'll wear my palla modestly over my head. No one will look twice at another servant bundled-up against this cold weather. I'm worried that whatever the wise woman is doing to help will take too long. Can we afford to wait? We must get news. I'll just pop along to see Salvia, in case she has heard from Lossio. I'll maybe come past the fort on my way back.'

Nothing Julia could say was sufficient to dissuade Britta, and in truth she didn't try too hard. Britta was quick-thinking and capable, and clearly itching to do something. And she was right about Julia and Corellia being too recognisable in this small gossipy city. Plus, Julia suspected, Britta was anxious and guilty about Tiro. It would do her good to get out and feel she was being useful.

'Very well. But take Sextus with you.'

Britta nodded, and hurried away looking more cheerful than she had for many days. Julia resigned herself to a long wait. She went to see how Fronto was doing — fine, and impatient to be back in his job, which he patently feared Sextus had encroached on; then upstairs to visit baby Flavius, who was fast asleep and not at all interested in greeting his restless parent; and then down into the storerooms and cellars to check food supplies and linen — where she found all in order, and so little to quibble with that she left feeling resentful.

An age later, as she was getting up for the fiftieth time to peer out into the darkening street to watch passers-by, she heard Britta come in accompanied by Sextus. There were other voices too, including a familiar deep one.

'Lossio! How pleased I am to see you!' Julia rushed to greet the tall Veniconian at the door. She stopped, transfixed at the sight of his companion. A correct young officer, with burnished copper hair outshone by an immaculately polished cuirass and shiny greaves, was removing an impressive helmet with transverse horsehair plumage. He placed it carefully on a table. Julia fell back in astonishment, and sat down abruptly in the nearest chair. 'Marcellus?' she said, uncertainly. 'How…why…?'

Britta laughed. 'I told you she would be surprised, Marcellus.'

'Surprised! I — I can't believe it. What magic is this? Lossio, how did you bring Marcellus to Eboracum so quickly? You must have had the wings of Mercury on you.'

Lossio looked amused, his hazel eyes narrowed. 'I wish I could take the credit, Lady Julia. From what Centurion Crispus tells me, the culprit is your insistent high priestess at the Serapeum. I have myself just arrived back in Eboracum from Vindolanda. I was at home with Salvia when Britta found me. I wanted to see you anyway, and was walking back with Britta along the river when we noticed a naval bireme docking. This pattern card of military show was disembarking with his troop.'

Marcellus broke into a shy smile, taking Julia's outheld hand. 'My lady, I am here at your service, and on the orders of Governor Rufinus. He has kept me informed of reports from Quintus Valerius, and some time ago ordered my cohort to Londinium, to be on standby to support Quintus if the need arose. We became concerned when no further reports beyond Carumabo came from your husband. Then we saw the report from Lossio Veda that the praefectus castrorum here, Antonius Gargilianus, had been killed in suspicious circumstances. I was sent by naval liburnian to Eboracum. The seas were favourable for once, and we made a fast voyage.'

Julia turned to Lossio Veda. 'But, Lossio, how did you know about Antonius? Only my friend Corellia, Britta and I knew Antonius had been murdered. I examined him myself, and found the hidden stab wound under his arm. We allowed the cover story of a hunting accident to continue, fearing we would be the next targets if we broadcast the truth. I don't understand how word got to Aradius Rufinus.'

'You are too modest, Lady Julia. Your influence with the high priestess is obviously substantial, and she seems to know everything that happens in Eboracum. She herself is held in high regard across the British sisterhoods, and so when she sent word by the official post, our governor acted immediately.' Marcellus drew himself up, almost to formal attention. 'I have with me authorisation from Governor Aradius Rufinus, the most senior official in Britannia, to relieve Legate Marius Crescens of his post and take him into my custody. It will be for Senior Beneficiarius Quintus Valerius to examine Marius Crescens himself when he returns. Quintus will recommend to the governor what legal action to take.'

Lossio was no longer smiling. 'How many men have you brought, Centurion? I ask as I believe Crescens has suborned many officers of the Sixth Victrix legion, as well as some at the Aelian forts.'

Marcellus frowned, picking up his helmet. 'I have a vexillation of twenty or so men. Enough from our Aquae Sulis station to provide me with official escort. Together with the governor's signed and sealed authorisation, I do not anticipate any great difficulty in carrying out my duties.' He nodded respectfully at Julia, smiled at Britta, who was an old friend, and saluted the speculator. Positioning his helmet carefully on his head, he left, looking the very embodiment of Roman might and justice.

Lossio looked at Julia in dismay. 'That lad may meet more resistance than he expects. I'd better see what I can do. I must catch him up quickly.'

He hurried out after the Aquae Sulis centurion. Julia blinked, wondering what on earth Marcellus thought he was doing. It was a very long way to Londinium. And Quintus was not here, either to lead or advise his deputy.

'Well, mistress, this could all blow up in our faces and no mistake. What would your noble husband make of it, I wonder? I wish he was here! And that Londoner alongside of him.'

'So do I, Britta,' said Julia with feeling. 'So do I!'

As Julia was sitting down to dine, a scrappy message from Lossio was delivered by messenger.

Lady Julia Aureliana
The arrest will take place tomorrow morning. I persuaded

*Marcellus Crispus to wait for daylight, as an arrest after dark
might be misunderstood and lead to unnecessary confrontation.
He will take his warrant to present to Crescens at the praetorium
after breakfast. I will accompany him, having taken what hasty
measures I could tonight. Please attend if you feel you can. Come
veiled, and in company.*
   Senior Speculator Lossio Veda

At dawn Julia emerged from her townhouse wrapped in a
voluminous mantle that covered her head and disguised her figure.
With her was a similarly attired Britta, and Sextus, carrying a
heavy cudgel on display.

Corellia and her husband came too. Julia had not expected her
friend, but she was secretly relieved when a carriage drew up in
the courtyard to disgorge Corellia into the frosty cold of dawn.
Corellia's status as a leading citizen of Eboracum would be a good
thing this morning, she thought. Even better, Corellia's stout,
confident husband Aurelius Mercurialis was with her.

'This is very good of you, Aurelius,' Julia said in greeting.

Aurelius smiled above his neatly trimmed beard. 'Nonsense, my
dear. It is my place as a merchant of standing in this town to bear
witness. And you may find others gathered at the fort when we get
there. Now hop in!' He nodded at Britta and Julia, indicating
dismissively to the unfortunate Sextus that he would have to run
behind, as the carriage was now full. Sextus tucked in among the
tail of clients, followers and slaves Aurelius and Corellia had
brought along, finding himself in good company.

Marcellus was waiting at the centre of the palace courtyard of
the Sixth Victrix legionary fortress. His men fell into place around
him, and on his command stood to attention as they waited. The
sun had risen, and several interested soldiers from the fort were
filing past, openly wondering what the vexillation was, and why
they were stationed in the courtyard. Legate Marius Crescens
emerged from his house. He was in company with two or three
officers, but stopped in his tracks when he saw the strangers facing
him. Marcellus saluted, and broke the seal on a scroll. He unrolled
it with a flourish, to read aloud in a ringing voice that carried
clearly across the large square:

THE LOYAL CENTURION

Marius Crescens, legate of the Sixth Victrix legion, and governor of Britannia Inferior, by the authority vested in me by Emperor Alexander Severus, I hereby suspend you from all your ranks, status and powers, both civil and military. You are under suspicion of treasonous dealings with declared enemies of Rome, together with other associated crimes. This suspension is valid until a formal arrest and investigation can be carried out by the senior investigative officer in Britannia, Beneficiarius Quintus Valerius. These proceedings will take place on his return to Eboracum, until which time you will be held under house arrest in the custody of Centurion Marcellus Crispus, presenting this declaration.

Aradius Rufinus, governor of Britannia Superior and legate of the Second Augusta and Twentieth Valeria Victrix legions.

Julia was watching Marcellus, awed at his composure, when Britta jogged her hard with her elbow. Julia turned to expostulate and saw excitement and trepidation on Britta's face. 'Look, Julia! Look around the square!' Julia lifted her palla away a little, and slowly turned her head to look. Corellia and Aurelius glanced round in surprise.

A file of uniformed soldiers, at least three deep, was gathering in disciplined silence. They stood in straight ranks on all four sides, surrounding the outraged legate. More men were moving silently into place. The legate yelled at his men, 'Take this traitor, men! This is insurrection, with the discredited Londinium governor behind it. Officers, do your duty!'

This last command was directed at his young tribunes, who had emerged rather late from their breakfast and now stood blinking at the sight of the legion rapidly deploying around them, directed by the more experienced centurions. Julia noted sadly the two missing senior officers: broad-stripe tribune Gaius Laelianus, who now lay in a lonely grave outside Vindolanda; and Camp Prefect Antonius Gargilianus, whom she had last seen as a corpse dragged over his own horse. She blinked, not because of the growing light.

Crescens looked furious. He took a step forward, and was halted by a vine stick planted in his chest. It was held by a senior centurion, the primus pilus of the First Cohort, who knew the legate well. The primus pilus was a burly middle-aged man whose cuirass was so smothered with awards for valour that the leather underneath could not be seen. He said something in a menacing tone. Julia guessed he had been looking forward to this little chat for some time. The legate fell back, spluttering and red-faced.

Another soldier approached, carrying a light spear. Crescens apparently realised today was not his day. He trailed back into the house, legionaries on either side, while Marcellus and his men followed. Leaving a guard at the door, and others posted by the windows, Marcellus accompanied Crescens into the praetorium. He shut the doors firmly.

All Eboracum was aghast and fascinated by the gossip rapidly sweeping the city. It was whispered that Legate Crescens had been arrested for treason, and that the Londinium governor was sending both his legions, the Second Augusta of Isca Silurium, and the Twentieth Valeria Victrix of Deva, against the Eboracum legion. No, insisted others, the legate was suspected of murdering his own senior officers, and was in custody pending trial. After all, everyone knew the popular base commander Antonius Gargilianus had died in suspicious circumstances. Hunting accident, indeed! The prefect was known to be wedded to his duty. He rarely took time off, and hunting was not a pursuit he enjoyed. Others said, more quietly, that it was the sudden death of the legate's young, beautiful wife that had been his downfall. 'She was the cousin, or sister, of Emperor Alexander Severus himself. Fancy, she was killed during Saturnalia. Such bad luck and sacrilege! Woe to the city where such dreadful things happen.'

Whatever the good citizens believed, it was certain the temple of Eboracum saw a pleasing rise in donatives and mouthwatering burnt sacrifices, such as had not occurred since the old emperor' obsequies years before.

The people of Eboracum were definitely worried.

Julia was relieved that both Marcellus and Lossio had come to Eboracum. Quintus would be proud of his deputy, she thought, swallowing a lump in her throat. Wherever Quintus was, at least his back would be safe now.

She did not see much of Marcellus, who was kept busy taking charge of an awkward high-profile prisoner, together with running a prestigious fortress manned by a large garrison. Fortunately, as Lossio was able to report the following day, he was getting a good deal of support from a staff of NCOs who were more loyal to the city and their dead camp prefect, than to their short-term legate.

'I think we can keep matters under control here, my lady,' he told Julia. 'But I wish we had word from Quintus Valerius. You have heard nothing from him recently?' he asked.

'No. And with the apparent theft or destruction of all Antonius's papers, including the latest report from Quintus, I am very concerned. I fear — Lossio, I very much fear — it's too late for Quintus. Surely if matters were going well in his embassy to the Pictish king, we would have heard from him by now?'

Julia's voice quavered as she asked this, and she hated herself for sounding weak. But Lossio looked away, pretending to busy himself with straightening a strap on his baldric. Corellia kindly stepped into the breach. She had taken to coming every day to see how Julia was, and to offer any help she could. She knew full well Julia had a fast-track into the current management of the city, which was another reason to keep in close touch, as Aurelius Mercurialis had sagely noted. Corellia had bridled a little at the implicit suggestion she should take advantage of her friendship with Julia, but she saw his point.

So did Lossio, who knew very well that Aurelius and Corellia were keeping the city's commercial and business interests informed. This suited Lossio very well, but he shrewdly began with other news.

'We've more evidence confirming Crescens had illicit dealings with the Picts. Marcellus's men found a huge amount of silver coinage stored in the legionary strongroom, separate from the normal paychest. It's money with no reason to be there. Marcellus told the paymaster that he would be charged with collusion if he didn't cooperate; the man quickly owned up. Crescens has been diverting into his own coffers the silver payments intended for our old allies in Caledonia, who have been guarding the lands between the Aelian Wall and the Bodotria river for many years. Those regions are now emptied by the threat of the encroaching Picts.'

'But why would the Picts not want the money?'

'Good question, Julia, and my best guess at an answer is worrying. From the intelligence I've been gathering for some time, I think Crescens agreed to turn a blind eye to Athair's amassing power and sweeping rivals away on his path south. In return, the Picts would forego the silver, which I am told Athair has no value for. So Crescens, the fool, would get rich, and Athair would gain unfettered access to the fertile lowlands as he moves south to threaten our Wall.'

'But the weapons, Lossio! You know about the weapons being traded to the Picts, don't you? Ah, no, you haven't seen Placidia's journal yet.' She quickly explained to the shocked speculator the meeting Placidia had secretly witnessed. He looked serious now, and she saw that the notion of Roman-grade weapons in the hands of Athair's warriors had him worried. She gave Placidia's journal to Lossio, to share with Marcellus. Lossio looked grim. 'This makes my latest news even more pressing. The primus pilus here at Eboracum fortress is gathering volunteers to go to Cair Pol. Whatever forces Athair has amassed to threaten the old fort, at least we can now send a sizeable defence force north.

'Plus, while I was at Vindolanda, I discovered that the beneficiariate troop there had apparently deserted. The commandant was furious, wanted them tracking down and disciplining with decimation. But as his own name is near the top of our list of arrests, I doubt that will ever happen. My contact tells me they have gone north, to follow their centurion to Cair Pol.'

Julia took little notice of this. She supposed these few men from Vindolanda would be some help in manning Cair Pol, if indeed Quintus's mission had failed and they were holed up in the old fort. But her face fell at the suggestion of sending troops all the way from Eboracum to the Tausa.

'I'm sorry, Lossio. I'm sure you want to cheer me up with the news of the Sixth sending volunteers north, but it's far too late! We must face the facts: Quintus will be dead long before any help can arrive from here, especially marching on winter roads.' She fought to keep her emotions under control as she said this, but knew she must sound hopeless.

But Lossio was looking brighter. 'You are right, of course. Any forced march over such distances in winter would arrive too late. But Cair Pol in its day was known as Horrea Classis, the storehouse of the navy. There's a large fortified harbour there, purpose-built to disembark large ships. So I have another plan, which involves your good friend here.' He nodded at Corellia, who had just risen to accept a tray of wine from Britta.

He went on, 'We've had a surprising number of volunteers. It seems Quintus Valerius and Tiro made a positive impression during their time here. Over a thousand men of the Sixth Victrix have stepped forward to help.' He paused to let this number register with his listeners. Together with the Vindolanda company, this was a substantial force for any native chieftain to deal with, Julia acknowledged. Then she thought again, and her mood dropped back into her shoes.

'How could we possibly transport all these men from Eboracum? With their weapons and supplies? There is no naval base here.'

Lossio looked at Corellia, who was looking upbeat too. 'Well, Julia, Eboracum is a major trading city with a navigable river. I would need to check with Aurelius, but I believe I know several merchants of this city who would be amenable to hiring out their ships for transport. Many of us have ongoing contracts with the army. I know of at least three corbitas currently in port, and others due to dock soon. The last thing this province needs is another threat of war, and the prospect of barbarians, armed with our own weapons, breaching the Wall would be very bad for business. Money and ships shall be found, and quickly!'

She stood, shaking out her skirts, and came to Julia to kiss her. 'Goodbye, my dear. We'll get your man the help he needs, and in less time than you might think possible. Lossio, come and dine with us tonight. We'll have something worked out by then.'

Chapter Twenty-six

Castlelaw hillfort

Quintus said and did nothing, awaiting events. His only weapon was the ivory pin, which would not serve him well against three longswords. The next move was Bedwyr's. The Pict looked at him shrewdly. He seemed to have an old head on his young shoulders.

'Give him your cloak,' he evidently said to one of his companions, who stripped off his colourful but rather soiled plaid and threw it to Quintus. Once Quintus was suitably covered up, Bedwyr said in his strange, fluent Latin, 'Roman, we must talk. Will you agree to a truce with me so we can discuss matters?'

Quintus thought he had very little to lose, given his situation, and assented with a nod. The taller of Bedwyr's two friends led the way to a hut set off to one side of the compound. Inside was a small fire which provided the only light, and there was nothing but the earthen floor to sit on. But it was private, and gave some shelter from the bitter night.

'We will speak in Latin, as I think you know little of the British language?'

Quintus nodded.

'My friends here have been my dearest companions since boyhood. They came with me when my uncle took charge of our tribe, and have been faithful to me ever since. They do not understand your tongue. If you try to betray me by telling anyone of our conversation, they will deny everything and immediately dispatch you to your gods.'

That was fair enough, thought Quintus. He nodded a third time. Bedwyr's mouth twitched, and he sat down to talk.

'My father was a well-regarded warrior, married to the daughter of the chieftain of our tribe. In those days, we Picts were still a loose confederation of small tribes scattered along the north coast, in and out of the northern glens. We shared a common tongue and way of life, but were separate tribes who occasionally fought over grazing and fishing rights. While I was still a child, we heard of he arrival of a strange people into the lands south of us. They were called Romans, and they came in mighty force, on huge ships, with more men than could be counted. Their armour and weapons shone to heaven. My grandfather deemed them too far away to trouble us: they had come to settle matters with the Caledonians and Maeatae in the lands to the south of us. But some of our young men were eager to fight, my mother's younger brother Athair being among them. Against my grandfather's wishes they went away to war, and although a few came back to tell of mighty war machines, huge forts and stone roads, my uncle was not among them. It was said the strange Romans had left, emptying their many forts, leaving their straight roads deserted, taking their terrible weapons. They had gone away for ever.

'My grandfather died a few years later and, as chosen by our people, my father became chief in his place. Time passed, and I grew up hunting, fishing, learning the lore of our people, our symbols of writing and the way of life of a chieftain-in-waiting. Then Athair returned. He said he had been captured and enslaved by the Romans. He was taken far south to a wide land of huge farms, where he was forced to work till he dropped. One day he struck down the slave-driver, and escaped. It was a long road of many months, but he eventually arrived home.

'But Athair was a changed man. Cruel, driven, full of resentment and an overwhelming desire for revenge. He told us we must alter our ways. He said the Romans would never let us live in peace, and that we must join together all the tribes to create an overwhelming force to defend our land. I learned he meant not only our ancestral lands in the north, but the whole of Caledonia, as far as the Stone Wall many days' journey away. My father disagreed, but some of the younger men listened. It began to be whispered that the chief was a coward, one who refused to defend his people against a usurping foreign enemy.

'One day, my father was found dead in the forest with an arrow in his back. No one ever confessed, but my uncle seized power. By rights, the next chief should have been me, but I was too young. Athair bowed to the will of the tribe, and let me live. I quickly realised I could stay alive to protect my mother and sisters only by ensuring that my uncle trusted me. So I became his right-hand man, his deputy. In due course, when it seemed that none of the many women he bedded would provide Athair with a son, he adopted me as his heir. I continued to serve, but quietly gathered some few about me who were still loyal to the memory of my father and grandfather. Thus you see me today.'

Quintus nodded. 'I came in good faith to parley with your uncle. My governor, Aradius Rufinus of the southern Roman province, is a wise man who understands that this island has room enough for both the Romans and the northern tribes, including you Picts. Our Roman way of life is best suited to the southern parts of Britannia anyway, and since the old emperor died, we have no desire or need to take any land further north. As a young man I came here to fight the Caledonians. Neither side won that war. This time I come to prevent more bloodshed.'

Bedwyr nodded. His blue eyes were alert and intelligent, and conveyed a certain pride.

'And yet you keep many warriors along the Stone Wall, and in forts behind it.'

'Yes,' said Quintus, keeping his tone steady. 'The Aelian Wall and the soldiers manning it are there to protect our people, who wish only to live in peace. It is not our intention to cross the Wall unless we are forced to. And yet certain of your warriors have been coming through the Wall. And we have found young women of your kingdom smuggled into our lands, sold into abuse. Do you know about this trade?'

Bedwyr flushed, and his mouth hardened. 'This is not the true way of our people. My uncle has taken his own path, punishing those nobles and leaders who defy him with death, and by sending their young women into shameful captivity. In return he acquires Roman weapons, intending to use them to raid your forts and breach your Wall. This policy angers many, including me. If I had my way, I would retreat to our own lands and, rather than threat and bloodshed, I would work at creating productive alliances with other tribes. The day of an enlarged Pictish kingdom across all this land will come, but it is not yet.'

Quintus nodded, feeling the final pieces falling into place.

Bedwyr had confirmed his suspicions: Athair's aim all along had been to acquire superior Roman weapons. He had no need for the silver diverted to pay off greedy, stupid Legate Crescens. Why would he, when soon all the fertile lowlands would fall to his massed well-equipped warriors? Then he would pour his men into a vulnerable northern Britannia, through a Wall no longer guarded, with the only remaining protection a somnolent legion under the command of a heedless traitor. The traded women were a useful red herring, he realised, just a means for Athair to terrify the opposition in his own territories into submission, while bribing the Wall garrisons to turn a blind eye to the steady breaching of the Wall. It was a terrible affirmation of his worst fears, but the telling afforded him some relief. He could work with this man, if what he heard was honest. He believed it was.

'Will you help me, Bedwyr? I have companions in the old Roman fort — you came across two of them getting away. They are all innocent of any wrongdoing here in Caledonia. I have tried and failed to negotiate peace terms with your uncle. One of my friends has already been lost to Athair's bloodlust. Will you allow me to get back to Cair Pol, so at least I can fight for my friends with a sword in my hand?'

He looked Bedwyr full in the face. The young Pict, blue eyes locked on his, nodded. 'Yes, I will. And more, although I fear it will be useless. I will try to persuade my uncle to leave your fort unscathed, to allow you to depart our country unharmed. Aila has been spreading the word that the Ban Sith are warning of terrible vengeance should we attack the Roman ghosts' fort. Athair has one weakness. He is fearful of vengeful spirits; rightly so. I will mention the risk of that fear spreading to our men. Watch for me to intervene if I can, although I must not be seen to speak to you again. Now you must go. There is a great army coming from the north, and if you are to escape ahead of it, you have very little time.'

He spoke quickly in the Pictish tongue to one of his bodyguard, who bowed and left the hut. As he opened the door, a few fat wet snowflakes drifted in to melt slowly on the floor.

'I am sorry about your other companion,' said Quintus. 'I was forced to kill him to get my friends away.'

Bedwyr waved a dismissive hand. 'He was no companion of mine. He was a sneaking rat set by my uncle to spy on me. You have done me a favour, Quintus Valerius.' The young warrior gave a brief wintry smile. Quintus wondered whether, had they met in better times, they could have been friends.

The door opened to re-admit the bodyguard. He was carrying a pile of tartan clothing, a black cloak, and a tall spear. He spoke excitedly to Bedwyr, who grimaced and said to Quintus, 'Put these clothes on over yours, and take this spear. I will accompany you to the main gate. From there you must make your way home as fast as you can. Our army has just been sighted, and will soon be encamped around Castlelaw. The snow will cover your tracks, and all eyes will be turned to catch the first glimpses of our kinsmen, so there is a good chance you will attract no interest. But make haste!'

'One more thing, Bedwyr,' said Quintus. 'Does the name Aine mean anything to you?'

Bedwyr's face darkened. 'Yes. She is a princess of a tribe my uncle took over. In fact, a close relative of your Aila. I wasn't there when Aine's family was broken apart. I believe it was in retribution for something said that Athair took to be disrespectful. I later heard Aine had been sent south along with other young women. Have you found her?'

Quintus briefly told of discovering Aine's body at Lagentium, and what Nicomedes had said of his friend. Bedwyr sighed, and rubbed a hand across his face. In a moment of compassion, Quintus said, 'Athair may have ordered her journey into darkness, Bedwyr, but we believe she was equally the victim of the Roman legate at Eboracum. If we survive the encounter with your army, I promise you the Romans involved in her kidnapping and death will be punished. We will honour her memory in our Roman style, if you permit?'

Bedwyr said nothing, but stood to grasp arms with Quintus in a parting gesture of mutual respect.

Swathed in plaid, coated in snow, and leaning on the great spear given him by Bedwyr, Quintus slowly forced a path to Cair Pol through growing snowdrifts. Night had fully fallen, and what faint light there was to guide him reflected eerily off the white mounds building around him. He was weary, his mind full of the approaching battle, and his bad leg itching with cold. The path ahead was obscured and confusing in the whirling snowstorm. In the end it was the snow that stopped him missing his way. As he emerged from the tree cover, unable to distinguish the great river or any other landscape features, his eye was caught by sharp white edges in unnatural shapes. By good fortune, he was looking directly at the Roman fort, its walls and towers outlined by the newly fallen snow.

Once again Quintus had good reason to thank his gods, and to be grateful that Tiro had insisted on bringing Nicomedes with them. As he neared the fort, making his way around the east side to approach the river gate, he heard a shout in a voice he didn't know.

'Halt! Drop your weapon!' Two soldiers muffled in red cloaks, swords drawn and pointing at him, came running out of the gate. As he was unwinding his large cloak from around his chin to speak, another voice, younger, familiar, broke out in excitement behind the men.

'Quintus Valerius, sir! Look out, it's the boss!' Then a dark shadow nearly knocked him off his feet, and a warm wet tongue licked his cold hand. It was Camilla, with Nico struggling behind her through the snowdrifts heaped up against the walls of Cair Pol.

Chapter Twenty-seven

Cair Pol

Tiro was feeling downhearted. He knew he shouldn't be, but it was so hard.

Marcus, good man, was doing his best to keep spirits up. He'd got his men busy too, integrating the newcomer Caledonians into the troop. He was running intensive training sessions, teaching the eager young men how to maintain and use the Roman swords, shields and knives they had inherited, together with odd bits of armour and even a slingshot or two. There was no shooting training, not so much because they had no bows, but because they were all well-used to bows for hunting anyway.

He turned as Aila came into the room and smiled at him. That was one good thing, Tiro thought: the crazy rescue of Aila and Kian had worked. He swallowed, trying not to dwell on the loss of Quintus. *Damn you, Boss! You just* had t*o do the brave thing and go last. I suppose that's what happened — someone saw you before you could get over the palisade and climb down the rope. So I have to carry on trying to be you, trying to fool Marcus and all of them that I know what I'm doing. But how much longer can I fool myself?*

'Horses all sorted,' Aila said. 'I've sent Nico for supper and an early night.' She looked at him closely, her face warm. 'Ye've been sitting in here moping too long. Come on out, let the cobwebs blow awa' before bed.'

He nodded, took a lantern and followed her outside. They climbed the steps up to the top of a wooden tower facing south. From here there was normally a good view of the Pictish hillfort. Tonight, as the snowfall diminished, the dark crag was revealed only by the tiny pinpoints of campfires.

Tiro was suddenly aware of a small figure, dark against dim lightness, approaching the south tower. What? He squinted, trying to focus on a plaid cloak swirling in the evening breeze. Tiro had very good eyesight; for a moment he thought he was looking at a

Pict, a lone warrior on a daredevil solo mission to infiltrate the fort.

'Gate! Enemy approaching!' he shouted to the guards. By the time they'd grabbed spears and stepped hastily through the gateway to halt the incomer, Tiro had recognised the slight limp of the cold, tired soldier in Roman boots. He cursed, torn between instant joy and sudden concern, and hurtled down the tower steps to find Camilla and Nico — not so fast asleep, it seemed — already ahead of him.

Something else caught his sharp eye. A good mile or more behind Quintus, in endless straggling lines lit by torches, a crowd was forming. Too far away to tell what sort of boots they wore, but he reckoned they wouldn't be Roman. They kept on coming, steadily forming a thickening skein of manpower weaving to and fro between the hillfort and Cair Pol.

The Pictish army had arrived.

There was nothing more to be done that night. Anyway, the boss needed to be fed, warmed and dried out. Then Quintus needed to greet Marcus, and listen while Aila, Kian and Nico all told their side of the big escape. Quintus said little, only nodding when Aila, almost in tears, told him how afraid she had been.

'We shouldn't have left you there, Quintus. I knew why those crabbit druids were coming — aye, and what the boggin' Pict had in store for you. I've seen the…bones, in my ain hame. What they did with their little knives to make people talk, or just to punish them…' Aila began to cry, silently. Kian had entered while she was speaking. He went straight over to Aila, put his arms round her and walked her out of the room, saying in gruff aside to Tiro and Quintus, 'She'll be all right. Just tired. I'll look after her.'

Tiro brought Quintus a hot meal, and some native beer. Rough on the back of the throat. Quintus ate and drank in gulps. He yawned hugely. The room emptied, as everyone but Tiro moved off to their own sleeping quarters. Tiro stood, too, but stopped when Quintus spoke.

'Don't go yet, Tiro. Sit down. I need to tell you what Bedwyr said, before he helped me escape from Castlelaw.' Quintus paused as if to gather his thoughts, then began.

'We've been wondering how the seemingly disparate parts of this conspiracy fit together, haven't we? The sudden increase in weapon-making at a time of peace. Pictish warriors seen moving unhindered through the Wall. The attacks on us at Vindolanda when we came north to find Gaius. Why Aila was kept captive at Vindolanda, instead of being sold at a slave market. The killing of Aine, who had escaped the Picts and yet was still afraid for her life. Antonius's dying soldier's "silver turned into swords". Talking of silver — the payments from Rome that never reached the Votadini. Above all, *why* would Athair and Crescens come to an agreement? Again, I think of Cicero: what does each have to gain from the other?'

He paused, and Tiro for once let his boss ruminate without interruption. Eventually Quintus looked up. His grey eyes looked weary and his expression was subdued.

'What Bedwyr told me made it clear there was not just one, but two deals made between our noble legate and the Pictish king. The weapons and the girls are part of one trade. Athair used terror and the kidnapping of women to still dissent among his opposition, and to remove the next generation of nobles that might attract a following among his warriors. Perhaps, as Aila suggested, he knows himself to be unable to father an heir, and was ensuring no one else's bloodline would take power in the future. Aila told us that Athair threatened those who opposed him; and Bedwyr confirmed the trade as a political weapon against his noble rivals.

'On the Roman side, the trafficked girls are forced to supply free sex for the remote garrisons along the Wall, keeping the commandants happy, and Crescens happy too. The Roman forts trade newly-forged weapons in exchange. Athair intends to conquer the whole of Caledonia, and to do that with his limited manpower he needs overwhelming force. Our weapons would give him that edge.

'I don't yet have definitive proof of this, but I suspect the second trade is the allies' silver, in exchange for a blind eye turned to actions behind the Wall. I believe the agreement was for Crescens to allow the Picts to take over all the lands of the friendly tribes right up to the Wall. With those tribes killed or swallowed up into the Pictish state, there would be no need for Crescens to continue paying them to be buffers between us and the Picts. Thus Crescens could take delivery of the silver from Rome, and send it direct to his own chests. Once he has what he needs, he sails back to Rome, leaving Britannia to sink or swim without him.'

Tiro stared at Quintus in horrified realisation, and leapt to his feet. 'Sir, I know exactly where that silver is! It's in the sacellum at Eboracum, with the soldiers' paychest. I wondered why there was such a strong guard outside. I saw them myself, eight legionaries standing guard at once. I'm so sorry, sir. I noticed it, and never thought to tell you! I'm a fucking idiot!'

'I saw the guard too, Tiro. That makes us both idiots.'

'But how would it benefit Crescens if the Wall was breached, and the northern province overrun by Picts before the Sixth Victrix — who he commands, *deodamnatus!* — before they could do anything, even if they decide to disobey his orders? And, sir — what about the danger to Eboracum? Lady Julia, Britta, little Flavius...' Tiro paused in his raging. His legs felt wobbly. He sat down, breathing hard. The boss's quiet voice penetrated his despair.

'He has everything to gain, Tiro. At first I too thought he must realise he is risking the security of an entire province, which would end his career spectacularly were the Picts to invade on his watch. Only a very stupid man would trust Athair to halt at the Wall, once he was armed. But I judge Marius Crescens to be both stupid and venal. He is so focussed on himself and what he wants, he doesn't care. You don't imagine he came to Britannia to serve, do you? To do his duty as a Roman patrician? No! He came here to make his fortune. How long do you imagine it took him to discover that the largest supply of silver in the province was flowing out to our old allies north of the Wall? He wanted that silver; all he needed was a partner who would help divert the flow to Crescens, and be happy to be paid in other ways to do so.'

'That just leaves one more part of the puzzle, sir: Placidia Septimia. Why was she killed at Saturnalia? We know her husband was out on the streets, the bastard. Was it jealousy? Did he find out about Gaius?'

'I don't know, Tiro. And there's a bigger problem. So far we have only circumstantial evidence against him. No Roman court will accept the statements of barbarians like Bedwyr and Aila, or even what Aine told Nicomedes. When we return to Eboracum' — Tiro lifted his head at "when we return" not "if we return" — 'we'll need, somehow, to get corroborating evidence good enough to satisfy the highest court. Crescens must not escape Roman justice!'

Quintus nodded once, a fierce look on his face. Then he stretched himself out by the fireside, and quickly fell asleep. Tiro reckoned the Pictish army could wait this night before he and the boss came up with the morning's plan, one that would thrash them Roman-style and send the tattooed barbarians running back to their mountains and glens. He fetched a blanket, taking it to the other side of the fire. Then he lay down to sleep, after quick thank yous to Jupiter, and Mercury, and Mars and Hercules, and …

It was a bright morning of sunshine, reflecting off the crisp snow mantling the river meadows and woods between Cair Pol and Castlelaw. The Picts were up early. Tiro wondered what these raw recruits thought of their job. Well, he reckoned the boss would have a few tricks for them up his sleeve. And Marcus, his troop, and the half-Roman lads were certainly up for it. He glanced at their own Ninth Hispana descendant. Kian had a softer look than usual on his face. Tiro was happy for him; happy for both of them. Young love.

But now to business.

'Sir?'

Quintus was up and breakfasted. He'd been out at dawn looking carefully at what could be seen of the enemy: mostly smouldering campfires and men moving about.

'Have you set a watch on the river, Tiro?'

'The river, sir?'

'Yes.' Quintus frowned, rubbing his right leg. It was a gesture Tiro recognised, meaning the boss was worried. *Why does he want the river watching?*

'Okay if I send Nico? I mean, we might need every spear and sword here, sir.'

'Yes. Do it. Then get Marcus and Kian in here.'

Uh oh. The grim look is back. Tiro thought over the times he'd seen that face before: at Corinium, before the battle with the Second Augusta; in the imperial palace when Chief Minister Ulpian was assassinated; after Quintus had watched his mother die of poison by the man she loved. It wasn't a good look, and Tiro desperately wanted not to see it again. But here they were.

Marcus came in and saluted Quintus.

'Take a seat, Marcus. I'm promoting you to centurion, pending confirmation by Governor Aradius Rufinus.'

'Sir — thank you, sir! And Centurion Pacatianus?'

'Will not be coming back. We will mark his sacrifice fittingly later.' Marcus visibly swallowed. Kian walked in cheerfully, took a look round and sat. Quintus rose, stretching his leg, and began to walk around the room as he spoke.

'Right. I want your views. Athair now has a large army at his disposal. I can't tell his numbers for sure, as he may have more warriors hidden away on the further side of Castlelaw. But from those we can see, as well as the twenty or so of his royal bodyguard, there could be two thousand Pictish warriors encamped between us and the hillfort.'

The happy look vanished from Kian's face. 'And we have — what? Fifty, some of us with little or no training in warfare. We'll have no chance against the Picts if they choose to attack us. Of course, they may just sit back and starve us out. Either hunger or the cold will finish us off.'

Tiro was annoyed at Kian. He was so ready to give up. It seemed the Roman blood had run thin in recent generations, despite his Mediterranean looks. Aila came in with hot drinks, and at a nod from Quintus, joined the circle. Tiro, still looking at Kian, now saw that his despair was entirely for her. He had a flash of memory, seeing again a glimpse of the pale face of Vibia as she lay dead at the foot of the Tarpeian rock in Rome. He suddenly felt sympathy for the lad.

Quintus had been watching the young pair, too, it seemed.

'You're right, Kian, We have only fifty or so fighters. For now. But we do have several things going for us. One of them is the fort and its position on the river. We have strong Roman walls here, built to last.' He did not add that they could hardly defend such a large fort with so few men on the walls, strong or not.

'Aila, you're a Pict, and you did a wonderful job of gaining Athair's confidence. What can you tell us of the Great Pict and his men that might help us?' A shadow passed over Kian's face, but Aila held her head high as she spoke.

'Athair is a strange man, unlike other leaders of the Painted People. He craves only power, over enemy and friend alike, and cannae be bought by aught else. I dinnae care to describe what he does to those who do not instantly obey, but I think ye know.' She nodded at Quintus, then carried on. 'His strength lies in fear and intimidation, not the love of his people. Fear is a strong weapon, but mayhap it can be turned on him.'

Quintus looked thoughtful. 'Tell us about the Ban Sith, Aila.'

She laughed. 'Och, there is a weapon of fear indeed! I sowed a few seeds among Athair's men, about Cair Pol and its supposed malign spirits. With luck those seeds have sprouted, and will spread into the arriving army too. With the Ban Sith on our side, we have more hope.'

Quintus rose and beckoned to Kian. 'There are other, even more powerful spirits here at Cair Pol. Fetch the eagle, lad.' Kian jumped up eagerly, and Quintus turned to Marcus. 'You at least will understand the hidden treasure of Cair Pol. I think our new friends from the locus meetings will be struck when we show them. I hope the Picts will be struck too.' Tiro saw the wry expression on Quintus's face, and despite himself began to feel more hopeful.

Kian came back shortly, cradling the old eagle still in its wrapping. As the gold bird was revealed, Marcus showed all the signs of awe Tiro himself had felt when he first saw it.

'An eagle — but…Can it be? It must be! The eagle of the Ninth Hispana, sir? I can't believe it, it's…a miracle. We've always believed at Vindolanda that the Ninth were lost in Caledonia. But where did you find it? Where, how…' Quintus laughed, saying

'You will need to ask Kian for the full history. It is his tale to tell. But for now, Marcus, can you get one of your carpenters to make a proper standard for this noble bird? It may get the chance to spread its golden wings once more in battle.'

Marcus still looked troubled. 'The eagle will be a help indeed, sir, but how are so few of us to stand up against their numbers?'

'I have one or two ideas, Marcus. Aila, am I right in thinking that among your people a challenge to ritual single combat may not be denied?'

Aila looked puzzled, but answered readily enough. 'Aye, sir, that it is. Once the challenge has been issued, a champion from each side steps forth. The fight is to the death, and straightaway must end the conflict between the tribes.'

'Right. Now, tell me — how likely is it, from what you know of Athair, that he would let someone else be his champion in such a challenge?'

Tiro felt alarm growing in him. Surely Quintus wasn't planning to go down this route again? Only good luck, and a timely puddle, had saved him at Corinium. Tiro hadn't yet seen the Great Pict, but from what he'd heard of him, this would be a challenge too far for the Governor's Man.

'Sir!'

'Not now, Tiro. Well, Aila?' Quintus was gazing intently at the girl, who had gone paler even than usual. She said in a quiet voice, 'Athair would never do that, even if he were dying. He would think it a slur to his manhood to let another fight in his stead.'

Tiro leapt up. 'No, sir! You are our leader. You are a father, and a husband. You must not put yourself at such risk, trying to kill the Great Pict!'

'Sit down, Tiro! Only I can offer challenge to Athair. I am the leader of the hated Romans; he will accept the challenge only from me. Besides, I don't need to kill him. Do I, Kian?'

Kian seemed reluctant to answer. After a long pause, he said, 'No. A maimed warrior may not continue as leader. Our tribes will follow only a perfect, whole man. If Athair is damaged beyond normal healing, say by blinding or losing a limb, his leadership will fall to Bedwyr. But, sir, Tiro is right. It would be madness to

209

challenge the Great Pict.'

Aila broke in, 'Aye! The man has ne'er been bested in a fight.'

Quintus had a smile on his face. 'There's a first time fo everything.' Only Tiro recognised the white-faced tightness behind the fixed smile.

Tiro spent the next few hours in increasing despair. Nothing he could say would sway the boss's resolve in the slightest. Every suggestion he made for alternative courses of action was batted steadily away. He paced up and down, while a young lad eagerly burnished Quintus's sword and polished the eagle till it shone. The bird was mounted onto a stout new standard, and fixed securely into place. The honour of being standard bearer fell to Kian by unspoken agreement. A meal was prepared and given out to the men, and signals passed round for calls to action. But, as Tiro told anyone who would listen, this was all a waste of time. Barring a miracle.

'And perhaps I *am* awaiting a miracle.' Quintus wa maddeningly calm. 'We've had miracles before. Always trust in the gods, Tiro. The time is right.'

'What miracle? What do you mean, the time is right?' Tiro said in exasperation.

Quintus looked at him, then shook his head in warning. 'Tiro, asked you to watch the river. That's an order.'

As Tiro, fuming, strapped on his long dagger, one of Marcus' men burst into the room. 'Sir! The Picts — they're on the move Coming this way.'

Quintus reached for his gladius. 'Right. Tell Marcus to deploy the men outside the fort gates as we agreed.'

He handed the eagle standard to Kian, and left the room looking every inch the perfect Roman officer.

Tiro could not bring himself to believe the truth: that he would never see Beneficiarius Quintus Valerius alive again. His vision blurred. Blazing with anger and mortification at being left out o the battle, he stalked through the north gate and slogged through melting snow to take up post on the river shore. The only thing he had managed to his own satisfaction was to send Nicomedes on Pegasus further along the shore, where the Tausa dramatically widened to embrace an island before emptying into the Mare Germanicum. More to give the boy something to do and to keep him away from the battle, than any forlorn hope. Tiro stood with his hand unconsciously grasping the hilt of his pugio, miserable and shivering and straining to hear what was happening on the landward side of the fort.

What he did hear came from an altogether different direction. It was the sound of hoofs, thundering along the shore. Julia's hunter was stretching his legs into a pace he had never before achieved, with Nicomedes mounted and shouting uselessly against the squally wind. The boy was pointing behind him, and as he neared Tiro could make out a lopsided smile on his thin face. Peering past the horse into the squally spitting north-easterly that swirled the waters of Tausa into white caps, Tiro saw something he had not dared even to dream of. He stared along the shoreline until his eyes watered.

There was no mistaking it: a naval bireme of the classis britannica was running up into the estuary, rushing along the flooding tide. Behind it was a string of merchantmen, corbitas of Eboracum, with sails strained tight against the following wind. Even from where he stood, Tiro could see the decks crowded with soldiers.

I bloody hate that man! He's always sodding right. Bless you, Quintus Valerius. I don't know how you've brought about this miracle, but by Jupiter, the time was *right!*

The liburnian docked first in the fort's harbour. Sailors jumped onto the dock with hawsers; then emerged a longed-for figure. The tall man's auburn hair was flattened against his skull, his hood drooped damply onto his back. Lossio Veda looked tired, but there was the ever-ready grin on the senior speculator's face as Tiro ran to greet him. But Nico, leaning down from Pegasus, beat him to it. Lossio reached up a hand to Nico, greeting the boy with a quick arm grasp. 'I see there's no keeping you out of trouble, my lad. Where is everyone?' the spymaster asked in a cheerful voice.

Chapter Twenty-eight

Cair Pol

Quintus surveyed the battle-lines. Marcus had his score of Vindolanda men tightly gathered in front of the fort. Above, on the battlements, the locus volunteers waited in hiding with only Kian in view. The newly-furbished eagle was also concealed for now.

The Picts had advanced across the water meadows to within a few hundred paces of the Romans. They were arrayed in irregular lines, many rows deep, with Athair and his royal bodyguard in the centre. There were no visible horses. Good. Quintus's one fear had been of chariots drawn by tough highland ponies, being sent spinning and crashing to wreak ruin among his own unmounted and largely untried men. No, that wasn't right. His actual real fear was of open battle. Their own numbers were so tiny that they could not repel a full-on attack. He prayed to Mithras his ruse would work.

Athair stepped forward from his host. Bedwyr was at his side, his expression inscrutable. Was he fooling himself, Quintus wondered. Would Bedwyr prove true? No way to find out except to risk everything on a single throw of the dice. He opened his mouth to speak, but the Great Pict beat him to it.

'Roman! So you've crawled back to your old castle. No doubt with that filthy little whore to help you. And the mongrel; I see him shivering on your walls. Not enough guts to come down onto the field to oppose me?' Athair turned to his men, laughing, inviting his army to join in. A dutiful roar of amusement rose behind him. Before he could speak again, Quintus plunged in. 'Athair of the Painted People. I offer you the traditional challenge: to fight me in single combat to the death. As your own custom dictates, I, Quintus Valerius, challenge you, Athair of the Picts. Advance to meet me.'

Athair laughed again, perhaps with less assurance. Bedwyr turned his arrogant words into Latin. 'A feeble attempt, Roman! In the face of my massed army, you bring a tiny handful of farmers

212

and guards. You have the effrontery to challenge, when the battle is already won by me!'

Bedwyr stepped close to his uncle, saying something in his ear. The chieftain brushed him aside, looking angry. Before Bedwyr could say more, a macabre wail arose from the Roman battlements. It was not clear where the eerie high-pitched noise came from. It swept across from one side, then the other, rising all the time in strength and potency. The Pictish warriors looked startled; some twisted and turned, clearly trying to see the source of the noise. A strong female voice rang out from the high tower at the front of the fort. It was Aila, dressed in flowing black robes.

'Warriors of the Painted People! I, Aila, one of your own, speak. I warned your lord, Athair, of the ghosts that linger here in the old Roman fort. He would not listen. Now, hear the Ban Sith!'

The wailing rose anew from behind her. Some of the Picts in the front row dodged away to hide behind their fellows; many lifted hands to their ears, in fear of the high message of death. One or two of the chief's bodyguard came to whisper to him. He pushed them away.

Aila persisted. 'If you keep disturbing the Roman ghosts, the Ban Sith will haunt you. You know of them; their job is to protect the dead. Their curse will be laid on your kin. Someone from each of your families will die, because of you!' She raised her hand in a dramatic gesture, and a sudden hush fell on the Picts as they saw the dread ghosts materialising. The gateway opened, and through it stepped a dead Roman, a warrior bearing the fabled sign of the legions. It was an eagle, a long-dead eagle. Gasps arose from the Pictish lines, as Roman after Roman came out, all dressed in old kit, bearing ancient short swords, following the ghost eagle as it led them onto the battlefield.

Bedwyr spoke urgently to his uncle. Athair looked around at his bodyguard, which had fallen back in dismay at the sight of the ghostly parade. The wails of the Ban Sith still echoed around the battlements. Athair made an impatient movement of his head, and strode out. He stood with longsword drawn, between his army and the small knot of Romans.

'I will accept your challenge!' he roared. 'Come forth, Roman, if you dare. You were already mine by rite of sacrifice; now I will claim your death by rite of combat.'

Quintus needed no further invitation. He stepped up to meet Athair, stopping a few feet from the big Pict. He held his buckler tight in his left hand and drew his gladius, shuffling around so the slanted sunlight was not shining directly on his face. As he did so, he caught a flicker of movement from the side of the fort. He hoped he had seen Tiro, but had no time to look longer. He narrowed his concentration onto his opponent.

Athair was taller and heavier than Quintus, and perhaps a year or two older. He moved catlike despite his great height, holding his longsword menacingly. Quintus knew himself to be a talented swordsman, but hampered by old damage to his right leg. It would not show yet, but he needed to settle this fight sooner rather than later.

On the other hand, two things cheered him: firstly, that the big man would need both hands to swing the long heavy sword, which gave him reach but denied a quick stab; secondly, that the Pict's sword was native-made. Quintus's gladius was older yet far stronger, the very finest Roman worked steel. It had been his father's precious sword, and felt perfect in his hand.

There was some initial feinting by both men, as they weighed each other up and shifted around in a circle, each seeking the slight advantage of the light. With every move, Quintus was looking for a way to end the fight with a wound that would put Athair out of action. He remembered what Aila had said about the tribes refusing to follow a maimed leader. A bad slice that severed a tendon would do the job. He carried on circling, parrying the savage two-handed strokes the big man aimed at him.

But Athair was ferociously strong and moved with surprising speed for such a big man. The edges of his sword, normally of little use against Roman scale armour, would be lethal for the unarmoured Quintus. Increasingly, he had to dodge side slashes as well as Athair's thrusts. It was soon borne in on Quintus that Athair was too fierce an opponent to offer him the luxury of a choice of strokes. *So I'll just have to kill him,* he thought, *no matter the consequences.* His fear was the Picts might rise with renewed

214

bloodlust to avenge their dead leader. But needs must.

The temptation was to stay out of reach of that lethal longsword, moving around to keep the Pict guessing and shifting his footing. But Quintus knew this waiting game was one he would certainly lose. Already he could feel prickling along his scarred thigh. At all costs, Quintus thought as he continued his grim dance, he must not let his opponent see the first signs of tiredness in that leg. If he flagged, even for a moment, he would die, slashed into bloody ribbons by the Pict's huge sword.

Resolutely he kept all his attention on his enemy's face, until he saw what he had waited for -- a flicker in Athair's eyes. The Pict leapt at Quintus, sweeping his sword upwards. It was a deadly stroke, delivered with great power. Quintus caught the swing on his buckler shield, giving way to the attack. This encouraged Athair to come in closer, on the offensive. He swung high again.

But now Quintus had him where he wanted him: close in where both his buckler and short sword were more effective. Quintus stepped forward, stooping low, his lesser height coming to his aid. With difficulty he again deflected Athair's cut with his buckler, using all his strength to thrust it straight up to the Pict's face. The great swing of the longsword was deadened, flattened by the little round shield and so losing much of its force. Quintus quickly brought the buckler to bear again, smashing it forwards to force Athair's sword flat across the man's own body. There, there was his chance!

He thrust his gladius up, feeling the soft give of flesh as his sword tip pierced the Pict's throat. With his full weight behind it, he carefully-sharpened sword slid unhampered, deep into his enemy's neck. A great gout of blood poured out, and Quintus leapt back out of range.

But Athair was already dead. His body whirled and fell, sliding across the frozen ground.

Gulping for breath, Quintus raised his gladius one final time. Turning so all could see him, he shouted to the crowd of warriors. By rite of mortal combat, I claim victory over your chief, and over your army. The fighting must cease.' A stillness fell on the men. Quintus stood, sword still raised, his eyes seeking and finding

Bedwyr. The young man stepped forward into the circle of combat. He saluted Quintus, who lowered his sword.

His enemy's blood ran down his hand, sticky and unclean. Suddenly he felt nauseated. This man, this lump of dead meat at his feet, had been a cruel dictator and unfit to rule. But how had he become so?

Because of Rome, because of what we did to him and his people. I was there, a soldier of Rome, helping the killing. I helped to cause his descent into madness and savagery.

Quintus let the gladius drop. He bent his head. He wondered at himself, the person he used to be. The Praetorian soldier. Then the imperial investigator who moved from case to case, murder to rebellion, province to city to palace, all without concern, with no sense of emotion. Impervious. Cool. Untouched.

He heard a commanding voice. Bedwyr was telling his people that the battle was over. That he, his uncle's appointed heir, would now lead them. That they would leave this place to the Roman ghosts, and go home beyond the Earthen Wall to their own lands where there was room and to spare.

Quintus was vaguely aware of more Romans filing out in front of the walls, many more. Where had they come from? Were there really Roman ghosts at Cair Pol? More people spoke. He listened as if through a fog, to Tiro almost sobbing with excitement. 'What a fight! I thought for sure you were a gonner, sir. That killing stroke you did, never seen anything like it…' Tiro's voice faded away. Quintus lifted his head, noting dully that Lossio was there. He was leading a large cohort, maybe a thousand men. Where had he magicked up all these soldiers? As he watched the Romans firmly urging the Picts away, he saw a vexillation standard bearing a bull. *Ah, the Sixth Victrix, from Eboracum. Of course Lossio got my report. But where is Antonius Gargilianus? Does Julia know?*

Suddenly he needed to lean on his sword. How he wished he could go back to being the remote person he once was. The soldier with no regrets, no conscience, no longings, no pain. *Julia,* he thought, *this is what you've done to me. You, and Aurelia and now little Flavius. I've learned to care, and it hurts like hell.* A small figure limped eagerly towards him, offering water in a helmet. He took the water, smiling as best he could at Nico. Behind the boy came Kian, with Aila. The young man held out the eagle standard proudly to Quintus.

At this moment of triumph, all he could feel was exhaustion. But he saw the bright eyes and excitement all around him. The young men of the old Ninth poured into the fight circle, all wanting, needing to celebrate. Tiro was still there, too, standing slightly off to the side with Lossio and Marcus, a huge grin plastered across his face. They were all waiting, watching him. So he stood up straighter, took the eagle to hold it aloft, and pretended for their sakes.

Later, round the fireplace in Cair Pol, he remembered to ask what had become of the Picts. Had they really just given up and gone away?

'Och,' said Aila, 'it'll be the Ban Sith they're feart of. I made sure many of the warriors in Castlelaw knew about the spirits at the auld Roman fort. All those unburied Roman soldiers of yesteryear.'

'What unburied soldiers?' asked Tiro. 'We never leave our dead unburied.'

'They don't know that. They think youse drink baby's blood too.'

Tiro laughed, but Lossio leaned forward, saying, 'I have a message for you, Quintus. I think you have made a friend, one who will be important for Rome.' He handed Quintus a piece of fine white leather, on which was written in careful Latin:

To Quintus Valerius

I will withdraw my people from sight till you are gone. We will re-occupy the empty lands as far as the old Earthen Wall. You have my word we will go no further. There will be peace for our lifetimes. Beyond that, I cannot tell, or make promises.

You have my gratitude. I salute you.

Bedwyr, King of the Painted People

Quintus sighed, and said to Tiro, 'Our mission here is ended. We must go back to Eboracum, where there is still work to do.' Tiro nodded, looking sober.

'You will find things have changed there, too, Quintus,' said Lossio. He explained that Marcellus had Marius Crescens under house arrest, and that Julia had uncovered the legate's crimes, thanks to Placidia and her journal. 'There is much more to tell, my friend, but it can wait.'

Quintus realised his fatigue must show. He made an effort. 'What of you, Kian? Where will you go? Do you stay here, with the eagle?'

Kian looked at Aila, taking her hand. 'Aila and I have talked of going together to Dál Riata. Aila has agreed to give up her own people to join mine. The eagle goes with us. But, sir, what will become of my brothers of the Ninth? Should we think ourselves Roman?'

Quintus shook his head. 'That will be for you to choose, and your children and your children's children, Kian. It is for you all to determine your own future. But I believe your fate lies on this side of the Aelian Wall.'

On their last morning in Cair Pol, Quintus and Tiro took a final walk along the battlements and around the barracks of the old fort.

'It's a wonderful place, this, sir. I wish somehow we could keep it Roman.'

'I don't think so, Tiro. This is not our land. These people have their own ways, and we must let them live so. Perhaps one day, someone will come across ruins buried here in the river sand, and wonder about the soldiers who once lived and fought here.'

Kian and Aila, cloaked, packed and with horses saddled by a tearful Nico, came to say goodbye. 'Farewell, Quintus Valerius. I wish you a safe journey back to your Roman province. Give my regards to your wife, and to your governor.'

'Go with speed and safety, Lucius Saturninus. You and Aila, I thank you both from the bottom of my heart for all you have done. I will never forget you and your beautiful harsh land.'

Aila surprised him by leaning forward to kiss him on the cheek Then the couple turned and led their horses out of the fort, not looking back. They passed Marcus, who had gone to the hillfort to look for signs of Litorius. Tiro looked enquiringly, but Marcus simply shook his head, a sad look on his face. Quintus felt for the new centurion.

'He was a noble soldier, and a great heart, Marcus. At the end he acted with honour. I owe Litorius Pacatianus my life. He will be remembered in Vindolanda. He was a truly loyal centurion.'

Chapter Twenty-nine

Eboracum

Quintus and Tiro went south by naval liburnian with the Vindolanda troop, taking Nicomedes and Camilla with them. Much to Nico's chagrin, the ship's master would not allow Pegasus on board — 'Not taking that whacking great stallion on board my nice neat galley!' — so Pegasus voyaged home with the Eboracum vexillation. He actually got home ahead of his master, as the naval bireme called in at Arbeia first. Marcus and his men disembarked there, and were issued with horses to replace those taken to Eboracum. Tiro, too, left the ship at Arbeia. He'd polished up his phalera, and looked ready for a jaunt.

'Permission to pursue investigations at Magna, sir? I've got a bone to pick with those archers!'

'Permission granted. I'm sure Marcus can spare you a few large lads. The archers from Magna are prima facie murder suspects, but who knows what else they've been up to? Don't be too gentle with your interrogation. And Marcus —'

'Sir?'

'Get those traitors at Vindolanda and Vercovicium into chains. Anyone you don't fancy the look of, including officers. Wait for Tiro, then bring them all under armed escort as fast as you can to Eboracum. I suspect there will soon be a very senior officer wanting to prosecute them, in connection with the illicit trading of weapons over the Wall. Not to mention the trafficking of the Caledonian women.'

Marcus said with a tight grin. 'I already know who to round up, courtesy of Litorius Pacatianus. He kept thorough notes.'

'Good man. If you ever fancy a job in the south, just get in touch.' Marcus saluted, and went off smartly to get his men gathered before he lost them to the taverns and brothels of Arbeia. Tiro threw a salute, ruffled Nico's hair in farewell, and rode west with some of the Vindolanda men along the Wall, ready for some fun in Magna.

So it was just Quintus and Nico, trailed by Camilla, who arrived at the Eboracum townhouse on a dreary wet afternoon, in time to meet Marcellus Crispus coming out.

'Sir!' The look of delight on the young centurion's face made Quintus smile in return. 'Lady Julia will be so happy to see you. No Tiro?'

Quintus explained Tiro was busy bringing justice to the whole suborned Wall command structure. 'I don't expect it to take long. He has the help of the Vindolanda beneficiariate troop, bent on revenge for their lost commander.'

'Well, sir, it's a relief to have you back, right in the nick of time.' Marcellus showed him a message from Londinium. It seemed Governor Aradius Rufinus was indeed coming north, to take personal control of Britannia Inferior. 'The legate being still under house arrest, you see, sir. So there's precious little going on in the city, or the province for that matter. To tell the truth, I was getting tired of holding things together here.'

Quintus laughed at Marcellus's rueful expression; civilian governance was not on the training programme for station commanders.

'You must allow me the rest of today before I let you off the hook, Marcellus. I suspect I have an irate wife to contend with.'

Marcellus bowed to Julia's prior claim and turned to leave as Fronto, hearing their voices, came to the door. He, too, was delighted to see his mistress's husband back in Eboracum.

But not as delighted as Julia. She had been going down to the docks every day since she heard from Quintus that he was alive, free, and on his way home. But today being dank and damp, she had decided to wait for a break in the rain before venturing down to the riverside again. Thus Fronto, hastening to open the door, and Sextus, very full of his new position as steward, were both gratified to enter the vestibule to find the dominus and domina locked in a heated embrace: the former travel-stained and damp, the latter flushed and wet-eyed. The two servants discreetly withdrew, taking an interested Nicomedes with them to the kitchen.

After quite a while, Julia untangled herself to look round. 'Where's Tiro?'

Before Quintus could answer, Britta bustled in. 'Yes, where is Tiro? Left him in a tavern somewhere, Dominus?'

Quintus managed to stifle his laughter as he answered the indignant woman. 'He's carrying out imperial duties at the Wall, Britta.'

She sniffed. 'Typical. That man is always late!' She swept out, leaving Quintus to raise an eyebrow at his wife, who was openly laughing.

'I'm sure Tiro will tell you all in due course. But I believe Quintus, that my worthy housekeeper and best friend has decided to marry, and was determined to let Tiro know at the first opportunity.'

Quintus's heart sank. 'Ah,' he said. 'Tiro will be very upset to hear that. I think he was working himself up to propose again to Britta.'

'That's where you're wrong, my darling. This time Britta is going to propose to Tiro!'

The next urgency was to spend time with his son. Quintus was amazed at how much the baby had grown, how strong his limbs were, how loudly he screamed when hungry, how much — everything. The screaming certainly brought Veloriga hurrying into the nursery, and she soon showed her charge's father out of the room, saying to Julia, 'I'm sorry, my lady, but Master Flavius must be fed in a peaceful environment. Perhaps the dominus could visit again later?'

Quintus was led meekly downstairs, having been brought to realise how low his stock had sunk over the past weeks.

Tiro was back with his unhappy prisoners in less than ten days, but before then Quintus had gone with Marcellus and a clerk to interview Legate Marius Crescens. The legate's custody was at the luxurious end of the scale, thought Quintus, as they were smartly saluted by their own Aquae Sulis men, and led into the palace

They had already passed by the principia, where more of the Aquae Sulis troop were guarding the shrine and the embezzled silver.

The house was large and cool, perhaps overly so for British tastes, as all the rooms faced on to a shady internal garden. They entered the reception room to find Crescens, also under guard, and looking dishevelled and somehow shrunken. The arrogance had been sucked out of him. His beefy red face had turned pallid, and the abundant chestnut hair that had once flopped generously onto his forehead was thinning. His stained toga hung haphazardly. But he made an attempt to look imposing when they arrived, standing to receive them with hands on both hips.

'Wait outside,' Quintus said to the guards. The room was very quiet. It was hard to believe this place was the centre of a large legionary fortress, at the heart of a bustling city. He looked at the clerk, a nervous man with a tall stack of tablets, stylus at the ready. 'You may begin recording.'

Crescens said pompously, 'Officers, you have no jurisdiction here. I am the senior judicial official in Britannia Inferior, and you have no right to keep me prisoner in my own home. I demand you release me immediately. I shall make a formal complaint to my colleague Governor Rufinus in Londinium.'

Quintus ignored this. 'Legate Crescens, in the name of the emperor, as authorised by your superior, Governor Aradius Rufinus, I charge you with murder, embezzlement, corruption, treason, conspiracy to kidnap and traffick, and obstruction of justice. Those you murdered or ordered to be killed are your wife Placidia Septimia, Tribune Gaius Laelianus, Aine known as Sacra, and Camp Prefect Antonius Gargilianus.'

Marcellus interrupted, 'What about the attack on your own home, Beneficiarius?'

'I think we'll just roll that crime in with all the others, as Fronto was fortunately not badly hurt.'

Crescens began to gabble, spitting out dislocated phrases '...no evidence ...those whores, nothing to do with me...betrayal by my own wife...disobedience and collusion with my enemies. I was keeping the silver safe...you can check, it's all there...' until

Quintus wearied, and said to Marcellus, 'Shall we gag him? Or simply add disrespect for imperial investigators to the list of charges?'

Marcellus looked with severity at the piggy-faced gibbering prisoner. It took a lot for Marcellus to display emotion, but Quintus could understand his hard expression on this occasion. He was relieved that Tiro had not yet returned; he suspected his short-fused optio would have quickly become judge, jury and executioner, especially with regard to the murders of Aine and Placidia. Fortunately, Tiro wasn't here, so due process would be observed. If Marcellus controlled himself. Quintus pulled out Placidia's journal, and showed it to the prisoner.

'You will be relieved, then, to hear that Governor Rufinus is en route to Eboracum. We expect him shortly. I am here to interrogate you; when he arrives, he will judge you, and sentence you to the appropriate punishment. I should warn you now that we have gathered sufficient evidence and witness statements, including your wife's journal, here — enough to find you guilty on all counts.'

This wasn't strictly true, as some details were still lacking. Such as who had ordered Aine to be tracked down, and how the weapons trading had been organised. Quintus liked to be thorough about judicial process. By the time Aradius arrived, he wanted to be able to present him with a nice, neat, tied-off case.

'For murder, the punishment is beheading or strangulation, but for treason, you will be subjected to the agonisingly drawn-out death of crucifixion. In public, of course,' he added, trying to look unconcerned.

Crescens slumped, terror in his face. 'I beg you, Quintus Valerius, help me. I'll do anything. You can have the silver, all of it.' He turned his bloodshot piggy eyes up in desperation. Quintus looked at the expression of disgust on his colleague's face. He could not stop his own lip curling. Crescens really was despicable. But the man had cracked — they had him at their mercy now.

'I *will* help you, Marius. I can make things much easier for you, if you cooperate. Just tell us everything, from beginning to end. For the record.'

Crescens had fallen to his knees, swaying a little. He moaned softly, then began his confession. 'I — I needed the money. They were after me, the sharks in Rome. That's why I came to this dreary little island. I thought with Placidia's dowry, and the opportunities the governorship would offer, I could straighten out my affairs and get those crooks off my back. But the little bitch had no real money to speak of, and I came here to find nothing but mud and savages. So when my commanders on the Aelian Wall told me the Picts wished to negotiate, and the silver payments to our former allies could be diverted to me, I was all ears. I went north to meet their king — a brutal painted man, ugh! But all he asked was room to move south, in exchange for the silver. I could see no objection.

'He started sending girls of his tribe, and others, south to Vindolanda. He told me they were to be disgraced as punishment for those who defied his rule. That suited me; there's a constant shortage of whores to service the Wall garrisons. Two things only are needed to keep soldiers happy: silver and girls. Now I had both, with a big bonus to me. In return for the girls, Athair said, he wanted weapons from our armouries. His own men were to collect them and take them north in wagons, at night. It seemed reasonable to me. The man needed to defend his own position, after all.'

Quintus stared at him. Was Crescens really that gullible? He managed to keep his voice measured as he asked, 'It never occurred to you that Athair was stocking up weapons to attack us? To break through the Wall and use our own arms against us?'

Crescens gazed in sudden shock, as if this notion had never crossed his mind. Marcellus drew a sharp breath, but was silenced by a swift glance from Quintus.

'Where are the weapons now? Have any been shipped yet?'

'N-no. Athair has seen samples, collected from Magna and Vercovicium and taken across the Wall by his men. But the supply isn't yet fully flowing.'

Quintus nodded. They had been in bare time to stop this danger. He thanked Minerva for the wisdom and watchfulness of Lossio Veda. But for him and his speculatores, Britannia might have been invaded and overrun before anything could be done to repel the northerners.

'Tell us about the girl, Aine.'

'I know very little. My commander at Magna took charge of monitoring that trade. I only know he reported that a girl had escaped. He sent archers to catch her, before she could spread alarm in the south.'

'So Aine was caught and killed on your orders. I see. And Placidia?' Quintus felt nauseated at the careless evil this man displayed. He managed to keep his face still, and his manner unruffled. He must squeeze the man till the pips sprang out.

'She — well, you must know neither of my previous wives had produced an heir. Nor did Placidia. But I had my suspicions when she resumed her childhood friendship with Gaius Laelianus. He wangled his way onto my staff, and they began to see each other in secret. My spies reported their meetings. Then she told me, just before the holidays, that she was pregnant. One night during Saturnalia I followed her myself, saw them kissing in an alley… I just couldn't bear the shame. I would have been a laughing stock. He left her momentarily, I don't know, maybe to fetch a horse or something, and there was my chance. She was so easy to kill…Please, I'll do anything, anything at all. Just tell me what to do, Beneficiarius.'

'Not yet. There is more, isn't there? Gaius Laelianus, and Antonius Gargilianus.' Quintus waited, remorseless.

Crescens sighed. 'You may as well know the rest. Gaius came back to find Placidia lying in the street. He ran. I couldn't have him spreading rumours, so I had the archers from Magna track him down. They did the job at Vindolanda, but messed up getting rid of your nosy man, I heard.' Quintus couldn't trust himself to speak; he merely nodded. 'They reported that you got away with a witness, heading north. I was sure you were intending to meddle in my arrangement with the Picts, and were secretly sending reports south through that disgraced centurion at Vindolanda. He left before we could catch him, but meanwhile I discovered my own camp prefect was the go-between here. He was got rid of, I don't know how. My men saw to that.'

Quintus nearly spat in disgust. He'd suddenly had enough. He looked at Marcellus, who nodded, hard-faced. His hand was on the pommel of his sword. Quintus unsheathed his own gladius, regretting the need to sully it.

'Here is the mercy you begged for, Marius Crescens. We'll allow you to do the honourable thing. If you commit suicide here and now, in front of us, you will be saved public humiliation and strung-out agony. We will inform Governor Rufinus that the law has taken its course. Your estate, of course, will be confiscated. The governor in his wisdom will decide what to do with it, possibly support some of the poor girls you conspired to traffic as prostitutes.' He laid his gladius on the floor in front of Crescens, indicating to the white-faced clerk that he could go. When the slave had scuttled away, he frowned at Crescens.

'Be swift, now. I am sickened by you; I need fresh air.'

They left the palace shortly after. Quintus said to the guards, 'You will find the legate has taken his own life. Remove his body for ignominious, but recorded, burial. I will inform the governor.'

Then to Marcellus, 'Come on. Let's get a drink.'

JACQUIE ROGERS

Chapter Thirty

Eboracum

Quite a crowd had gathered to greet the Governor of Britannia
Superior, Aradius Rufinus, and his lady Servilia Vitalis, as they
arrived in Eboracum. The governor's palace had been cleaned,
painted, refurnished, and emptied of anything reminiscent of either
the disgraced Crescens or his unhappy young wife. The Sixth
Victrix was fully assembled in the fort, with the volunteer
vexillation now returned from Cair Pol. Uniforms had been
spruced up, armour polished, and weapons sharpened for the
honour guard lining all four sides of the principia courtyard. This
was the first visit by the senior governor of Britannia in over a
decade, and who knew when another would occur? So the
citizenry of Eboracum, determined to make the most of such an
occasion, had dressed in their finest to pour into the fortress.

In front of the headquarters building, gazing across the crowded
square, stood most of the remaining principal players in the recent
drama, in varying degrees of discomfort. Senior Beneficiarius
Quintus Valerius, with Lady Julia Aureliana at his side, was in the
centre of the receiving line, Julia moving her too lightly-clad feet
around and wondering if the roast meats she had ordered would be
enough for all the guests coming to dine after the ceremony. Next
to them stood the elegant Corellia Velva and her richly-dressed
husband, Aurelius Mercurialis, hitching now and again as the
purple-bordered toga slid off his shoulder. The high priestess of
the Serapeum, suitably veiled, was seated in deference to her age
and seniority. The veil did not dim her sharp gaze as it swept the
crowd with satisfaction. Optio Tiro, Senior Speculator Lossio
Veda and Centurion Marcellus Crispus stood in a huddle with
Centurion Marcus, newly arrived from Vindolanda after arranging
a handsome memorial stone for Litorius Pacatianus. The four
soldiers shuffled their boots, exchanging news and banter. The
only major player in Eboracum missing from this line up was
Nicomedes, but as he much preferred to be at the front of the

228

crowd with Britta, Fronto and Sextus, Quintus was sure he felt no dissatisfaction with his lot.

Quintus watched the four soldiers enviously, wishing he could join them, until Julia slid her hand into his. 'It won't last long. Then we can fetch Aradius and Servilia and our friends, and take them home for spiced wine and, hopefully, a dinner to do us proud.'

He squeezed her hand, then let it drop as the gubernatorial carriage rolled through the gateway.

After the speeches, kept mercifully short due to the weather, the governor welcomed Quintus, Tiro and Lossio into his office in the headquarters building. Lossio muttered aside to Quintus before they went in, 'Quintus, I've just received a strange report from the far north. A party of prisoners was apparently seen going by sea to the Cave of the Dead, sent by Athair before his fall. I don't know who they were, but the rumour is that a Roman officer was among them.'

Quintus was not really surprised. He had feared this ending all along. There was no time to reply before they were greeted and led into the office. A slave poured warm mulsum for them and left. Aradius looked as pale as ever, and rested his club foot on a stool near a brazier, but Quintus recognised his expression as that of a pleased man.

'I don't know which of you to thank first,' the governor said, looking at them. 'Lossio Veda, without your professionalism and quick-thinking, we could have lost a province here. We all have much to be grateful to you for.'

'Sir, thank you. I was doing my duty.' The tall Caledonian looked happy.

'What are your plans now, Lossio?' asked Aradius.

'If I may, sir, I'd like to return south. I'm bringing Salvia with me, who was a faithful servant and friend to our poor Placidia. With your permission, I will take her to Londinium for us to be married.'

Aradius Rufinus directed his gaze at Tiro.

'Ah, Optio. Yours was perhaps the hardest task. You had to keep up the morale of all at Cair Pol, when you had apparently lost your senior officers, along with two valued Caledonian allies, all dragged into that dreadful hillfort.'

Tiro looked up, flushing and stammering that he had little to do with anything. 'But, sir, if I may, it was all the doing of my boss here. He gave himself up to try to save Centurion Litorius Pacatianus, and our young friends. And it was his clever plans that held off the Pictish army, until our own men could arrive.'

Quintus broke in. 'Nonsense. Sir, you have grasped the matter correctly. Tiro kept spirits high and planned our escape, when all could have been lost at Cair Pol. I am immensely proud of him.'

'Well, Beneficiarius, I have more to say to you in private. For now, I wish to make an announcement. For services rendered, and leadership beyond his duty, I now appoint Tiro to the rank of centurion in the beneficiariate.' He clapped once, and a slave came in bearing a very handsome centurion's swagger stick, which Aradius presented to Tiro.

'Congratulations, Centurion,' murmured Quintus, grinning at Tiro's red face. 'Whatever became of that disgraced drunkard I once found in a Londinium gaol?'

Quintus stayed behind to brief the governor on all that had happened. Aradius was especially interested in the agreement he had brokered with Bedwyr, now king of the Picts. 'That will be a useful relationship, I hope. Quintus, this is exceptional work. I, and all Britannia, are once more in your debt.'

'Yet, sir, I believe the real hero has left us,' said Quintus.

'Ah, you are thinking of Litorius Pacatianus.'

'Yes, sir. Just now Lossio brought me news which I fear means he is truly lost. He sacrificed himself with great gallantry to save our young part-Roman friend, Kian mac Dougal of the Gaels. It is not my story to share, but I know he suffered under a heavy burden of guilt that he longed to atone for. His was a noble act. I hope you will approve the memorial stone I have ordered set up at Vindolanda in his name.'

Aradius nodded, holding up his wine glass to toast. 'To Litorius Pacatianus, the loyal centurion. May he find eternal peace with the gods.

'Well, Quintus, I have one more thing to say to you before we leave this draughty palace. Your achievements at Cair Pol are likely to keep this province safe and at peace for a generation. That is no mean feat, and I believe only you could have achieved it. I have in mind another such mission for you and Tiro later in the spring, hopefully without as much danger. If you will accept it.

'But first I think you will want to go home to Bo Gwelt, to catch up with that remarkable daughter of yours. Please pass on my regards to her. My wife has been to meet your new son, by the way, and is all envy. And now, Quintus, I think we should join our womenfolk. Servilia tells me that Julia has a notable cook, and that your Eboracum home is much snugger than this freezing old palace.'

The following morning found a subdued gathering at breakfast in Julia's kitchen. The previous evening's party had lingered on into the wee hours, and they had slept late. Tiro was telling Julia about Aila and Kian.

'Imagine, my lady, he's both Lucius Saturninus, bearer of the Eagle of the Ninth, and he's a Gael, Kian mac Dougal. And now he's partnered with a true Pict, Aila, a fighting painted lass who stands no nonsense. I'd love to see them again in ten years. I hope they will be safe and happy.'

Quintus looked at Britta, who for once had sat at table with them rather than supervising the kitchen staff. He saw she was, in her turn, intently watching Tiro with her mouth curving at the corners. It was a fond look, he thought.

It was Julia who took the bull by the horns. 'Not heartbroken over any young ladies this time, Tiro?'

Tiro shrugged. 'I must be getting older, my lady.'

'Or wiser, perhaps', she said, smiling.

Britta still had that soft look on her face, and Quintus knew for sure.

He settled into Julia's bookroom to write his final report for Aradius Rufinus. He was unsurprised when Tiro knocked and came in. Tiro stopped in front of the big oak desk, looking awkward.

'Well, Tiro? Worrying about how to look like a proper centurion?'

'Oh no, sir, I'll get me a big shiny helmet and some of those ostrich feathers, I reckon. It's something else…'

Quintus waited, barely repressing a twitch of the mouth as Tiro continued to stand there, looking uncertain.

'Something to tell me?'

Tiro nodded. 'It's like this, sir. I've asked Britta again, and she didn't answer at first. She just gave me a letter she'd written while I was away, and never sent. Long and short is, we've asked each other, and we've both said yes!'

Tiro stopped, beaming. Quintus burst out laughing. 'I take it this means you'll want your own married quarters when we get home.'

Tiro's eyes shone. 'Yes, sir, if you're sure that will be okay. And sir…?'

'Yes?'

'Sir, could Nico live with us, too? Poor lad, he's scared silly we'll leave him behind. We both want to give him a good home.'

'Of course. Now go off and find out what that bossy woman of yours wants by way of housing, furniture and so on. I have work to do. And Tiro?'

'Sir?'

'Congratulations. You'll be very happy together.'

'I hope so, sir.' The touch of doubt in Tiro's voice was barely discernible. But Quintus heard it, and had to acknowledge theirs was likely to be a stormy marriage at times. A bit like his own, he supposed ruefully.

Quintus turned back to his report, but after barely a moment he laid down his pen again. When Julia came into the bookroom later, carrying an oil lamp, the room was almost dark. The only light was the glow of firewood on the stone hearth. Quintus was still sitting at the desk, his gaze turned to the window. Outside in the shadowed garden a hardy finch poured out a silvery song. He glanced up as she came in. He must have looked as sombre as he felt.

'What is it, my darling?' she asked. For answer, he stood and took her into his arms, holding her tight to his chest. 'Is it the eagle?'

'No.' He held her still a moment longer. Then he reluctantly released her and resumed his seat at the desk. 'No. The eagle is in good hands, exactly where it should be. I must just finish this report for Aradius Rufinus before dinner, that's all.' She nodded, smiling, and moved round the room, tidying and lighting lamps. He watched her, wondering afresh at his fortune in life: this beautiful woman, his soulmate; the enduring wonder of their children; a career he loved under a governor he respected and admired; his friend and colleague Tiro; the remote green island of Britannia, his home.

'Julia?'

'Yes, my love?'

'I wonder what you would ask for, if I could give you your heart's desire? I owe you so much. You've played a key part in this drama of Eboracum, and went through much danger to do so.'

'I like to think we all helped, Britta and Corellia as well. And the high priestess. We women can be effective, you see.'

'I've always known that. But what *is* your desire, now it's all over?'

She took his hand, and smiled. 'I have it already: you being back with me.' She was quiet for a moment, then said, 'Actually, there is something I long for.'

'Yes, my lovely one?'

'I want to go home, Quintus.'

'To Bo Gwelt?'

'Yes.'

'So do I.'

He thought of the lovely golden farmhouse in the Summer Country, and their daughter Aurelia riding over the Polden Hills with her friend Drusus. For a brief moment he felt intensely homesick.

He did not notice Julia leave the room, but the crackle of collapsing logs drew his attention to the hearth. His imagination was taken back to Cair Pol, the empty fort so far away. His

thoughts went on, leaping out into the crisp northern air, to the
dark bubbling burns and bottomless lakes, the bare bleak
mountains, and the impermeable mantle that dropped at night over
the land of the Painted People. Again he wondered at the old
emperor's strange obsession, trying fruitlessly to cage the raw-
boned warriors of that land. Pictland remained a place of glens and
summits, of sudden blinding mists and far distant pale skies. It was
a landscape where too much blood had already soaked into the
earth. That highland country belonged to its own people, he
thought, and no Roman should seek to change it.

Despite himself, his mind flicked to his younger brother Flavius,
pleading on the battlefield for Quintus to save him from the
Caledonian and his fatal longsword. But no, that was not right.
Flavius had not been pleading; he had been acknowledging
Quintus, blessing him with a last gaze before death veiled his eyes.
He must remember that, at all costs. The other path led only to
madness and terrible grief. He shook his head in rejection.

His thoughts settled on Kian mac Dougal instead, the likeable
young man with dark eyes and russet hair. A hybrid son of two
warlike peoples, born of two tribes. The proud scion of his remote
Roman ancestor, that loyal centurion of the Ninth Hispana legion
whose dangerous bequest he had guarded so well. Quintus hoped
with all his heart that Kian was now sitting by his own fireside in
Dál Riata, with his fierce little Pictish wife and perhaps soon a son,
the next Lucius Saturninus.

Slowly and inevitably, his mind's eye turned to the other loyal
centurion: Litorius Pacatianus. They might never hear what had
become of this man, so flawed and so brave, who had risen at the
end from darkness and despair into the light of Mithras. All the
more reason, Quintus vowed, to make sure the centurion's name
was known and honoured wherever Roman soldiers served.

When Tiro came back in with details of the departure to Aquae
Sulis of Marcellus Crispus and his troop, the lampblack-dipped
pen was back in Quintus's hand. His graceful script rapidly formed
across the papyrus. He looked up at his own new centurion.

'Well, Tiro, I'm afraid we've lost Litorius. But now at least the
authorities know of his sacrifice.'

Tiro nodded. 'I was thinking of him too, sir. On the way to the garrison, could we stop to make an offering at the temple of Mars?'

Quintus smiled and nodded, knowing how taken Tiro was with the gilded statue of the god of war, arrayed in elaborate Greek military costume in his Eboracum sanctum.

For himself, he would be content to carry Litorius in his heart, and to share him silently with his god at the temple of Mithras.

Epilogue

The Cave of the Dead

After they had been pulled out of the boat, eyes bound and hands tied behind them, they'd trudged across the shingle shore for what seemed an eternity. At length they were halted, and rough hands pulled off his blindfold. He looked around. The other five prisoners were still blindfolded, awaiting further commands. All were dressed in native clothes, and all had blue coiled and curling pictures on their skin, even the two youths. They looked faintly familiar; he thought they must be Picts, perhaps the family of a noble opposed to Athair.

He ceased to wonder. It was no matter — nothing mattered any more.

In front of them was a cave with a double entrance. It was a liminal place, a threshold between the world of the living — the bright sea-crashed strip of stony shore behind them, smelling of seaweed and ozone — and the world of the dead — the dark, double-mouthed cave whose maw gaped ahead.

The Cave of the Dead, crowded with ancient ghosts.

He turned to look north across the sea to Black Isle, and beyond to the far-off shore. He craned to peer up at the sea cliffs above them, squinting into the early morning light. There was no track down those forbidding crags. Now he understood why they had been brought here by boat, pitching and yawing in the currents of the ebbing tide. It was the only way to access this sacred place.

The dimly lit cave was the size of a grand hall. Now he noticed a druid was with them, long white robes damp and marked with seawater. He straightened to his full height, looking the druid in the eye. He could discern no expression on the man's face. It was as if he himself was already a fading ghost.

'May I pray one final time, to my god and to the spirits of this place?'

The priest held his gaze with a new respect. 'Our gods are unknowable. Even we priestfolk do not name them. But you may call on your own gods.'

Litorius Pacatianus stood, emptying his mind. He heard the sloughing sea, and the calls of the milling birds beyond the cave, shrieking in the hunt for fish. He heard his own breath, holding it smooth and calm, feeling a profound peace at last. He felt the presence of Mithras. The god of light and love was near. He bowed his head to the genius loci, the gods of this cave, the surrounding sea and the wandering winds. Lastly, he thought of Stella, his beautiful little daughter. He would be reunited with her very soon.

When he was ready, he knelt down on the damp sand, head bowed, not noticing a crescent-like symbol carved deep in the cave wall above him, leaping into relief as a glancing beam of low winter sun caught the rock face.

He simply knew that this death had taken a long time to come. Here it was now, at last; the gift of Mars Ultor, the god of revenge.

At the end, he heard the sighing sweep of the long Pictish sword.

Author's Notes

Rosemary Sutcliff's *The Eagle of the Ninth* has preyed on my mind since I first read it as a child. It is rightly regarded as the iconic book about Roman Britain. Recent research has reopened the debate about the loss of the Ninth Hispana legion, whose eagle is now known not to reside in Silchester. This is my homage to a brilliant and brave writer.

The Picts, or Painted People, do not appear in Roman records or elsewhere in recorded history until the late third century. Recent DNA studies suggest them to have been related to people already in Ireland and the west of Scotland. The heartlands of the Pictish kingdom stretched from the Firth of Forth to the Highlands, and further to Orkney and Shetland.

I have followed recent research which suggests that merging anti-Roman factions led by powerful warlords may have arisen in NE Scotland earlier than once thought, leading to migration. It seems to me possible that the creation of a wasteland further south, by Roman policy under Septimius Severus, may ironically have drawn this potent enemy into the vacuum thus created. For further reading about the Picts, I recommend Professor Gordon Noble's recent book *The Picts: Scourge of Rome*.

Recent research on the precise nature of the *speculator* role during the Severan period seems blurred by similarities with another body of detached soldiers, the *exploratores*. I have been persuaded by my research to assign covert military intelligence-gathering to *speculatores* like my Lossio Veda. He was a real Caledonian, buried in Colchester.

The character of Stella, the daughter of Litorius, is loosely based on an illicitly buried child's skeleton uncovered at Vindolanda.

Sculptor's Cave (called the Cave of the Dead in my book) is a fascinating place on the Moray coast. In this sea cave archaeologists have uncovered honoured burials from the Bronze Age. Much later in AD 220-235, a small group of adults and teenagers were apparently brought in as prisoners and executed by decapitation. Their DNA is local to Moray, but I have used fictional licence to include one person with some Roman heritage.

Finally, I have tried to give voice to some of the real Romans and Britons who we know lived in the places and time of my story. My portrayal of all characters and their doings remains fictional.

Acknowledgements

My grateful thanks to:

Fiona Forsyth, author of the Lucius Sestius trilogy, who graciously allowed me to use the name of a bar from her novel *Blood and Shadows* as my book title.

Dr Andrew Tibbs, for his well-timed book *Beyond the Empire* and his generous help with tracing the ancestors of the Picts.

Angus Macintyre at Abernethy Museum, for opening his museum specially for us during closed season, and regaling us with tea, shortbread, and much local wisdom about both forts Castlelaw and Carpow.

Andy Fenwick of the McManus Museum in Dundee, for valuable conversations and emails about Carpow (Cair Pol) and its artefacts.

Richard Luke, Specialist Information Officer and Cerebral Palsy Programme Lead at Scope, for a wealth of detail about cerebral palsy when I was developing the character of Nicomedes.

Historian Simon Elliott, who has mastered the knack of publishing a terrific guide on every point of research I need, just as I need it. For this novel, I leaned particularly on *Septimius Severus in Scotland,* and *Roman Britain's Missing Legion.* Simon please write a book about Roman Ireland next!

Fellow crime author and adoptive Scotswoman, Val Penny, and her Handsome Hubby, for suggesting dialect words for my character Aila.

The staff at Yorkshire Museum, who answered so many questions, and provide a handsome respectful home for the real Ivory Bangle Lady, whom I named Placidia Septimia. It was a pleasure to visit you again when I appeared at the 2023 Eboracum Roman Festival.

As always, Sue Willetts and team at the magnificent Hellenic and Roman Library, without whom Quintus and Tiro would go nowhere.

My gratitude to readers of early drafts: Pauline Ridel, Ian Walker, Louise Trafford, and my generous fellow authors, Lynn

Johnson and Fiona Forsyth.

I am very much indebted to my copy-editor/proofreader, Rhodri Orders, who gave the book a detailed, thoughtful and timely edit.

Thanks to my publisher, Sharpe Books.

Finally, thanks to my husband and first reader, Peter, who not only carried on with the cooking and bottle-washing while I wrote this book, but also organised two research trips: the first to York and Hadrian's Wall by motorbike in intense heat; the second by train and car to Edinburgh, Carpow, and Dundee, in extreme cold. You are amazing.

[For more material, go to https://linktr.ee/jacquierogers, where you will find links to my Substack blog, with map, cast list, and blogposts. Also links to author events and my Youtube channel, with supporting videos about places in the book.]

Place Names

Aelian Wall: Hadrian's Wall. Named after Hadrian's family name, Aelius.

Aquae Sulis: Bath.

Arbeia: South Shields, Tyne & Wear.

Bodotria: the Firth of Forth.

Cair Pol: the Brythonic name for the Severan Roman fortress at the confluence of the rivers Earn and Tay in Scotland. Named Horrea Classis in the Ravenna Cosmography; modern name Carpow.

Calcaria: Tadcaster in north Yorkshire.

Camulodunum: Colchester.

Carumabo: possible Roman name for the fort at Cramond, west of Edinburgh. From here it is thought a bridge (possibly a pontoon) was built across the Firth of Forth during the Severan campaigns.

Danum: Doncaster.

Deva: Chester.

Dunpeldyr: Traprain Law, East Lothian. The hillfort capital of the Votadini tribe.

Eboracum: York.

Fiv: the Fife peninsula.

Isca Silurium: Caerleon, South Wales.

Isura: the river Ouse, at York.

Lagentium: Castleford, West Yorks.

Locus Maponi: Clochmabenstane, on the north shore of the Solway Firth.

Locus Manavi: Clackmannan, on the Firth of Forth.

Londinium: London.

Luguvalio: Carlisle.

Magna: a sister fort to Vindolanda, a few miles to the west.

Mare Germanicum: the North Sea

Pons Aelius: Newcastle on Tyne.

Summer Country: Somerset, more or less.

Tausa: the river Tay, on which Severus built the large fortress and fortified harbour of Horrea Classis (Cair Pol).

Trimontium: Newstead, near Melrose in the Scottish Borders.

Vebriacum: Charterhouse in the Mendips, Somerset.

Vercovicium: Housesteads fort, midway along Hadrian's Wall. East of Vindolanda.

Vindolanda: a large fort on Stanegate, built before Hadrian's Wall. The name is thought to be local Brythonic, and may mean "white camp".

The Cave of the Dead: my name for the Sculptor's Cave, at Covesea on the Moray Firth. A burial site from the Bronze Age, in which several skeletons of people executed by decapitation much later in the 3rd century AD have recently been found. The reasons for such brutal execution in this ancient and sacred spot remain a mystery.

Glossary of Latin and Brythonic terms

Ban Sith: in Celtic traditions, Banshees were warning spirits whose wailing at night foretold a death in the family.

Caracalla: ankle-length hooded cloak worn by a *beneficiarius,* popularised by the Emperor Caracalla.

Classis Britannica: Roman naval fleet based in Gesiacorum (Boulogne) which patrolled and protected the seaways round Britain, and supplied armies on campaign.

Corbita: a large cargo vessel, with a high hull designed for ocean-going.

Dextra/sinistra: right/left

Genius loci: the protective spirit of a place.

Hasta: a decorative spear, the badge of office carried by officers detached on Imperial or Governor's business.

Mansio: a posting-inn with stabling for official travellers.

Latifundium: a great landed estate mostly worked by slaves.

Locus: formal meeting places and markets in southern Scotland, where Roman officials met regularly with local friendly tribes, to gather information, monitor tribal movements, and carry out diplomacy. Examples include Newstead (Trimontium) and Lochmaben.

Optio: normally second in command of a century; sometimes detached to serve as assistant to a Governor's Man, as Tiro is in this story.

Opus signinum: a form of Roman concrete, used to build floors in less prestigious rooms.

Palla: a mantle worn by well-off women.

Pancratium: mixed martial arts contests involving a combination of wrestling and boxing. Popular in the Roman army.

Phalera: a roundel of silver awarded for exceptional military valour, worn on the cuirass.

Praefectus Castrorum: the Camp Prefect, the most senior officer in a legion after the legate and tribunes. Usually an experienced centurion, promoted from the ranks.

Praetorium: the house of the commanding officer in a fort/palace of a governor.

Principia: the headquarters of a fort.

Pugio: large leaf-bladed dagger worn by Roman soldiers.

Sacellum: the strong room in a Roman fort, where the pay chest, legionary standards and statues of the gods were kept.

Serapeum: temple where Serapis, a Graeco-Egyptian god of fertility, wisdom, the underworld and healing popularised by Vespasian and the Severan emperors, was worshipped.

Speculator: a scout or spy, nominally headquartered at the Castra Peregrina in Rome and assigned to duties in support of governors in troubled regions of the empire.

Triclinium: the dining room of a wealthy home, or the officer's mess in a fort. Diners reclined on couches grouped round low tables, served food and wine by slaves.

Printed in Great Britain
by Amazon